Henrietta felt those eyes—felt them as powerful as a physical force, probing deep within her.

'I think it is ti[...]ached a clear understanding a[...]ing between us.'

His words confus[...]d to her senses and [...]et the physical desire she felt for [...]ed to ache inside her. A small, insidious voice whispered a caution, reminding her that any liaison with Simon would bring her nothing but heartbreak, but another voice was whispering something else, telling her not to let the moment pass, to catch it and hold on to it.

Still she hesitated, for what she was contemplating went beyond anything she had ever contemplated before. All she wanted was for him to hold her again and to kiss her into insensibility.

AUTHOR NOTE

I thoroughly enjoyed writing A TRAITOR'S TOUCH, which is set in 1745–6 against the turbulent issues that beset both England and Scotland at that time. The climax of the story is the Battle of Culloden.

Dark family secrets, hidden hurts, desperation and undeniable love—all these and more appear in A TRAITOR'S TOUCH.

Beautiful, clever Henrietta Brody flees London to escape a ruthless murderer. With little more than the clothes on her back she sets off on a lonely, friendless road to the wilds of Scotland, determined to find her uncle. She enlists the aid of handsome Lord Simon Tremain—a staunch Jacobite whose values and loyalties to the cause are against everything Henrietta believes in.

While the battle of Culloden and the issues of the time are real, the characters—with the exception of The Bonnie Prince—are entirely fictional.

A TRAITOR'S TOUCH

Helen Dickson

Published in Great Britain 2014
by Mills & Boon, an imprint of Harlequin (UK) Limited,
Eton House, 18-24 Paradise Road, Richmond, Surrey, TW9 1SR

ISBN: 978 0 263 90957 9

Harlequin (UK) Limited's policy is to use papers that are natural, renewable and recyclable products and made from wood grown in sustainable forests. The logging and manufacturing processes conform to the legal environmental regulations of the country of origin.

Printed and bound in Spain
by Blackprint CPI, Barcelona

Helen Dickson was born and lives in South Yorkshire, with her retired farm manager husband. Having moved out of the busy farmhouse where she raised their two sons, she has more time to indulge in her favourite pastimes. She enjoys being outdoors, travelling, reading and music. An incurable romantic, she writes for pleasure. It was a love of history that drove her to writing historical fiction.

Previous novels by Helen Dickson:

THE DEFIANT DEBUTANTE
ROGUE'S WIDOW, GENTLEMAN'S WIFE
TRAITOR OR TEMPTRESS
WICKED PLEASURES (part of *Christmas By Candlelight*)
A SCOUNDREL OF CONSEQUENCE
FORBIDDEN LORD
SCANDALOUS SECRET, DEFIANT BRIDE
FROM GOVERNESS TO SOCIETY BRIDE
MISTRESS BELOW DECK
THE BRIDE WORE SCANDAL
SEDUCING MISS LOCKWOOD
DESTITUTE ON HIS DOORSTEP
MARRYING MISS MONKTON
DIAMONDS, DECEPTION AND THE DEBUTANTE
BEAUTY IN BREECHES
MISS CAMERON'S FALL FROM GRACE
THE HOUSEMAID'S SCANDALOUS SECRET*
WHEN MARRYING A DUKE...
THE DEVIL CLAIMS A WIFE
THE MASTER OF STONEGRAVE HALL
MISHAP MARRIAGE

**Castonbury Park* Regency mini-series

And in Mills & Boon® Historical *Undone!* eBooks :

ONE RECKLESS NIGHT

Prologue

1734

On the discovery of a plot for the capture of the royal family and the proclamation of King James across the water, Andrew Brody was arrested with other malcontents and hanged at Carlisle. His body was brought home to Glasgow in a plain wooden box. To spare his wife and young daughter the sight of his blue and grotesque face, its tongue bulging from a rictus mouth, the lid was kept nailed down.

Maria, his wife, went mad with grief. She wept day and night and could not eat. She was terribly ill and there was no consoling her.

After two weeks, their seven-year-old daughter, Henrietta, went outside to look for her mother, thinking she might have taken a turn round the garden. When she failed to locate her she turned to go back to the house, but for some reason she did not fully understand herself, stopped and looked towards the river. Following a moment of indecision, she began to walk towards it. Perhaps it was to satisfy a sense of nostalgia, to recall happier times when the river had been a magical place. Or perhaps it was some other, darker sense that impelled her to get a closer look.

Whatever it was it led her along the bank of the gently swirling river. And that was when she saw a woman's body floating face down in the water, her hair forming a rippling halo on the surface.

It was her mother.

Henrietta's stomach lurched and she called her mother's name and drew closer to the edge, hoping she was not too late, but knowing that she was. She turned and ran back to the garden.

'Help me!' she cried to the gardener raking up leaves into a heap. 'My mother—she's in the river. I don't know what to do! Help me! Please help me!'

The gardener threw down the rake and ran towards the river, the girl following close on his heels. On seeing the body, he quickly assessed the situation. Wading into the water, he hauled his mistress onto dry ground and rolled her on to her back. He stared down at the lifeless form, at the woman's face that was so white, but still beautiful in death.

The gardener looked up at the child. She stood like a small frozen statue, her eyes wide and filled with horror, and he could feel the agony coming off her, sense the torment twisting her soul like a weighted rope. Slowly she got down on her knees, staring into her mother's bloodless face, her small hand smoothing her dark brown hair back from her forehead over and over again, whispering words the gardener could not hear.

The girl was remembering all the days spent with her mother, how they would sing and gossip. How nothing could touch them then. But now she was gone. The vivacious, spirited and delightful woman was gone. The girl told herself over and over again she would not see her mother again in life. But now she must not think of it, else she would lose her mind like her mother.

Eventually the gardener rose on stiff legs. 'It would seem your mother has had an accident, Miss Henrietta,' he said by way of explanation, while knowing otherwise. 'I will carry her to the house,' he said gently. The child did not look up, did not break the rhythm of her hand stroking her mother's hair as she whispered tenderly, as though they two were the only people left on God's earth. 'I will be gentle with her, I promise, but I think we should take her home now.'

The gardener waited a while longer, watching a swan with three cygnets in her wake sail stately by. Then the child got to her feet. Her face glistened with tears and bewilderment filled her green eyes as though she was desperate to understand why her mother had left her.

'Please don't hurt her.'

Swallowing hard with a resolute nod, for one heartbreaking moment, the gardener looked down into the young face. 'I won't.' And so, carefully, more carefully than he had ever done anything in his life, he bent and took the dead woman into his arms, trying not to look at her face as he carried her to the house.

The funeral coming so soon after her father's interment was too much for the child. She drew in a breath of panic. She did not want to be there. She did not want to be afraid all the time—afraid of death. Her father's brother, Uncle Matthew, came and took her in his arms.

Matthew shook his head in despair. Tears lit his eyes. He tried to explain. All this had happened because her father was a Jacobite. Matthew was of the opinion that men should be free to worship God as they chose, as long as they obeyed their king and did no harm by it. Tragically his brother had supported the wrong kind. The Jacobite cause had been his life. Even when he was condemned he saw his last journey to the scaffold as a veritable moment of glory, as though he were raised suddenly to celebrate for his good deeds, instead of hanged for his seditious acts against the Crown.

The girl could not get beyond the Jacobite word. This new knowledge of the circumstances surrounding her father's execution, followed so quickly by her mother's suicide, haunted her day and night. The anger and hate directed at the Jacobites entwined, swelling and blooming inside her, threatening to consume her body and soul. It was anger and hatred more acute and darker than anything she had ever known.

And then Uncle Matthew took her away—to London—putting as much distance between her and the event as was possible.

Chapter One

1745

Baron Charles Lucas and his wife Dorothy had embraced Henrietta in her hour of need and taken her into their lives and their home with the kind of easy, unconscious goodness that was born of good breeding and a happy life.

And now they were both dead. Along with their coachman, they had sustained fatal injuries in a carriage accident when they were travelling home from the theatre. Within the space of twenty-four hours, Henrietta was forced to grow up quickly and keep herself in control for the sake of the grieving servants. But beneath her calm exterior she endured a sickening and inevitable turmoil over the loss of the two people who had given her a sense of worth and for whom she had borne a real and unselfish love.

She closed her eyes as the enormity of their

loss made her realise how alone she was and she knew she would have to consider wisely how to make the best of her circumstances and to think about her future. After considering the advantages his niece would reap in London, including learning everything a young lady should be cognizant of, Uncle Matthew had placed her in the hands of Baron Lucas and his wife Dorothy, her mother's dearest friend. They had been delighted to become Henrietta's legal guardians. She was the apple of their eye, the child they had never had.

Uncle Matthew was the only family Henrietta had. As a youth and being a scholar with much intelligence and curiosity, he had sought to quench his thirst for knowledge and had gone abroad to enrich his education. He had been gone some time. When he came home, expecting to be welcomed by his brother, he had found unexpected tragedy. Never having married and seeming to have a dislike for all society following the terrible circumstances of his adored brother's brutal death, he'd acquired a crofter's cottage close to Inverness and, surrounded by his precious books, become something of a recluse. Henrietta knew she could be sure of a warm welcome there.

But maybe she wouldn't have to leave London. Dorothy had assured her that she would be well provided for. Henrietta remembered how the dear lady, who'd insisted she call her aunt, had smiled and said that Henrietta's mother had been a good friend to her—as close as sisters they had been—and that she honoured her memory in the best way she knew by honouring and taking care of her daughter to the best of her ability.

Remembering this, Henrietta swallowed and set her jaw.

Hearing carriage wheels on the gravel drive, she glanced out of the window. Her heart sank. It was dark, but she could see by the carriage lamps that her guardians' nephew, Jeremy Lucas, had arrived at Whitegates to claim his inheritance. Followed by his wife, Claudia, he breezed through the great entrance hall and into the salon where Henrietta was sifting through some correspondence, mainly letters of condolence from friends of the elderly couple.

The moment Jeremy entered the room with his wife flouncing after him the atmosphere thickened with tension. Tall and lanky and fashionably attired without prudence, he walked with a swagger as if he owned the world. He was a popular, much sought-after figure about town and could be charming when the occasion demanded it, but Henrietta had seen the cold, cunning heart behind the charm. He was inclined to call at the house unannounced. The last time had been the day after the accident. He hadn't seen fit to turn up for the funeral which had been a mere twenty-four hours ago.

Henrietta rose, smoothing down her black skirts as she turned to face him. Jeremy felt a deep resentment towards her and had never made any attempt to disguise the fact.

'Jeremy! You were not expected. However, you are welcome.'

While his mind noted the young woman's perfunctory courtesy to him, his mind catalogued the valuables in the room. 'I should damned well think so since it's my house.' His eyes gleamed overbright as he strutted like a well-preened rooster on the oriental carpet, eyeing and fingering precious heirlooms he had coveted for years.

Henrietta's face tightened with the effort of holding back a sarcastic rejoinder. She braced herself for what was to come, for after her dealings with this man in the past she knew it was not going to be pleasant. She glanced at Rose hovering in the doorway, a pensive look creasing her round face.

'Is everything all right, Miss Brody?' she enquired, glancing nervously at the visitors.

'Yes, thank you, Rose.'

Rose stepped back, but was not out of sight. Her faithfulness to her mistress remained as strong as the time when she had come to live with Baron Lucas and she had long ago proven her confidante in the most troubling times.

'Bring us some refreshment, will you, Rose?'

The maid bobbed a curtsy and hurried away.

Henrietta and Jeremy Lucas were isolated enough that they could converse in private in the salon, yet the servants were still close enough that Henrietta did not feel as if she was under any threat. It was indicative of her mistrust of Jeremy that she even thought of such things—that she was actually considering herself to be in possible danger in her own home.

'The servants are disrespectful,' Jeremy informed her as he sat down heavily on a chair, stretching his long legs out in front of him, unconcealed malevolence in his pale blue eyes as they swept insolently over her. 'But no matter. I have not come here to discuss something that can be replaced.'

Henrietta stiffened, all her senses alert. 'Replaced? What are you talking about?'

'Servants are two a penny. Now I've come to take up residence, if any of them want to remain they must know their place.'

'Quite right, Jeremy,' Claudia piped up in her shrill voice. 'You show them how you mean to go on from the start and that you'll stand for no interference from them.'

Henrietta looked at Jeremy's wife. During several visits, Henrietta's red-gold tresses had incensed the hard-faced virago, causing Claudia to berate the whole Scottish race as being slow-witted and to demean Henrietta as a heathen, a derogatory appellation many an English Protestant was wont to lay on the Roman Catholics.

True to form, Claudia was gaudily attired, her generous assets amply displayed. She wore too much powder and paint for good taste. Her dark hair was piled high on her head and a black patch dotted her cheekbone. With her nose tipped disdainfully high, her hazel eyes hostile, Claudia gave her a haughty smile as she doffed her gloves and tossed them aside. Prowling slowly about the room, her skirts swishing in her wake, she trailed well-manicured fingers across polished surfaces, lingering on a valuable figurine while eyeing other knick-knacks as if to assess their value.

'If you have come to discuss the will, Jeremy,' Henrietta said, trying to hide her aversion to the man, 'the solicitor is coming tomorrow.'

'I am aware of the contents, Henrietta. I called on Braithwaite earlier. As you know, Braithwaite has had the honour of being the family solicitor for the past ten years—'

'Who has been absent—America, I believe—for the past two years,' Henrietta pointed out.

'I am aware of that, but he has recently returned,' Jeremy retorted, irritated by her interruption. 'He made up my uncle's last will and testament.'

'Which you are telling me he has made privy to you. Clearly there has been some mistake and your uncle had not informed you—'

'Be quiet,' Jeremy snapped, shoving himself out of the chair and glaring down at her, his long, ungainly body quivering like a snake about to strike. 'I'm not interested in what you have to say. My uncle kept a copy of the will, which I will find in his study when I go through his papers—and which I intend doing this very night. But understand this, Henrietta Brody. Everything has been left to me. The house, the money—everything—and I aim to take immediate possession.'

A feeling of alarm began to creep through Henrietta. She had never discussed such matters with her guardians. Indeed, there had been no reason to do so. But she knew they had cared for her and would not have been so unconcerned for her that in the event of their demise they would have failed to make provision for her future. She had certainly not expected much, but she could not believe they would have overlooked the matter.

'You were not included,' Jeremy went on. 'But then why you should think my aunt and uncle should have left you anything at all defeats me. You were not a relative. You were nothing to them.'

'Jeremy's right,' Claudia's shrill voice piped up. Catching Henrietta's look of disdain, she bristled. 'And don't look at me like that. Jeremy will wipe that smirk off your face when he sends you packing. You think you're better than me, don't you, you stuck-up Scottish witch—you and your high-handed ways. Well, you're wrong. You're not fit to clean my shoes.'

Even after enduring the loss of her guardians and Jeremy's cruel words, Henrietta refused to yield to Claudia that very thing she craved most—an undeniable feeling of superiority. Highly offended by his words, though her anger and animosity rose up within her, she forced herself to remain calm. 'I do not believe that and I was certainly not expecting anything of value. Having lost both my parents and being alone in the world, I was extremely grateful when they welcomed me into their home. I was deeply devoted to your aunt and uncle and I know that over the years they grew attached to me. Your uncle was a methodical man about his affairs and I cannot believe that when the situation changed and my own uncle made him my legal guardian he would not have made provision for me—at the very least to give me time to vacate the house when you took possession.'

Jeremy smirked. 'Well, he didn't,' he bit back, thoroughly enjoying putting her in her place. 'I expect they were fed up with you mooning about the house and hoped to marry you off before their demise. Just who do you think you are? A lady?'

'If you knew your aunt and uncle at all, you would not have said that. They were good, kind people and would not brush people off so easily—especially those they cared about.'

Jeremy reached out and jerked Henrietta's face around, his long, clawlike fingers bruising her tender flesh. 'Where you are concerned they appear to have done just that. I own this house now. I am master here and as soon as the will has been read I want you out of it.' Removing his hand, he thrust her away.

Henrietta stared at him. She was now certain that he was not aware that his uncle had executed a new will, let alone changed his solicitor. It didn't augur well for the future. Displeased with the way Mr Braithwaite conducted his business—he was not a man noted for his discretion—both his uncle and aunt agreed that Mr Goodwin, a barrister in the city, was a man of probity, wisdom and common sense in equal proportions. She was surprised that Mr Braithwaite, who was a close friend of Jeremy's, had failed to mention it. Although why on earth he should not have done when he had nothing to gain by not doing so she could not imagine. She was on the point of informing Jeremy herself but when he began bearing down on her once more, his cold eyes conveying to her that if he became vexed or angry enough he would have her forcibly removed, her mouth went dry.

Recognising her fear, Jeremy felt a surge of power. He laughed, a thin, cruel laugh that chilled Henrietta. 'You, Miss Henrietta Brody, have been a drain on this family for too long, playing on my aunt and uncle's goodwill when they took you in, living in the grand manner you think is your due. You have got above yourself. Enough is enough, I say, so pack your bags and be ready to leave as soon as Braithwaite has read the will.'

'That's right, Jeremy. You tell her straight,' Claudia quipped while running her fingers appreciatively down the thick damask curtains and eyeing the crystal chandelier and Turkish carpet beneath her feet. 'Nothing but a beggar—an upstart she was. She doesn't belong here—never did. It's time she was put in her place.'

Henrietta thought that was comical coming from her. Hadn't Jeremy plucked her off the stage in Drury Lane? She would have laughed out loud had the situation not been so serious.

'She will be, my love. I guarantee it.' Jeremy looked Henrietta over, noting her trim figure, with its tiny waist, her prim beauty, the red-gold of her hair and softly rounded curves beneath her mourning dress. As much as he had intended exacting revenge on his uncle's ward, with her proud head elevated to a lofty angle and her eyes blazing defiance, as much as he might have wished otherwise, it was blatantly obvious that Claudia suffered badly in comparison.

'You cannot do this,' Henrietta said. 'I beg you to reconsider.'

'I suppose I could—for a price.'

'Now don't you go making any bargains with her, Jeremy,' his wife chided. 'She's going and that's final.'

'I suppose something could be worked out between us,' Jeremy said, his gaze dwelling on a rounded breast, giving no indication that he had even heard his wife.

Henrietta shrank as she felt the weight of his stare. She could feel his eyes burning into her flesh through the fabric of her dress. Her heart pounded and she looked up at him, suddenly wary. His eyes held a hard, predatory gleam and a confident smile stretched his thin lips that made her skin crawl. His thoughts were the kind a decent young lady would not invite.

'Of course there is the matter of your guardianship to consider, Henrietta. It cannot be overlooked. As the legal ward of my late uncle, I expect the responsibility has fallen on me. In which case I have legal ownership of you. You must obey me. Obviously you have not yet come of age whereby you can make lawful decisions on your own. I am duty-bound to provide for you.'

It was the smugness of his expression which finally brought Henrietta's senses to life. 'I am not your ward,' she retorted, seething at his arrogant assertion. 'I do not believe there is the mention of any guardianship being transferred to you in any will. A moment ago you were prepared to throw me out on the street. That was hardly an act of solicitude.'

Jeremy's eyes became less threatening. 'I acted a tad hastily, I admit. As I said, I will allow you to remain for the time being—'

'But for a price,' Henrietta said, cutting him short, incensed by what he was suggesting. 'How dare you insult me so? To have made such suggestions at all is disgusting, but to make them in the presence of your wife is doubly so. How dare you come here prancing about like some arrogant lord, you graceless fop? I would rather take my chances on the streets than remain here with you and your wife. I would rot first.'

Jeremy's eyes flared as her insults hit their mark. His face darkened to a motley red. 'And you will. I'll see to that, I promise you,' he flared, his whole body shaking with rage. 'Now go to your room and don't come down again until I give you permission.'

There was a warning in his voice which sent a shiver of fear through Henrietta. She backed away. 'Most willingly.'

She turned on her heel, leaving the room as two maids came in carrying trays laden with a silver tea service, fine china and a plate of sweet delicacies to tempt the palate.

She was halfway up the stairs when, having second thoughts, she decided to return to try again to inform Jeremy about his uncle's change of solicitor. The door was ajar and she paused, steeling her nerves for further confrontation, but on hearing Claudia's shrill voice she remained where she was.

'I thank the Lord she's going. She couldn't continue living here.'

'Don't worry, my love,' Jeremy said, biting into one of cook's delicious iced cakes, scattering crumbs down his fine silk waistcoat. 'You won't have to put up with her for long. Henrietta Brody no longer has any place here and, as soon as the will is read, one way or another she will cease to exist.'

'It's a pity we failed to get rid of her along with the old fools. But then we must be thankful that everything went off as we hoped, better even since they had the sense to die and leave you everything.'

'It had to be done. I couldn't wait any longer. With creditors baying at the door, it was either that or the debtors' prison.' A sudden vision of himself locked in a filthy prison cell at the mercy of other prisoners and the guards flashed into Jeremy's mind's eye. It was a vision that had haunted him too much of late for comfort. 'It's not too late for Henrietta Brody. I vow I'll see her hanged before I let her touch an object or a penny of what's mine.'

Henrietta listened in amazement and shock to this eruption of venom. Horrified, she saw at last the cynical calculation of these two, who had coolly set about playing on her guardians' goodness and her own innocence. Even more than their revelation was the contemptuous way this creature who was Jeremy's wife dared to speak of her guardians' memory that roused her anger.

'Not only that, the girl's a papist, isn't she?' Claudia added with scorn. 'They're likely to stab one in one's bed with the smallest hint of an uprising. Don't forget what happened to her father.'

Having heard enough and horrified at what their words implied—that they had been responsible for the death of her guardians and that she would have suffered the same fate had she not pleaded the onset of a cold, which had prevented her attending the theatre that night—Henrietta backed away from the door and, turning quietly, made her way to the baron's study. The desk where he kept his private papers was locked, the key kept in a drawer in a separate bureau, although the deeds to the house and other important papers he kept with Mr Goodwin.

Opening each drawer in the desk in turn, she sifted through some household accounts until she found what she was looking for. Jeremy was right. There was a copy of the will, but it was the recent will drawn up by Mr Goodwin. Hearing Jeremy leave the morning room and cross the hall to the kitchen where he proceeded to bark orders at the staff, clutching the will in her trembling hand, gingerly she closed the study door. Afraid of making a sound, stealthily she tiptoed across the hall and flitted up the stairs to her room.

With shaking hands she opened the copy of the will and scanned what was written. She read enough to know that if she valued her life she must get away immediately. As Baron Lucas's sole heir it was natural that Jeremy would expect to inherit his entire estate, but he had excluded Jeremy in favour of her.

Caught in a nightmare, she realised she was completely alone, at the mercy of demons that were intent upon destroying her. Who was to know what Jeremy would be tempted to do if he found out she had knowledge of the terrible crime he'd committed, one he would hang for? And on the morrow when he discovered his uncle had changed his solicitor and made a new will, leaving her everything, the knowledge would elicit terrible repercussions from Jeremy and she was not strong enough to stand against him.

Briefly she considered throwing herself on the mercy of her guardians' friends, but dismissed this immediately. Jeremy had always been a golden boy and, because of the shocking events in her family's background, they had quietly resented the position she had acquired in the Lucas household. No one would believe the conversation she had overheard between Jeremy and his wife and that he had murdered his uncle and aunt to get his hands on their money to keep him out of debtors' prison. It would be her word against his, and were she to seek out Mr Goodwin, he would ensure the inheritance came to her, but he would never believe she was under threat from Jeremy.

So, with no one to whom she could turn to for help and with only herself to rely on, knowing that if she was to save her neck she had to do something, she acted on pure instinct. She would not be beaten. She would not sit and wait for Jeremy to destroy her with the same vicious cunning as he had his aunt and uncle. She had to get away and get away with all speed.

A concerned Rose followed her into her room, where Henrietta lost no time in telling her what had occurred and that she must leave the house with all haste. That Jeremy and his wife had admitted to killing her guardians she kept to herself. The fact that Jeremy could have done something so horrendous was difficult for her to take in, but if he could take the lives of his own flesh and blood without a qualm, he would not turn a hair in getting rid of her.

Sending Rose to find her some clothes suitable for riding a long distance, preferably male attire since she didn't want to attract attention to herself and her very gender rendered such an undertaking dangerous, she also asked her to instruct Robbie to saddle her horse and bring it into the yard at the back of the house, and not to say a word to anyone. When Rose had disappeared to do her bidding she snatched up some small items she would need—the copy of the will, a purse containing several coins and some of her jewels, so that she could sell them if it became necessary. She also had the presence of mind to arm herself with a small dagger to defend herself from vagabonds and highwaymen. It had belonged to her father and she prayed she would not have occasion to use it. Rose returned with some clothes she'd commandeered from the young groom.

'Robbie won't miss these,' she said, handing her the breeches.

They were ill-fitting and stained with saddle oil and other distasteful substances, but they would serve their purpose. The shirt, which came down to her knees, she tucked into her breeches, and her youthful breasts she bound flat with a snug-fitting chemise. Shoving her arms into the sleeves of one of her old jackets, she thought she was beginning to look the part, but how Lady Lucas would have admonished her ward for riding in such an immodest and unladylike style.

Glancing in the mirror, she considered her features for the hazard they might pose. Was there something that might betray her: the pert nose, the large green eyes that slanted upwards, her long silky black lashes and the soft, too-pink and delicate mouth? Small and slender, she would have no trouble passing herself off as a youth—not even Jeremy would recognise her dressed like this, but she would have to do something about her hair. The long, soft, curling tresses would become a liability she could ill afford.

'I hope you know what you're doing,' Rose said, deeply concerned for her safety.

'I don't, Rose,' Henrietta said, handing her the scissors. 'All I know is that I cannot stay here with Jeremy. What I heard tonight gives me reason to fear for my life. I have to get away and it's imperative that I look the part, which is why I want you to cut my hair.'

Rose was appalled at what she was being asked to do. 'But—your lovely hair? I can't do that.'

'Yes, you can. It's necessary. This is a time for survival, Rose, not girlish longings. It will soon grow again. Now hurry. I have to leave before Jeremy comes looking for me.'

When Rose had completed her task and disposed of the shorn hair, Henrietta heard Jeremy down below, his voice raised in anger. Hearing the noise of the study door banging shut, the noise reverberating through the house, she trembled with fear.

'Where is she, damn you?' he shouted to a terrified servant, having decided to take a look at his uncle's documents and being unable to find the key to his desk. 'In her room, is she? Get her. She will not hide from me.'

Suddenly Henrietta felt Rose's arms around her. A sudden tug of emotion made her hug Rose in return. Before the feeling could turn to tears, she pulled away and stood upright like a soldier.

'This is just terrible,' a tearful Rose said, wiping her wet cheeks. 'That you are being forced to leave your own home without a place to go. Where will you go?'

In her present terrible plight, there was only one place Henrietta could go, only one person who could help and advise her—her uncle—and he was hundreds of miles away in the wilds of Scotland. She was in no doubt that it would be a monumental undertaking for her to get there safely. Fearing that Jeremy would interrogate Rose and demand to know her whereabouts, Henrietta considered she was better off not knowing. 'I can't tell you that, Rose, but I mean to leave London. I'll write to you when I reach my destination. I promise. Wish me luck, Rose.'

'I always do, miss. God keep you safe,' Rose whispered. 'I will be praying for you.'

Shrouded in a black woollen cloak, her cropped red-gold hair dulled with a smidgen of soot and hidden beneath a wide-brimmed hat, hearing Jeremy's loud, harsh tones, with hate beating a bitter note in her breast, Henrietta hurried out of a back door to her waiting horse. She shivered as the reality of what she was planning to undertake hit her. It would be wiser to wait until morning, to set out on her journey in the light rather than in the dark, but she could not wait. Without a backward glance, like a shadow she slipped away on to Hampstead Heath without encountering a living soul.

As she rode on to the heath, Henrietta looked around with renewed spirit and saw that no black clouds hung in the sky to mar her plans. There was no hampering wind, either, and, since it was late August, the air was warm. Fortunately for her, she knew the heath well and there was no lane or byway with which she was not familiar. It was a rambling, hilly place embracing ponds and ancient woodlands. Unfortunately Hampstead Heath had a sinister reputation for criminals. There was no doubt that there were major hazards to crossing it at night and that ordinary dangers were compounded by those threatened by highwaymen.

Driven by some compelling need to put as much distance as she could between her and the threat Jeremy Lucas posed, digging in her heels she rode off at a gallop, the horse's hooves thudding over the turf. Approaching woodland, fearing she might be knocked from her horse by low branches, she slowed her horse to a walk and entered the interior. Every now and then she paused to listen, straining her ears for every sound. All was silent in the darkness. The moon and stars were hidden behind thick cloud.

She picked her way through the undergrowth and stopped when she came to a clearing, staring at the dark silhouette which was the tumbled ruin of a cottage. There were no lights showing. Intending to ride on by, she looked ahead. As she did so, something flashed in the corner of her eye. She swung about—a lantern had been put out and she realised there was someone outside the building. Afraid that if she rode on whoever it was that lurked there would come after her, dismounting, she tethered her horse to a branch. With her heart thudding in her chest, she crept forward and ran the last few paces, crouching against a side wall and creeping towards the corner of the building. Pressing herself against the wall, she realised only then that her legs were shaking beneath her. For a panic-filled moment, the mere awareness of her fear threatened to collapse her self-control, but she pressed trembling fingers to her lips, resolving to overcome her trepidations by her own will and fortitude. Though the full moon gleamed brightly overhead and cast a strip of moonlight over the ruin, deep in the shadows along the walls the blackness was almost palpable.

Holding her breath, she peered around the corner, seeing that she was several feet from what had once been the door. A man was skulking in the gloom, long and dark like the shadows. She waited until her heart had slowed and her breathing had steadied. Somewhere on the heath she heard an owl calling, the haunting sound echoing in the silence. Hardly breathing, soundlessly she pressed herself against the wall and waited.

Suddenly she heard the sound of horses, the thump of their hooves on the ground and the clink of their harnesses. Retreating along the wall, she stood in the shadows. Three men rode up and halted in front of the building. They slid to the ground and the man in the shadows stepped forward to greet them.

Her curiosity getting the better of her, Henrietta crept forward once more to observe them more closely, straining her eyes in the darkness as she wondered at the reason for them meeting so furtively. She could see the outline of the horses and the shape of the men. They stood close together, murmuring in consultation. Two of them broke away and walked in her direction, pausing to converse. Straining her ears, she was just able to hear what they said.

'Good to see you, Jack,' the man who had been waiting said.

'Have you been waiting long, Simon?' asked Jack.

'About half an hour,' Simon replied in low tones.

'You have come from Dover?'

'I met with the agent. He's a reliable source—a Frenchman and a friend. He deals in commodities and is of great use to us.'

'Just one of our brave liaisons. You've a long ride ahead of you before you reach Edinburgh.'

'Aye, but a necessary one. I mean to stop at my home over the border. I have arrangements to make should things not turn out as we hope. I've one or two loose ends to tie up here in London, but I hope to be heading north long before dawn. It appears Prince Charles has arrived in Scotland with only a handful of men. It will be common knowledge soon. Convinced the English Jacobites will stage an uprising, he is already planning to invade England. I mean to ride north to assess the situation.'

'I'm loyal to the cause, but planning a rising to put his father on the throne is foolish in my opinion.'

'I couldn't agree more,' Simon said, 'but he had his head set on it. The proclamation states that by the ordination of Almighty God, King

James, VIII of Scotland and III of England and Ireland, asserts his just rights to claim the throne of three kingdoms, and to acknowledge the support of these divine rights by the chieftains of the Highland clans and Jacobite lords—and various other such loyal subjects of His Majesty King James. We need soldiers, weapons and money, which we don't have.'

'Then he will fail. We need the French to succeed.'

'If we wait for the French to help us, we'll be waiting a long time. But then again, with the British at war with France and all the armies fighting in Europe, perhaps now is the time to act.'

Simon shook his head. 'I have my doubts. I fear support in Scotland may be lacking. Some clan chieftains will rally to the call. Others who are loyal to the British government will not. There are many who consider it a better place since the Stuarts left. It has become a proud nation—united with England. The people have grown richer, more powerful and more respected throughout the world. They fear the return of the Stuarts will bring fresh misery and have no stomach for war. What of you, Jack? Are you afraid to continue? Does he have your support?'

'Certainly. We've come too far to retreat. I will inform our men here in London of events.

To bring about the change there is nothing that I would not do on behalf of Charles Stuart. If he succeeds, I will know I played my part. Few men will be able to claim as much. What do you think, Simon?'

'I agree, but it would be better if King George could be removed by diplomatic coercion.'

'That won't happen. The part you play in this drama is great and heroic. You are to be just one of our liaisons in the north. We could not have chosen a man who knows that part of the world better.'

'True, I know it well enough. But if the rebellion is to succeed, there are grave times ahead. Those who support Prince Charles will be branded as rebels and as traitors to the English Crown.'

'It will be nothing to what our fellow Catholics have already endured. If they have been safe for a time, it is only because they—we—have learned to be silent. You, Simon, rebel in the name of the Stuarts, I in the name of the Catholic martyrs. We have suffered for over two hundred years. This will be just one more test of our resolve—I pray it will be the last.'

'I agree, but I cannot imagine that Prince Charles's arrival after so many years of darkness and despair for the Jacobites is about to allow the sun to break through the clouds.'

Realising her curiosity had unwittingly placed her in danger, Henrietta followed this exchange with amazed disbelief. Beyond a doubt, everything that had happened to her in the past few hours had the incoherence of a bad dream. She was shaken, for in this day of Jacobites, of plots and counterplots, imprisonment and treason, it would seem she had stumbled across a nest of Jacobite conspirators. Somewhere in the dark chambers of her mind a memory stirred—not a pleasant memory—and her father's tortured face flickered for a moment in her mind's eye, which she quickly shoved away. A cold shiver travelled down her spine.

As a Catholic, she had followed the Jacobite cause with reluctant interest. James Stuart's court, the exiled king of Scotland—or the Pretender to the throne, depending on one's loyalties—was in Rome. He had mounted an abortive attempt to regain his throne in 1715 and had failed through lack of support. Since then he had worked ceaselessly at trying to gain support from fellow monarchs, reiterating his son Charles's legitimacy to the throne of Scotland and England.

What she had just overheard suggested that Charles Edward Stuart had come to claim his father's throne, prepared to resort to armed rebellion to restore the Stuart monarchy. As she adjusted her position her cloak brushed against the wall, dislodging a loose stone, which fell at her feet with a soft thud. It alerted the men and they fell silent. She stood stock-still, her heart drumming in her chest, and cold sweat trickled along the side of her face and down her spine. She knew that her breathing must be deafening—she was certain that she could be seen and heard in spite of the darkness.

A long moment passed. Hearing the men exhaling ragged oaths, she also heard footsteps coming closer. She shuddered and swayed slightly to keep her balance. She was sure that they would find her. She had to get away. Cautiously she began to retreat backwards. A man stepped round the corner of the building—a formidable silhouette bent on bloody murder. He stood motionless, staring at her. The moon chose that moment to slip from behind a cloud, haloing his tall, powerfully muscled form with its brilliance. His hat was slung low over his face, shadowing his features, but she thought she saw his eyes, and ironic ones they were. His gauntlets were made of fine leather, with gold thread trimming the edges. While she wore one of her old cloaks, this man wore a cloak of fine black cloth interfaced in gold. He said not a word as their eyes clashed across the distance.

Like the prey entranced by the predator, Henrietta was momentarily transfixed. She remembered then of the harm he might do to her. He did not speak, but the second he moved towards her, she whirled around and fled in the direction of her horse. She raced with all the stealth at her command, but when her foot caught in a hole she nearly tumbled headlong. Recovering her balance, she rushed on. She could sense the man coming after her, feel him gaining on her, and then he reached for her, but in the blink of an eye, she ducked under his arm and fled.

'Oh, no, you don't,' he growled. Pivoting round, he reached out and grabbed her, wrenching her arm up her back. 'I wouldn't struggle, if I were you, boy. Stay put,' he coolly ordered.

Letting out a cry Henrietta struggled to free herself, but she was no match for his strength. With one hand he grasped her arm, and with the other resting on the hilt of his sword he hauled her back to the others.

'Keep still, you little savage. It will do you no good. Lower your weapons,' he said to his comrades. ''Tis naught but a youth.'

The sound of his voice sent a thrill down Henrietta's spine, and she trembled for some unknown reason. Glancing at the men, the one called Jack brandishing a dagger, told Henrietta that they wanted blood. Suffering the painful grip, she began to fear for her life. When she had come to live on the edge of the heath, one of the old grooms, who loved to tell stories, had told her a host of gruesome tales about the fearsome things that had happened to people who had been on the heath after dark. She would never have believed that such things could happen to her. But one cannot be confronted by four dangerous men and not fear for one's life.

Little by little, she was learning the hard way that most cruel of all lessons—that if she were to survive, she would have to use all her wits to do so. But she guessed she was not going to be good at deception. It did not come naturally to her. She had no experience of it and had never had reason to resort to dishonesty.

Though she held her chin high and glared in a show of grand defiance, she knew she was defenceless. But when she glanced at her captor, big, black and fierce and for all the world like some fearsome being from Hades itself, a strange, murderously tranquil smile on his face, she blanched and, when he released his hold on her arm, she spun around, seeking any escape route. Unable to see a way past the men who had formed a ring around her, there was nowhere to flee. Her heart pounded. The man called Jack reached out to try to grab her, and Henrietta reacted in self-defence, reaching for the knife in her belt, the blade flashing wickedly in the moonlight. Jack fell back with a garbled curse.

'Why, you young pup, I'll gut you for that.'

'Try it if you want my blade in your own,' she replied with admirable self-possession, pitching her voice low, while inside she was trembling with terror, knowing she would never have the courage to use the weapon.

Simon looked her over. It was clear the lad could take care of himself, but he was insane if he thought he could take on the lot of them. He held out his hand. 'That's a nasty blade you have there, lad. Hand it over.'

Henrietta's eyes were wide, filled with fright. She swept the surrounding men with a nervous glance. 'And get myself killed?'

'You're already in trouble and you can see you can't escape. Don't make this any worse for yourself than it already is.'

She wetted her lips with a nervous flick of her tongue and again eyed the men. 'But they—'

'I'm the one you'd better worry about,' he warned in a low voice. 'Give me the knife,' he coolly ordered. 'And do that very slowly, for I am not at all amused.'

Henrietta grimaced at the man's unintentional pun, but she did not relinquish her weapon.

He waited immovably, the men looking on in

palpable tension as the fierce youth dared refuse Simon's order.

Simon flicked his fingers impatiently, beckoning her to hand the knife over—he stretched out his waiting palm, watching her intently. 'Hand it over,' he said in a hard tone. 'You've got no choice.'

Henrietta agonised over the decision, the war of emotions transparent on her face, but after a long moment, she slowly yielded, handing it over.

Simon clasped the weapon and thrust it into his belt. 'There. That wasn't so difficult, was it? Take my advice, my fine bandit, and study your craft more. You are a most inferior footpad.'

Henrietta found herself meeting dark eyes set in a face of leanly fleshed cheekbones. There was a cleft in his strong chin, his nose was thin and well formed, slightly aquiline, and beneath it were generous, but at the moment unsmiling, lips. There was an air of the professional soldier about him, a quality that displayed itself in his crisp manner and rather austere mien. The handsome features bore the look of good breeding and those eyes, glinting with a sardonic expression and blue, she thought, seemed capable of piercing to her innermost secrets, causing a chill of fear to go through her.

'For pity's sake! Do not kill me,' she pleaded,

having no idea of the kind of men she was dealing with.

An evil laugh was the answer. 'No witness—that's the first rule in this business.'

'Who—who are you?' Henrietta demanded, feeling most uneasy.

Simon raised his eyebrows at her question. 'Who am I? I might ask the same question of you—and with considerably more justification.' He looked the youth over disapprovingly, taking in every detail of his clothes. His eyes quickened as he studied him with the keen glance of a man accustomed to noting the minutest detail around him. The lad was no country boy, though he might dress like one. His voice gave him away. Simon was secretly intrigued. 'Explain what you're doing here, lad. Why the devil are you wandering about the countryside by yourself?'

'That's my business.'

Simon's eyes gleamed coldly in the darkness. 'Not any more.' The hard line of his mouth tightened and the crease at the corner grew deeper. 'The person who sent you cannot have done so merely for the pleasure of visiting the heath after dark.'

'Why should you think anyone sent me?'

He stared at her intently. 'If you are indeed here on a mission, the most likely supposition is that you're an agent. But whose? Did you follow us here?'

'No, I swear I didn't. I—I saw the light and I was curious.'

'Perhaps you are on a mission, which argues a high devotion to duty, and I must congratulate whomever employs you on their ability to inspire it.'

Henrietta stared at him, beginning to realise what he was implying and that he was accusing *her* of spying on *them*. 'No one employs me. I work for no one.'

'And we are to believe that?' Jack grumbled. 'What are you running away from, lad? Maybe the law, eh? Likely you're a thief, I shouldn't wonder.'

To hear herself accused of theft was more than Henrietta could bear. 'I am no thief,' she retorted fiercely with a fine and cultured accent, 'and I forbid you to insult me!'

'Forbid? Listen to me, laddie, you're in no position to *forbid* anything. I'd watch that tongue of yours if I were you. There's nothing to stop me taking you by the scruff and tossing you in the river.'

Henrietta was too angry to be frightened. 'If you wish to throw me in the river, feel free to do so. You will be doing me a service. I regret that I was mistaken in you. I took you for a spy. It seems, however, that you are a murderer!'

'Hell and damnation!' Jack, seething with fury, was about to throw himself at the insolent young pup, but Simon cast himself bodily between them and thrust him back.

'Let it be, Jack. Can't you see he's only a lad? He's scarce out of breeches.' He turned to Henrietta and gradually his stern visage softened as he stared at the worried figure. When a smile tugged at the corners of his mouth, he quelled it as quickly as it came. 'I'm sorry, lad. My friends are a long way from home. I fear their manners need as much improvement as their judgement. How old are you?'

'Old enough to know what's what,' she replied sullenly. 'Not that it's any of your concern. I have not asked you questions—but after what I overheard, I imagine there are people who would be extremely interested in what you are about. Unpatriotic activities, they would say, of which gathering support for Prince Charles Edward Stuart, Young Pretender to the throne, is one.'

Simon nodded slightly. 'You heard right. We meet in secret. 'Tis dangerous for us to meet like this.' He glanced at his silent friends who remained motionless. 'You must understand,' he went on, 'that if you fear for your skin, you will keep your mouth shut.'

'And if I don't?'

Anger glinted for a moment in Simon's eyes, then receded. 'It would be a dirty deed I would have to undertake—regrettable since you are but a lad—on that you must accept my word. What have you to say?'

Henrietta bit her lip, the words sticking in her throat. The men gathered before her, silent and antagonistic as they awaited her response.

Chapter Two

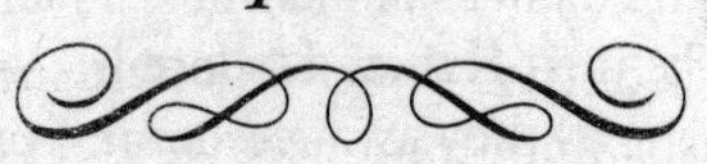

Henrietta's eyes flashed defiance as she held Simon's stare. There was a self-assurance about him which was unmarred by arrogance. It inspired her confidence and she relented.

'You have my word that I shall not speak of what I overheard. I have my own reasons for remaining silent.'

He nodded, satisfied. 'That is all that I shall say on the matter.'

'Thank you. When your friends turned up I was about to go on my way, but I was afraid of what you would do to me if you heard me.'

'So if you aren't a spy, what are you doing here?' Simon demanded.

She gave him a scowl that suggested he mind his own business, but then thought better of it. With four angry men glaring at her, she was in no position to argue. 'I'm going to my uncle.

I—I've moved out of the house of the people I was living with.'

'Do they know where you are?' Simon watched the youngster thoughtfully.

'They'd turn over in their graves if they did,' she answered quietly.

'I see,' Simon said, beginning to understand her plight. 'And your uncle? Where does he live?'

'In Scotland.'

'That's one hell of a journey for a lad to undertake alone.'

'I have no choice. There—are reasons why I have to leave London.'

'You make it sound like a matter of life or death.'

'It is.'

She shivered and sent a furtive glance over her shoulder, as though expecting something terrible to materialise out of the darkness, her gaze scanning the impenetrable blackness among the trees, cocking her head, as if listening for something, some far-off noise.

Simon was sorely tempted to dismiss her remark as wild exaggeration, but by rights he could not do so unless he had a chance to delve into the matter. His gaze softened at the lad's plight and he instantly suffered a pang of compassion. He couldn't be any older than fifteen and he didn't think he had known much kindness. He reminded him for all the world of some little prey animal, his preternatural senses alerted to the imperceptible sound of some fierce predator's approach. His curiosity for this unfortunate youth was beginning to grow.

'Do you have a name?'

Henrietta squirmed uneasily and glanced around her.

'You do have a name, don't you?' Simon enquired with a hint of sarcasm.

A brief, reluctant nod gave him an affirmative answer. 'Henry,' she prevaricated evenly. 'My name is Henry.' There—her first lie. It wasn't so bad.

Fixing her eyes on the man's face, she studied him as much as she was able in the moonlight. She had heard him say he was to go to Scotland. Hope surged up in her. He was on a mission—a dangerous one, too, if what she had heard was to be believed—and could not be too particular in the matter of formalities. For her, this meant safety, luck beyond hope which she could not afford to lose. If he were willing to take her with him, she was prepared to offer any service she was capable of giving—within reason, that was—in exchange for a helping hand.

Henrietta became set on a course of action and, in spite of a very reasonable fear of rejection, she continued. She was on a tightrope with an obligation to move forward, not backwards. Having come this far, she had to speak the words she had rehearsed in her head.

'Since you are to go to Scotland, will you take me with you?' She had no qualms about making the request. She was desperate. Overwhelmed by a sense of her own audacity, she braced herself for rejection.

Simon stared into her hope-filled eyes, thought of his vital secret mission, and let out a sigh. 'No.' He shook his head. 'Absolutely not.'

'But why?'

'Because it's a mad idea.'

'No, it's not.'

'Yes, it is. I might be about to let you go, but I have no intention of playing nursemaid to a quick-tempered lad.'

Undeterred, Henrietta took a step towards him, her chin jutting belligerently. 'I'm past the stage of being in need of a nursemaid. I can take care of myself. You're going to Scotland anyway—I heard you say so. At least if you take me with you, you'll know your secret is safe.'

His eyes narrowed on her expectant face. 'That sounds like blackmail to me.'

Henrietta allowed herself a smile. 'Not really, but I suppose it must look like that from your position.' Her smile faded. 'I do know that the content of your discussion can be classed as a treasonous act for which all of you could be hanged if caught. But I don't care who you are and what you are about is your business. All I know is that I stand a better chance of reaching Scotland unmolested if I do not travel alone.'

Jack stepped forward, not at all happy about the lad's suggestion. 'Don't be swayed, Simon. Think about it. Time is a luxury you can't afford. The lad will hold you back.'

'You're right.' He looked at the youth, his expression uncompromisingly hard. 'As I said, it's out of the question. I've important matters to take care of and I've no desire to saddle myself with a troublesome lad. Now away with you. Think yourself lucky we're letting you go with your life.'

Henrietta went on her way across the heath, heading towards Highgate, feeling angry and mortified as well as bitterly disappointed. Everything that had happened to her seemed so improbable. She had, to be sure, a little money, but so very little it would not enable her to subsist for more than two weeks. She had her jewels, but they were not worth very much. Of sentimental value since the pearl necklace had been her mother's and the rest given to her over time by Aunt Dorothy, she would be most reluctant to part with them.

* * *

It was way past dawn when she reached Hatfield, thankfully without mishap. Saddle-sore and starving hungry, there was a weariness in her eyes as she dismounted and pushed her woollen cloak back over one shoulder. Leading her horse, with her mind on finding something to eat, she walked along the street, glancing into alehouses as she went. Never having entered such establishments, she was reluctant to do so now.

Was it only yesterday that Jeremy had turned up at the house? It seemed an eternity since she had left. It had needed only a few hours to make her first an outraged young woman because of the injustice meted out to her by Jeremy and now a fugitive who would soon be hunted down by that same man when he discovered the truth about his uncle's will. She prayed he wouldn't think of looking for her north of the border. But when she thought of Jeremy, who had treated her so cruelly, no remorse troubled her mind.

With an effort of will, she drove out these gloomy thoughts. She was young and strong and determined with all the force that was within her to overcome the malign fate which dogged her and to do that, it was necessary to remain in possession of her wits for the long trek to Scotland. Tethering her horse to a post, she glanced about her warily, feeling terribly conspicuous in her masculine garb.

There was a bustle in the street as the town was coming to life. An assortment of rustic-looking folk went about their business. A loud curse made her jump swiftly aside and she waited as a couple of huge, plodding horses, their foam-flecked sides heaving, drew a large wagon piled high with casks. Intent on staying out of their path she heedlessly stepped backwards into a loitering group of youths. Their presence was first noted when a voice called loudly, 'Young fool! Look where you're going.'

Spinning round in alarm, she stared at the youths, the eldest of whom was about sixteen. He stepped in front of her, his feet spread, his thumbs hooked in his belt and a tattered hat askew on an untidy thatch of brown hair. He towered over her, looking her over suspiciously.

'Can't say I know you. What you doing here?' he demanded boldly.

'I—I'm just passing through,' she nervously stammered, lowering her voice to fit in with her masculine attire. Uncertain and dismayed at this unexpected confrontation, she glanced uneasily towards the others who were circling around her. For the most part, they seemed only to be seeking some diversion from boredom. She could not be too careful and sought to make them more cautious.

'I'm supposed to be meeting someone—my uncle,' she lied in an attempt to make them back away. 'He—he should be here…' Her voice trailed off and she looked around expectantly.

One of the youths laughed loudly and gave Henrietta's shoulder a shove. 'Hope he'll come to your rescue, do you?'

Hands seeming to come from every direction reached out to shove and push. The next instant her hat was snatched from her head, baring a mop of shaggily cropped hair. Henrietta threw her hands over her head, at the same time opening her mouth to vent her outrage. For some reason she thought better of it and clamped her jaw shut, angrily making a grab for her hat, only to see it passed from one to the other. Incensed, she stood there with her fists clenched, refusing to show her fear. 'Give me back my hat and I'll be on my way.'

Immediately one of the youths shoved her shoulder and she found herself stumbling backwards, but not before she'd made another grab for her hat as it went sailing through the air. Jamming it on to her head, she glowered at them, ready to do battle if they attempted to take it again. Her jaw slackened as she stared amazed by the sight of the three youths suddenly backing off and pressing themselves against the wall.

A tall figure in a swirling black cloak strode into their midst. Large and powerful, a cocked hat set jauntily sideways on his head, she recognised him as the man Simon she had met on the heath the previous night. Henrietta was more unsettled than she was prepared to show by his sudden appearance. Now, in broad daylight, he bore a striking resemblance to the pirates whose exploits she had relished when safely between the covers of a book. This man had no black patch over his eye or gold rings in his ears, but these details apart, he seemed the living image of a gentleman of fortune.

'On your way, the lot of you,' he barked, brushing them aside as best he could. 'I'm sure there must be chores to occupy you other than abusing others.'

He watched the scrambling departure of the youths before turning to the individual who found herself meeting eyes of deep blue set in a hard and unsmiling face.

'I thought it was you,' Simon remarked sharply. 'You appear to be in a spot of bother.'

Henrietta's heart lurched in her breast. She was torn between resentment because he'd refused to let her go with him to Scotland and relief that he'd rescued her from possible harm at the hands of the three youths.

Observing the lad's expression of concern, Simon said, 'You need to watch lads like that. They clamour around and then they'll suddenly disappear—along with your purse. I don't doubt that half of them will end up dangling on the end of a hangman's rope one day. I was about to get myself a bite to eat. Would you care to join me?'

Having recovered her composure, Henrietta raised cool, bright eyes holding more than a measure of distrust to his. She hadn't forgiven him for abandoning her on the heath. Having witnessed her humiliation at the hands of those louts, he was infuriatingly sublime in his amusement. If her situation weren't so dire, she'd cheerfully tell him to go to the devil.

'You don't have to do that,' she replied sullenly. 'My mother told me never to talk to strangers.'

'Your mother was right, but you were happy to talk to me last night when you thought I could be of use.'

'That was last night. Things look different in daylight. I don't want any handouts.'

'I wasn't offering to pay for your breakfast. I merely thought you might like some company, but it seems I was mistaken. The least you could do is thank me for getting you out of a scrape.'

'I didn't ask you to,' she retorted ungraciously. 'I can take care of myself.'

'Is that so?' His eyes did a quick sweep of the small, slight form in ill-fitting garb before him, noting the pathetically shorn hair of an indeterminate colour and badly stained breeches. There was an air and manner about him that held his attention. 'By the looks of you someone needs to take you in hand.' His jaw set squarely, he turned away. The lad was proving to be a headache. And yet…those snapping green eyes…the soft mouth and curve to the cheek…

Simon! an inner voice commanded. *Enough! It will be your downfall if you pursue this train of thought.*

It was indeed enough—but even so he found himself turning back. He glanced at her horse. 'Get your horse and come with me if you want some breakfast—before those young ruffians come back and finish what they started.'

Turning on his heel and leading his horse, he headed for the back of the nearest inn. Racked with indecision, Henrietta glared at his retreating broad back, the hollow ache in her middle reminding her how hungry she was. Seeing her three abusers loitering on the street corner still eyeing her with malicious intent, though it chafed her to do so she grabbed her horse's bridle and hurried after him.

Leaving her mount to be fed and watered in the tavern's stable, she was almost treading on his heels when he crossed the threshold into the large and welcoming common room. It was adorned with gleaming copper and brass with a number of tables disposed around the room. A good fire burned in the hearth and a number of serving girls tripped about bearing loaded trays.

There was a stir of interest among them when their eyes lighted on Simon's handsome form and their eyes boldly appraised him. His expression softened as his gaze swept over one of them—a pretty young girl, her loosely laced bodice barely containing her ripe breasts—and he inclined his head in the briefest of bows. The way he regarded them told Henrietta that this was a man who enjoyed female company. From the flirtatious fluttering of the women's eyelashes, it was obvious they had fallen prey to his charm.

'What it is to be so popular,' Henrietta commented without bothering to conceal her sarcasm as she followed him across the room.

'Being reasonably handsome—or so I've been told—has its advantages, Henry.' There was something about the amused tilt of his eyebrows, the way the serving girls melted a pathway before him and the sudden mischievous twinkle in his eyes that made her laugh.

'And I have no doubt many of the ladies surround you like moths around a candle.'

The liquid blue of his eyes deepened. 'Many moths, but no butterflies—and I have to say that I am not partial to moths.'

The landlady of the inn paused in her work to watch the two cross the room where they settled at a table in the shadow of the wide chimneypiece, where they ordered breakfast and cold beer.

'You've ridden quite a distance,' Simon said, removing his hat and cloak and dropping them on the seat beside him.

Reluctantly Henrietta did the same before sitting back and availing herself of the chance to take account of her companion. His vigour seemed to fill the room with such robust masculine virility that it took her breath, because she had grown accustomed to a life with her guardian, a diminutive older man. Her gaze leisurely observed his lean yet muscular thighs and she allowed it to wander upwards over his breeches to his narrow waist and powerful shoulders, her eyes settling on his dark features. He had nothing wanting in looks or bearing. He wore a blue jacket and black breeches above his riding boots and his tumble of raven-black glossy curls was secured at the nape.

Settling back in his seat, his long, lean body

was stretched out at the table pushed slightly forward to accommodate his long legs. But there was nothing ungraceful about him. The muscles of his arms and legs were sinewy and strong, and finely honed. He regarded her with some amusement, smiling, his teeth very white against the tanned flesh of his face, but there was a disturbing glint in his blue eyes.

She noticed that he was studying her with intent and she was aware of the tension and nervousness in herself. Of course anyone else might have seen past her disguise and laid bare her secret, but with this man, she could only surmise that he was contemplating the disgusting state of her shaggy hair—the soot she had rubbed in to darken it having run and stained her face—and dirty breeches. She avoided his eye and vowed to remember her false identity at all costs. So far there had been no hostility in his voice when he addressed her and she must take care not to raise his suspicions. As a man of the world, he would be familiar with the subtle differences in bone structure between men and women, and he might have noticed that she was abnormal. If he did, fortunately he did not press the matter.

Simon idly watched the serving wenches go about their business, his eyes lighting on a particularly buxom redhead giving him the eye. His mind turned over possibilities and began sketching scenarios in which he would take her somewhere private where their coming together would end in some climatic terminal.

Thoughts of climaxes brought vivid, full-colour visions of Theresa to mind, the last woman he had made love to in the twilight of her father's French garden—her heavy breasts perfectly round, her face beneath his washed by his kisses, eyes closing tight in pleasure, then opening again to look with delight into his, her mouth stretched wide in a permanent gasp of pleasure. The daughter of a French nobleman, she had meant nothing to him and had receded into the past like so many before her. Still, she had been a beauty all right and he would probably never see her again.

He did not normally permit himself the indulgence of sentiment. There was in his nature a very cold streak and he cultivated it because it protected him. And now, with a rising and rebellion imminent, it was imperative that he did not relax his vigilance. But he was restless, cursing the imagination which sent him thoughts the like of which he had not suffered since he had left Theresa. But he often thought the imaginings were so much better than the disappointing real thing.

His relationships with the fair sex often left him puzzled—where was the blinding ecstasy that came with the mystical fusion of two bodies into one? He was a good lover, he had been told. He found sex interesting, as well as physically pleasant. He rarely had to seduce a woman—for some women he was a highly desirable man—and the thrill of conquest was not what he wanted. He was also an expert at giving and receiving sexual gratification. But over time he had formed the view that ecstasy came not from a man's pleasure in a woman, but from their pleasure in each other, which was something that seemed to elude him.

Shifting his gaze from the serving wench, he studied his young companion more closely. With short hair and small heart-shaped face accentuating the large green eyes and slim, fragile features and high delicate cheekbones, the youth looked much younger than he had originally thought.

'We shall have refreshments and discuss what I see lurking in the depths of those eyes of yours.'

Simon waited for Henry to make the opening gambit. But it seemed his expectations would come to naught for Henry volunteered nothing of himself. 'Since we are to eat together, we might as well get better acquainted,' he said in an attempt to draw the lad out of himself. 'My name's Simon Tremain. I already know you are called Henry. Your family name eludes me?'

Henrietta met his gaze and immediately the shutters came down over her eyes and her expression became guarded. She had the uneasy thought that her companion was like a tall, predatory hawk and that she was a small, disadvantaged animal about to be pounced on. 'That's because I didn't tell you,' she retorted, not wishing to become too familiar with an active Jacobite whose sympathies were akin to those of her father.

He, too, had been a Jacobite agent, and his scheming and conspiracies against King George had led him to the gallows, leaving his wife and Henrietta to carry the burden of that crime of treason. Nothing would ever lessen the deep bitterness she felt towards the Jacobites. It was a bitterness that burned inside her with an all-consuming intensity. Henrietta didn't like talking about herself, especially not with strangers. Andrew Brody was a name remembered and still talked about by many.

Simon's curiosity increased. He arched a brow and peered at his companion, shrugging casually. 'Just curious.'

'You ask too many questions.'

'It's a habit of mine. You do have one, don't you?'

When Henry made no further comment Simon did not pursue it. But with this in mind he looked again at the lad and felt drawn to him. He sat erect, his small chin in his heart-shaped face raised, and Simon could see him putting up a valiant fight for control—a fight he won. Despite his ragged garb he looked incongruously like a proud young prince, his eyes sparkling like twin jewels. Simon's granite features softened and his eyes warmed, as if he understood how humiliated the lad felt on being brought low by a situation that had obviously driven him from his home.

'I ask your pardon, Henry. It was not my intention to intrude on your privacy. Being a private person myself, I respect it in others, so you can relax. You were serious when you said you were going to Scotland? To your uncle, I believe you said.'

Henrietta nodded.

'Where in Scotland does he live?'

'Some miles from Inverness. It's—quite inhospitable, I believe.'

'I believe it is.'

They fell silent when the landlady arrived at their table, skilfully balancing a huge tray on one hand. She placed the steaming plates of eggs and ham and wedges of warm bread and butter and freshly made succulent fruit tarts before them, telling them to enjoy their meal. Unable to override the demands of hunger before the landlady had retreated from their table, Henrietta began munching on the bread, savouring the delicious taste. Simon watched her in amusement until the object of his scrutiny became aware of his attention. Suddenly abashed, she slowed down. Simon laughed, then turned his interest to his own breakfast.

Henrietta hadn't eaten since dinner time the previous day and ate heartily at first, but once her hunger was satisfied, she ate slowly while her companion consumed his portions more leisurely, savouring each taste fully. She felt much better after the meal and, with warmth and nourishment having restored some measure of elasticity to muscles chilled and stiffened by hours on horseback, a gentle drowsiness crept over her and slowly her eyelids began to droop.

When Simon had finished his meal, he wiped his mouth on a napkin and once more fixed his attention on the youth. His head had fallen forward and his eyes were closed. Clearly the long ride was beginning to take its toll. He frowned. The more they were together, the more curious he became about his young companion. He'd already decided that he was a young person of no ordinary cleverness and intelligence. He noted that he ate much too daintily for a street urchin and there was a refined quality to his speech and in his manner that did not tie in with his outward appearance. His breeches and shirt were of poor quality, the breeches having seen much service, and his hair and face were clearly in need of soap and water. Yet his boots and cloak were of good quality and he had also noted that his horse was no ordinary nag, but a valuable blood horse, clearly out of the stables of a gentleman.

'What—or whom—are you running away from?' he asked suddenly.

All at once Henrietta's eyes snapped open and she sat up with a start, wide awake on the instant. 'Who said I was running away?'

'You did—on the heath?'

After a moment and lowering her eyes, Henrietta nodded. 'I am obliged to go to Scotland.'

'And it's a matter of life or death, if I remember correctly.' She nodded. 'Like to tell me about it?' he said, ignoring what he had said about intruding on her privacy.

She shook her head. 'I'd rather not talk about it.' If he were to find out her true identity she wouldn't be able to deal with the repercussions, and after her unpleasant encounter with those youths, she realised she had a better chance of reaching Scotland with this man to protect her—if he could be persuaded to take her with him.

'And your parents?'

'A hint of tears brightened the light green eyes as she spoke. 'Both my parents are dead.'

Simon felt a pang of pity for the lad. 'I'm sorry.'

The sympathy in his voice made her study him. He had a warmth of manner which made her feel as if she had known him a long time, and she decided she liked him. 'Don't be. It was a long time ago.'

'But you still miss them.' She nodded. 'Well, you'd best eat up if we're to reach Scotland.'

Henrietta's eyes shot to his. 'Are you saying that you'll let me travel with you?'

Simon's mouth softened into a lazy smile. He amused him, this youth. Simon smiled at the confidence he displayed in front of him. It flowed out of him. As he met the green eyes he saw the eagerness there. 'I'm thinking about it. But if you lag behind I won't think twice about abandoning you. Is that clear?'

At once, Henrietta felt her spirits revive. Now that he'd agreed to let her travel with him, hope and courage returned and she was able to fight with all her strength against the insidious counsels of despair. The prospect of being alone with him made her shudder, but, she reasoned, the protection of such a man while ever she was on the road would be invaluable. She refused to think this man might do her harm.

'Thank you. I am grateful,' she said, remembering her manners, unable to conceal her excitement. 'I will not dawdle. I cannot afford to. I can ride as well as the next—man. I could even act as your squire—or whatever term you care to use—and do it well. I will not be a burden. But if you think you've got something to fear from a defenceless youth, well, sir, you'd just better not hire me. And how do you know I'm not a thief who will rob you blind when I get the chance?'

Simon laughed aloud at the youth's audacity. 'Call it intuition. I like your spirit. I trust you, Henry.' He'd already come to the conclusion that the lad was as blunt and honest a youth as he'd met in a long time—and twice as unkempt. He was also beginning to think Henry could be completely exasperating, yet there was something about him that was likeable, too.

'I expect you'll be suggesting wages next.'

Her eyes brightened. 'We could discuss it. How much will you pay me?'

'Nothing. Meals all found along the way. Take it or leave it.'

'I'll take it—and I'll pay for my own bed. I like my privacy and have a penchant for sleeping in my own room.'

Simon's lips quirked. 'I don't snore, if that's what you're afraid of.'

'Never crossed my mind. As I said, I prefer my own room.'

'That's settled, then,' Simon said, half-amused. 'But you'd better be worth it. I can only hope you know what you're in for. It's only fair to warn you that it's going to be a long haul to Scotland and many things could happen that you may not like. However,' he said on a more serious note, 'I find I must place one stricture on the pact.'

Henrietta glanced at him obliquely. 'And that is?'

'That until we reach Scotland you will speak to no one of what you overheard on the heath.'

'I thought I'd already given you my word on that.'

He nodded. 'I just wanted to make sure.'

Henrietta nodded, drawn to him by his sheer physical presence. For a moment she felt her resistance waver, but then she rebuked herself, bringing her mind to a grinding halt. For her peace of mind she must not let him get beneath her guard. She was grateful to him for agreeing to let her travel with him, but how long could she hope to hide her identity behind the guise of a grubby youth?

'And while we're at it,' he went on, 'have you not thought of cleaning yourself up?'

Henrietta's jaw clenched with indignation. 'Show me the way to Scotland and I'll be grateful. But keep me out of your plans. Untidiness and a little dirt never hurt anyone.'

The buxom redhead who had caught Simon's eye earlier came to clear the table, a provocative smile on her lips when her eyes settled on him. 'Will there be anything else, sir? More ale?'

'No, thank you. The food was good,' Simon replied, giving her a wink and returning her smile. Getting up from the table, he chuckled softly as the girl picked up the plates and went on her way, her hips swaying seductively from side to side. He glanced at his companion. 'Tell me, Henry, have you known the love of a maid? Is that what takes you to Scotland?'

Henrietta's eyes opened wide with indignation at the very suggestion. 'No, of course not.'

'No, you are still young. Whatever takes you there is not for the love of a maid.'

'How do you know?' she asked him, making no further attempt at denial.

'One's only to look at your eyes, lad. Not a spark of love in them. Take my advice and keep it that way. Women are every man's downfall and there are too many that are any good for the peace of honest lads like you and me. When I looked into your eyes just now, I saw just one thing. Fear! That's why I've decided to take you to Scotland. I've no truck with love. I came to the conclusion a long time ago that it's a waste of time. But fear! There's some sense in that. Now come. I'm at your service. I believe,' he said thoughtfully, 'that you and I shall deal favourably together.'

Donning his cloak and ramming his hat down on his head, he set off out of the inn with long, purposeful strides, leaving Henrietta to ponder on his words. After a moment she followed him, still wondering why this man who for all the world resembled a pirate and was capable of instilling fear into even the stoutest heart, should fill her with such instinctive trust.

Hoisting herself into the saddle with an agility that both astounded and impressed Simon, Henrietta gritted her teeth and steeled herself for the ride ahead, refusing to betray her trepidation, for she could only imagine the great distance they would have to travel before they reached their destination.

Henrietta's stout-hearted mare matched Simon's big black gelding stride for stride as they headed north. The road was wide and busy with travellers going north and south, some on foot and some on horseback, and the guards on the back of stagecoaches frequently blew their horns merrily as they went by.

But as the day drew on the journey began to take its toll of Henrietta. She tried not to let her companion see it, but she was exhausted with fatigue and her inner thighs were so sore that she felt as if she would never ride again. She could hardly remember the girl who would ride almost daily in the park, cantering on her horse. That girl was a lifetime away from her now.

As it grew dark they were approaching a large village which likely meant a good inn, a decent supper and a soft bed. Dismounting carefully, she ruefully rubbed her bruised posterior and wished she could groan her misery out loud and sink her tortured body into a hot tub. Averse to revealing any hint of her waning strength, she managed to drag her stiff and aching limbs forward with a modicum of dignity, which, as Simon observed her discomfort, brought a mocking grin to his lips.

'Sore, are you, lad? Too soft, that's your trouble. But worry not.' He chuckled infuriatingly, dismounting and handing the reins to a waiting stable boy. 'You'll harden before you reach the Borders,' he said, offering his wisdom freely.

'Or expire in the process,' Henrietta mumbled, having no difficulty imagining how pathetic she must look to him.

'If you would allow me to offer my assistance, I have some salve in my bags I could massage—'

'No, I couldn't possibly!' Aware of the colour flooding her cheeks, Henrietta shook her head.

'What's the matter, Henry? Afraid to pull

your breeches down in case I confiscate them?' Simon leisurely raised a questioning eyebrow.

Irritably Henry gave him a narrow look. 'No. I'm capable of doctoring myself if need be, that's all.'

Simon shrugged nonchalantly. 'Suit yourself, though I guess when a lad is as soft as you are, he might just as well take to wearing dresses.'

'Will you stop fussing about my looks?' she retorted crossly. 'I made the first day without complaint, didn't I?'

Slinging his bag over his shoulder, Simon smiled sardonically. He was becoming used to Henry's contrariness, but in view of the lad's youth, he translated it more as bravado. 'You did, Henry. The challenge will come in the morning when your muscles have stiffened up.' He glanced sideways at her, a devilish gleam in his eyes. 'We'll see how you fare then. Come tomorrow night you might be begging me for that salve.'

Henrietta wouldn't ask him for his precious salve no matter how desperate she became. Refusing to let him bait her, she bit back an indignant reply. Looking up at him, she saw his face in the deep dusk and the soft yellow glow of the buttons on his jacket as they reflected the light from the window of the inn. It sometimes surprised her just how handsome he was. Self-consciously she tugged down the brim of her hat and followed him inside. The contrast between them was excruciatingly painful when she allowed herself to forget that he was a man on a mission and she a young woman.

The inn was, in fact, commodious. Simon procured them two rooms, but before Henrietta had finished her meal, the effects of the warm fire and wholesome food began to take its toll. Her head nodded with weariness and her eyelids drooped. She had not realised until then the depth of her fatigue.

Relaxed into the corner of the settle across from her, his long booted legs stretched out to the hearth, Simon was not unaware of her exhaustion. Beneath the grime of the road her face was flushed to a soft pink glow and her eyes two sleepy orbs of emerald-green.

'It's been a long day,' he said softly. 'You look done in.'

'Yes, it has. Tomorrow will be no different.'

'Nor the day after that.'

Simon watched her comb her hair back from her face. Suddenly the lad looked so young, vulnerable and completely innocent, despite his air of bravado.

Henrietta looked up to see him staring at her, and when their eyes met, he looked away quickly. From that moment on she grew even more aware of his nearness to her. She sneaked a glance at him from under her lashes and saw that his face was flushed. It was the fire, she thought, because he was sitting so close, or perhaps a result of the ale he'd downed so quickly.

'Go to bed and get some rest while you can,' Simon said sharply. 'I'll give you a knock in the morning.'

Henrietta nodded. Bone-weary, having shied away from Simon's practical suggestion that they share one room, she went to bed and was soon drifting into the realms of sleep.

The sun was not yet up when she was cruelly wakened by the sound of someone banging on the door. Shaking the sleep out of her eyes and struggling into her clothes and boots, she opened the door to find her companion standing there.

'It's late,' he told her, his manner brisk. He was impatient to be on his way. 'Come and get some breakfast and then we'll get going.'

Mutely Henrietta followed him, aching in every limb from the effects of the long ride the day before. Snatching a quick breakfast, they continued their journey.

The sky was overcast, but it was not raining, and towards noon the sun beat down on them. Henrietta pulled a handkerchief from her pocket and mopped her face and neck, wiping away the dust. She shifted her weight in the saddle to ease her discomfort. The day was just like the one before, and the one before that. Apart from the occasional stop to eat and quench their thirst Simon gave her no respite. Not that she complained, for she was determined to show him she could stand the pace.

Though it gave her some assurance that he had not yet guessed her secret, she wondered if all he saw was the dirt on her face and ill-fitting clothes, for it was there his criticism thrived. He could not know, of course, the effort she took to smudge her face and hair every morning when he threatened to dunk her in the river and scrub her clean himself. As uncomfortable as she was in her disguise as a boy, she was unable to discard it.

The further north they got the quieter the roads. It was midafternoon and they had paused beside a stream to eat some bread and cheese they had bought at the last village they had passed through. Henrietta had removed her boots and was dangling her feet in the cold water as she ate, scooping water into her hands to drink every now and then.

When they were back in the saddle Simon broached a subject she would have preferred avoiding. Instead of setting off at a gallop he was silent and thoughtful as he kept his horse's prancing pace attuned to Henrietta's steadier gait. Then, thoughtfully, he turned and looked at her.

In the course of their journey, despite his assertion that he would respect his privacy, Simon had done his best to discover why the youth was hell-bent on going to Scotland, but with a skill beyond his years Henry had managed to avoid giving more than vague, generalised answers, remaining reserved in his friendliness towards him, leaving him no wiser than he had been at the beginning of their journey. In truth, he was concerned about what would happen to him when they reached Edinburgh and they had to part company. Without his protection he would be prey to all manner of dangers that beset lone travellers.

'When we reach Edinburgh and we go our separate ways, I can arrange for an escort to accompany you to Inverness.'

'Thank you for your concern, Simon, but I beg you not to worry. I am grateful that you have allowed me to travel with you, but I am fairly self-sufficient and able to take care of myself the rest of the way. You owe me nothing and I will take nothing from you.'

'You never did tell me why you were running away.'

'I have no wish to involve you in something that is not your concern. You have problems of your own to worry about.' She was as determined to remain silent as he was to drag it out of her. She had her pride and her reasons, which she would not discuss with him.

Simon sighed heavily. 'You are a stubborn lad, Henry.'

'The same could be said about you,' she said, directing the conversation from herself. 'All this time we have been together, not once have you let your guard down.'

'Not intentionally I assure you. My mind is somewhat occupied with what might be going on over the border.' He looked across at his companion. 'Unlike you, Henry, I have nothing to hide. What would you like to know?'

She shrugged. 'In truth, I haven't thought about it.'

'Well, I will begin by telling you that I was educated at a school in France which attracts children of Catholic families in England and Scotland. After that I trained in military arts and saw service abroad.'

'Do you have a wife?'

Almost immediately his gaze shifted once

more to the slight figure riding beside him. 'I do not.'

'So you are a bachelor and a soldier. That is a lot more than I knew a moment ago. And now?'

'Now I follow the dictates of my religion and my conscience.'

'Which is a dangerous thing to do.'

'In this present climate it is so. But I am always slow to voice my opinion. In this time of persecution against Catholics in England, since the king and his ministers have not the slightest intention of toleration for the old faith, it is prudent to be diligent, which is why we Tremains have kept our titles and our land. Few families can boast as much.'

She looked at him sharply. 'You have a title?'

Her surprised amused him. 'I'm afraid so.'

'What is it? How should I address you?'

'I am Lord Simon James Talbot Tremain—but I give you leave to continue calling me Simon.'

'So, you are a lord and you have inherited a fortune, yet you are unattached—uncommonly selfish of you.'

'How is that?'

'Having witnessed the way women fall at your feet when you enter a room—'

'That will be tavern wenches,' he interrupted with an amused tilt to his mouth.

Henrietta shrugged. 'What's the difference?

Women are the same the world over and, though it pains me to say so for I have no wish to feed your ego, you are a handsome man. I imagine not a woman in the kingdom will spare the other gentlemen a glance until you have been claimed.'

He cocked an amused brow. 'Why, Henry, what's this? Flattery?'

'No. I was merely stating a fact. But going back to what we were talking about, if the conversation I overheard between you and your fellow Jacobites on the heath is true and Charles Stuart is indeed in Scotland, it can mean only one thing—that some disorder is brewing—that some extraordinary event is anticipated. Is there to be a rising?'

Simon didn't answer straight away—when he did, he spoke thoughtfully, picking his words. 'Nothing is that simple, nothing is obvious. I am assailed with a multitude of questions but I will find no firm answers until I reach Scotland and Charles Stuart.'

'Do you think it will be concentrated in Scotland, if there is a rising?'

'I cannot answer that, but it has to be on a great scale for it to be of effect.'

'Will the Catholics win, do you think?'

Simon's mood had darkened and his expression was grim. Although he looked calm and in control, his mind was in a continual turmoil of conflicts. 'That depends on the support Charles Stuart can raise on both sides of the border.'

'What's he like? Have you met him?'

He nodded. 'He's young, with considerable charm and dignity.'

'And is that enough to bring him to Scotland to lead an army of restoration?'

'As to that, we shall have to wait and see. I was in Paris myself recently and, by and large, the prospect for a Stuart restoration did not seem to be preoccupying the aristocracy of France. One thing is certain. Whatever the outcome, it will bring about change for the Catholics. If it fails, the damage will do the cause no good and will be so great that both here and abroad they will be condemned. Anyone connected with the rising will be arrested. It would be a hard thing indeed to escape the full consequences if we were to be charged with rebellion and treason. Men have lost their heads for less. The Protestants did not scruple to send men to the gallows merely for saying that James Stuart had claim to the throne.'

Henrietta was scarcely able to grasp the reality of it all as Simon's words fell like hammer blows against her heart. Remembering the tragedy that had deprived her of her father, as she stared at Simon's hard profile a chill seemed to penetrate to her very soul. 'Then may the Lord save you all,' she whispered.

The prayer was heartfelt and Simon looked at her closely, seeing pain and panic in the eyes of this unusually assured youth.

'Are you in favour of rebellion, Simon?'

'In a word, no. But I am of the faith and must support it. Catholic fanatics have been conspiring for years to claim the throne for the Stuarts. They have a long tradition of subversive activity.'

Henrietta's lips twisted in a wry smile. 'That I do know,' she uttered quietly, thinking of her father's lifelong dedication to the cause.

Puzzled by her words, Simon glanced across at her. 'What do you mean by that?'

She smiled awkwardly. 'Nothing. I was merely thinking aloud.' She looked ahead. 'See, the clouds are gathering. I'm sure there'll be rain before nightfall.'

'I believe you're right,' he agreed. 'If my words have frightened you, I apologise. It was not my intention to upset you.'

Simon's voice was surprisingly gentle and the unfamiliar sound caused an embarrassed flush to sweep Henrietta's cheeks in a crimson flood. His head was turned towards her and for a moment she fancied there was a strange expression in his face she had not seen before. 'You have not upset me, and do not forget that my sole purpose for going to Scotland is to visit my uncle. But now you have spoken of what might be afoot, I can perceive the danger and act upon it should the time arise.'

'The picture may not be so bleak. I may be wrong.'

'And I am afraid that you may be right,' Henrietta whispered, nudging her horse to a gallop as the first drops of rain began to fall and a gust of wind swept the land.

Chapter Three

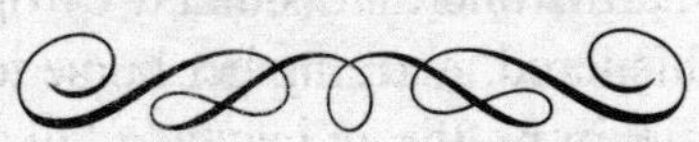

In London, just when he thought that everything he had ever wanted was within his grasp and relishing the thought that he would have his heart's desire at last, a sickening dread invaded Jeremy Lucas's dark soul. He had long coveted his uncle's wealth, but he was impatient. His uncle was in good health and likely to live another score years and ten. He could not wait and in the end he had triumphed and that was all that mattered. Until now. Everything around him had turned sour.

It had never occurred to him that there might be a problem, but on his search of the house, when he failed to locate his uncle's legal documents—his financial papers and deed to the house—he became frantic. His worries increased when Mr Goodwin presented himself at the house and asked to speak to Miss Brody. On being told that he was his uncle's solicitor and the late gentleman's entire estate had been left to Miss Henrietta Brody, without so much as a blink, Jeremy saw to it that the respected solicitor met a timely end at the point of his sword and his body was consigned to a watery grave in the River Thames.

Securing his uncle's documents from Goodwin's satchel and intending to destroy the new will and abide by the old held by Braithwaite, Jeremy stopped when he saw in bold print that the new will had a copy.

Of course there was a copy! Why hadn't he realised that? How could he have been so unfamiliar with legal practices that he had stupidly thought the will in Goodwin's keeping was the only one? But where was it?

Smothering a cry of pure rage, he sought out Braithwaite. After much deliberation they decided there was only one person who could throw some light on the matter and that was Henrietta Brody. She might even have absconded with the copy of the will. He should have searched her before he'd thrown her out on to the street. It was imperative that he got his hands on it before she handed it over to a lawyer and her case was heard in a court of law.

The calm Jeremy had felt after killing Goodwin reasserted itself. Hate welled up inside him as he thought of Henrietta Brody. The name was a curse. He was consumed with a vengeful quest to vent his wrath upon the girl. The chit would pay, and would pay dearly. Of that Jeremy was certain. Where would she go? She had no friends who would take her in and only one relative, an uncle in Scotland—Inverness or somewhere equally as remote. He'd find out. He'd leave no stone unturned to find her.

Simon and his companion had ridden through Northumberland, which lay between the Tyne and the Tweed, its countryside of rivers and forests, where Romans and Normans had left their own particular mark. Mile after mile they rode, over fell and vale, across long ridges to Cheviot and the Solway, where streams and burns meandered in timeless grace. Eventually they crossed the border into Scotland. It was a beautiful landscape of rolling hills which gave way to green and pleasant valleys. The historic abbey towns of Jedburgh, Melrose and Kelso bore witness to the cruelty and senseless destruction brought about by war and political reprisals down the centuries.

Unfortunately the weather, which had been warm and fine for most of the time, broke with an alarming savagery, and since leaving the hostelry where they had stopped for the night, the heavy mists of early morning had coalesced to a soaking rain. Leaden skies pressed down on them and the crude road quickly turned into a muddy morass. On the more exposed areas the gale-force winds went searching along the landscape in a frenzied dance, threatening to blow them off their horses and into the soggy turf alongside.

They pushed their animals hard, apparently attempting to outrun the storm, but the wind blew with an ever-deepening chill that made Henrietta shiver. A bolt of lightning seared the sky, closely followed by a loud clap of thunder. As she glanced at her companion silhouetted like some devil against the grey sky, the wind whipped his cloak out wide about him, lending wings to his form.

A groan of despair slipped from Henrietta's lips as she thumped her heels against the mare's flanks to urge her on in the punishing downpour. The horse responded readily, quickening her pace, but the heavy, wet soil clung to her hooves, impeding her progress. They could barely see, much less move any measurable distance. The journey was already taking its toll on Henrietta. She felt utterly drained both in body and spirit. Her whole body was battered and bruised from the nine days of riding, and now her clothes became so thoroughly drenched that they were soon plastered like a second skin to her body.

Seeing the youth's distress, Simon peered around for the closest haven and, pointing to a group of trees growing close together, he guided the horses towards them. There was another sharp crack of lightning and for a moment the scene was brightly illuminated. Unable to believe that they could be so ill-favoured by the circumstances, Henrietta fought an urge to weep, but the impulse to relent to harsh, anguishing sobs was promptly forgotten as a blinding flash of lightning ripped through the trees, hitting a tall pine a short distance away. The fiery bolt snapped the trunk in half as easily as a dried twig, sending a dazzling spray of sparks flying in all directions. Shaken to the core of her being, Henrietta threw up her arms to shield herself from the blinding flares and, in terrified trepidation, looked up as the top of the tree plummeted to the ground with a crashing roar, in its rapid descent stripping off branches of nearby trees and scuffing a blow on the side of her head.

Before it reached the ground, a deafening crack of thunder seemed to shake the land around them. The mare shivered in terror, letting out an anguished shriek, and heaved herself forward.

Astounded by how closely the youth had come to being permanently singed black by the lightning, Simon's breath left him in a rush as he came quickly to his aid, concerned by the blood trickling down the side of his face. He was trembling uncontrollably, soaked to the very depth of his clothes, straining desperately to bring his mount under control. Reaching out, Simon snatched the bridle. 'Easy, girl,' he murmured in an attempt to sooth the horse. 'Easy.' The mare calmed a trifle, but stood shivering beneath the dripping trees. 'Henry, are you all right?' he shouted to his companion above the noise of the storm.

Though the words seemed no more than a whisper in the pelting torrent, Henrietta's head snapped around. Now fully alert to Simon's presence, which was hardly more than an ominous grey shadow in the rain-shrouded gloom, she lifted a hand to shield her eyes from the downpour. Even so, the moisture dribbling down from her sodden hair forced her repeatedly to blink in an effort to clear her vision. She opened her mouth to speak, but words failed her. Frozen through and deeply affected by what had just happened, her body was all a-tremble.

Shifting his hat forward over his brow, Simon pulled the collar of his cape up close around his neck and swung down to the ground. Wasting no time, he reached up and dragged Henrietta from the saddle. Her strength had vanished, her senses dulled, her wits long fled. Unable to stand, she crumpled to her knees upon the sodden ground. She could no longer force her shaking limbs to perform. All she wanted to do was curl up somewhere, close her eyes and sleep. Drawing herself into a small, disconcerted knot, she hunched her shoulders against the deluge.

Without more ado, Simon's arm slipped beneath her shoulders and a hoarse voice murmured words that failed to penetrate her confusion as his strong, sinewed arms lifted her and held her close against a broad chest. Her head lolled limply against his shoulder and even the fear that another bough would descend on her could not rouse her from her darkening world.

Simon lifted her onto the back of his stallion. Taking the long rein of the mare, he tied it to a metal ring behind the cantle of his saddle. Swinging up behind the trembling form, he clamped a protective arm around her and reined the stallion back out into the open as the mare dutifully followed at the end of her tether.

They rode on for what seemed to be an eternity. Night crept in with its stealthy cloak of darkness. Suddenly a large house seemed to appear from nowhere in the dusk. Through a haze, Henrietta watched the welcome sight of the dark shape of the building come nearer. But at the moment she couldn't be awed by anything. The rain had seemingly spent its furore and dwindled to drizzling mist. Only Simon's arms holding her body stopped her from falling off the horse. She could hear him urging her to stay awake, but his voice sounded hollow and distant. He opened his cloak and pulled her snugly against him. Henrietta found no energy to resist, but rested her head against the solid bulwark. Vaguely she was aware of her body tilting back and her head bumped gently against his broad chest, but a dull ache began to throb there. In the next moments the heavy mists seemed to swirl around her, closing in upon her like a dank tomb, choking off her breath and pulling her down into a dark abyss as a numbing, uncaring oblivion claimed her.

Riding into the stable yard, Simon barked orders to the groom staggering out of the stable to see who it was that commanded attention. On seeing the master he hurried to do his bidding, taking the reins of the two exhausted mounts and holding them steady while his lordship came to ground with a single bound and dragged the inert form of a youth after him. Carrying him into the house, Simon strode through the hall as Annie Atwood, the housekeeper at Barradine, came hurrying from the kitchen to see what all the commotion was about. On seeing the master she gasped her delight on having him home again, but she looked worriedly at the figure in his arms.

'Oh, my goodness!' she gasped, gazing at the pale face resting against his shoulder. 'Is she badly hurt?'

'Nothing more serious than exhaustion and a cut to his head, Annie. The lad's also drenched to the skin. I'll take him straight upstairs. Have a bath prepared and some food.'

Annie watched him cross the hall and bound up the stairs, a thoughtful frown creasing her brow. *Lad?* Why, 'twas obvious to any who had two eyes and a wit in his head that that was no lad.

Emerging out of the darkness, Henrietta realised with some relief that she was no longer plagued by a feeling of discomfort. She was still wet, but indeed she was warmer than she had been, her body stretched out on a bed, a soft pillow beneath her head. She struggled to find a shadowed place from the radiance that shone on her eyes. The light was bright and intrusive in its boldness. Squeezing her eyes tightly shut, she tried to banish the glare, but unable to do so she finally yielded a cautious peek through silken lashes and found the culprit to be a brightly burning lamp on a table beside the bed. An indistinct shape loomed over her, a shape that took

Simon's form, his expression darkly aloof and pensively silent. Having removed her jacket, he was intent on the task of unbuttoning her shirt.

His hand hovered over the flesh at her throat, close enough that she felt the warmth of his skin. In an instant, her awakening awareness of what he was about to do rose to the fore and she felt the first tentative fingers of fear trail along her spine. As her thoughts became fraught with growing anxiety, a sobbing cry surged upwards from the pit of her being and she could not contain it.

'No!' she cried, and with a slash of her hand knocked his hand away.

'I'm glad to see that you're still alive,' he said, his voice deep and imbued with relief. 'You were sleeping so soundly, I was beginning to wonder if you would ever wake. Lie still and let me get you out of these sodden clothes lest you take a chill.'

Bent on removing her wet clothes, not to be deterred, his fingers swept hurriedly up the ties at the neck. He glanced up when Annie came scuttling in, her eyes wide with shock when she realised what he was about.

'Stop, sir. There is something I must say to you.'

'Well?'

'I—I find it difficult to form the proper words,' the housekeeper stammered.

'Fling convention away, Annie, and simply speak your mind.'

She plunged in. 'It—it concerns her sex… 'Tis a well-worn disguise that your young friend has adopted, and it has obviously fooled you… but…' As if embarrassed by her own verbosity, her words trailed off.

Henrietta's heart began to hammer as the shirt fell away. Knowing that she would soon be devoid of clothing, her secret no longer a secret, her panic was too great. Twisting around, she attempted to pull herself upright, but she was still weak.

His sculpted face grim, Simon ignored the hands that slapped him and jerked the shirt open. There was a glimpse of a pale rounded breast. His stare homed in on it—sharp, piercing, alarming, his mind rebelling in disbelief. No longer able to suppress the horror and the hideous suspicion that now assailed him, he retreated. For a moment he seemed frozen, then the windows of his understanding were suddenly blown wide open.

He stared in amazement at his young companion as the truth struck him deeply. The boy—his riding companion, whom he had believed was a boy, was not a boy. 'He' was a girl—a woman.

How could he have been so foolish, so blind as not to see it? he chided himself. And yet, how could he? She had kept her hat pulled low most of the time and had pitched her voice low, hiding her shapely figure in ill-fitting clothes.

And he had not expected 'him' to be a 'her'.

No, there had been no way to perceive the identity of his companion.

In two short strides he was in front of her, his face contorted with dark fury as he glared down at her. When she made to cover her exposed breast his fingers clamped down on her slim wrist, wringing a gasp of pain from her. She fought him, wildly twisting and writhing in an attempt to gain her freedom.

'Let go of me,' she cried. 'Please, Simon—let me go!'

Rage boiled inside Simon like fiery acid, destroying his tender feelings for the youth who had just revealed herself as a young woman. 'Damn your conniving little heart. Will you be still?' he rasped through gritted teeth, and when she would not, he increased the pressure of his grip on her delicately boned wrist. Stubbornly she resisted the pain until finally he gave up the tactic, not wishing to hurt her.

Henrietta stared at him, her mind in a complete turmoil. 'Release my wrist,' she begged, feeling the little strength she had draining out of her. 'You're hurting me.'

'Be still then,' he commanded.

Towering over her, his lean, hard face bore no hint of humour. Something had shattered inside him, splintering his emotions from all rational control. Slowly she quieted and Simon loosened his hold, but his eyes were relentless. This boy—girl—deserved to be taught a lesson. Frustrated that he'd been duped by a mere lass, the rage enveloping him knew no bounds.

'That's better. Now, I think we should talk. What the hell do you think you're playing at? What do you have to say to this deception?'

Biting despair seized Henrietta and she slumped against the pillows. 'I—I can explain,' she said, trying to draw her sodden shirt together, but failing to do so. 'But I'm really a fairly honest person. It—it's just that—there are times when it becomes expedient to hold back the truth.'

'What you're trying to say is that you're a liar when it meets your mood.'

'That's not what I'm saying at all,' she murmured dismally and heaved a sigh. She was thoroughly exhausted and her head was hurting where the falling branch had glanced off her flesh. She couldn't even manage a discomfited blush as Simon considered her taut breasts outlined beneath her shirt.

'Then kindly explain what you mean, Miss Whoever-you-are,' he urged, eyeing her coldly. 'I am all ears. I thought you trusted me. Why did you not tell me you were in disguise?'

'My name is Henrietta. I knew you would have no tolerance for a girl in boy's clothing. It would simply amuse you to discover this and to set it against me.'

His anger beginning to abate, Simon, much against his will, felt his heart warm to the words of the plaintive girl. She was right. Had he known the truth of the matter, he would not have tolerated the situation and ordered her to return home. He stared at her, suddenly on his guard. 'How old are you?'

'Eighteen.'

He heaved a sigh of relief. 'I feared you were much younger. Well, young lady, I don't know who you are, but you're no common sort. I'm not so much of an idiot to know a respectable young woman doesn't set foot outside her home without the protection of servants.' Henrietta glanced away awkwardly. 'I can only conclude that either you are not respectable—which I doubt—your manner is too fine, your speech refined—or you have fallen on hard times. I do not know the particulars that made you leave home and adopt such a mode of attire. Perhaps you wouldn't mind telling me *exactly* what you were doing on the heath that night?'

'For your information, I was turned out of my home. My guardians were dead and I had nowhere else to go. I've already told you that my only living relative that I know of is my paternal uncle, who lives near Inverness.' Granted, she was thoroughly exhausted and greatly in need of sleep, all of which hindered her ability to think straight, but even if she had been fully alert, she preferred not to tell him what had driven her from her home.

Wanting to know who it was that had forced her to flee her home and masquerade as a lad, yet sensing her reluctance to explain, Simon made every effort to smother the gallantry that seemed eager to escape when he considered her thoroughly exhausted condition. She was vulnerable, traumatised. He knew from experience that what she needed right now was someone she could trust, not someone who was bent on interrogating her. The thought that this naive young woman might have been alone on the journey to Scotland filled him with genuine alarm. She'd had no idea what she was getting into.

Shedding his wet cloak, he slung it over the back of a chair, from where Annie, tutting disapproval, retrieved it. By the time he faced Henrietta again without responding to her plight, she had risen from the bed and was swaying on her feet in a dazed stupor. He cursed softly under his breath, knowing the battle lost. At the moment she seemed ready to collapse in a crumpled heap.

Going to her, he shoved her back on to the bed and was immediately struck by how slender and delicate she seemed. Her features were drawn and, beneath her eyes, there were dark lavender shadows that made her cheeks appear sunken. In all, she was a rather pathetic sight, too pitiful for him to hold on to his anger.

'Now you know I am no youth, I beg you not to cast me out. I cannot go back.' Her voice was low, but Simon could hear it tremble with fear.

He knew she feared he would turn her out. Her hands were clasped in her lap and he could see her slight form shaking. How could he turn his back on her?

'Fear not,' he said at last and her head jerked as though he had somehow branded her.

'Fear?' She laughed now, an uneasy sound. 'You do not know fear, sir.'

'There you are wrong, lad…Miss Whoever-you-are. I know fear. I have ridden with it day after day and its shadow has leaned over my shoulder for too long. No. I do know fear. And I know that you fear.' He paused. 'I know not the reason why you do, but you have no reason to fear me.'

She met his gaze direct and Simon thought he saw a softening in her eyes.

'Thank you. Now please, Simon, I just want to go to sleep,' she pleaded.

'You'll feel better after a bath and something to eat. Hurry it up, will you, Annie—and a hot toddy would not go amiss.' Taking her chin, he looked closely at the slight wound on the side of her forehead, rubbing at the caked blood with his thumb. 'Nothing to worry about there. It's only a scratch and will soon heal, but you'll be left with a bruise. I have to get out of my sodden clothes and then I'll be back. Until then, don't move. Do you understand?'

Her smooth forehead creased slightly as if he had asked a difficult task of her. She nodded, taking the quilt and drawing it round her shaking shoulders.

Simon's pledge was confirmed by his swift return to the room. When he entered with a mug of brandy laced with lemon and hot water, a wave of perfumed air hit him in the face. A roaring fire had been built up in the hearth and she was already ensconced in the bath behind a screen, having managed to remove her clothes with the help of Annie and climb in without falling over.

Stepping round the obstruction that hid her view from prying eyes, he stopped short, unable to believe the sight of the naked young woman that met his eyes.

Her eyes were closed and at first he was sorely tempted to wake her, but it would have deprived him of the pleasure of watching her from his vantage point by the screen. He was transfixed—not merely by the sight of so much loveliness, but the lack of inhibition that was only possible in one who was bathing unobserved—and watching her thrilled and moved him to the core of his being. Until that moment he had never thought so much pleasure could be derived in simply watching a woman who was oblivious to being watched. Such a sensation was so rare. It was like an electric current passing through him. The mere sight of her, with the soapy water lapping those small twin orbs of femininity with infuriating, tantalising familiarity, was, for Simon, such a pleasurable experience that it made him ache.

Earlier, with a deep sigh of appreciation Henrietta had lowered herself into the bath and relaxed into the absolute luxury of the hot water enveloping her body before scrubbing her flesh hard with the scented soap and working it into the snarled thatch on her head. She felt as though she was washing away the hardships of the journey. Washed clean, she slid beneath the foam and rested her head against the high end of the bath. The tub was long enough to let her straighten her legs. Exhausted, she lay still and watched the snapping, crackling fire until her eyelids fluttered closed and her resistance gave way to sleep.

The sound of the door opening and closing caught her attention, but thinking it was Annie returning to assist her out of the bath, she sighed, too tired to respond. She was jolted awake by the intruding suspicion that she was being watched and a mild panic grew when she failed to recognise her surroundings. Candles bathed the area around her in a soft, golden light and she felt the warmth of the fire on her face.

Everything came back to her in a rush. With a gasp her head whipped round and like a flame the powerful awareness of Simon's physical presence scorched through her. His unheralded appearance startled her to a sitting position and Simon watched the soapy water sluicing off her satiny skin. The heat of his appreciative gaze ranged with deliberate slowness over her hair and face and down to her slender shoulders, pausing at length on the exposed swell of her breasts, leaving the frothy water to provide modest cover for the rest of her.

He was far too close for Henrietta's peace of mind, for in relaxed mode he stood with his shoulder braced against the screen, his arms folded across his broad chest, looking for all the world as if he had been watching her for some time. Having changed out of his wet clothes, he looked dapper in a dark green coat and grey breeches and waistcoat. He was close and Henrietta had no difficulty discerning his face's every detail. The soft, lazy smile it bore stirred feelings that, while thrilling, were also most disturbing. The shivery warmth that ran through her completely disrupted her composure.

Henrietta stared at him as if stunned, distressed that he should be a witness to her undignified position. As if through a haze it came to her that she should be angry at his intrusion, but before that urging took some direction, he casually relinquished his stance and, undeterred by her discomfiture, sauntered to the foot of the bath. Watching him, uncertain and silent, it was this action that caused panic and fear to course through Henrietta. Suddenly she felt intimidated and vulnerable. Her eyes opened wide in alarm. Had it been anyone else she would have screamed, but this was Simon and she knew she was not about to be cruelly ravished.

His gaze never wavered from her, but when it dipped downwards, she saw the light that flared in his eyes, making her conscious of her lack of modesty. Immediately the alarm she had felt vanished and she slid further beneath the suds and glowered up at him.

'How long have you been standing there watching me?' she demanded.

A slow smile touched his lips. 'Long enough to come to the conclusion that you were worth bringing all this way.'

'You should have made your presence known to me.'

'What! And deprive myself of the pleasure of watching you?' he murmured softly.

The warmth of his tone brought the heat creeping into her cheeks. Disturbed by his perusal and quite put out that he had been silently watching her and had made no effort to alert her to his presence, as if instructing an errant student slow to learn, she pronounced her words carefully. 'Simon, I would appreciate it immensely if you would leave me to wash away the grime of the journey. I feel as though I've been dragged through a swamp. Going without a bath on the journey was extremely tortuous for me, to say the least. I appreciate being clean more than I ever gave heed to before, which is why I shall enjoy a lengthy soak.'

'You were asleep. You looked so content, how could I disturb such a blissful state?'

Henrietta was in no mood for games. 'Well, you did. It is highly improper for you to intrude on my privacy. Do you make a habit of entering a lady's bathing chamber?' she asked in shocked tones, although she was so exhausted she didn't really care what he did. She stared at him, unconscious of the vision she presented as her short hair was beginning to dry and curl in soft, feathery wisps.

'That depends on the lady.' As he remembered the discomfort she had experienced on the journey, his expression became one of concern. 'I imagine the warm water comes as a welcome relief after the hard ride. Let me remind you again of the salve I mentioned.' The barest hint of a grin defied that predominantly sombre visage. 'I'd be happy to apply it to your...sore bits myself if you wish. It will soothe the redness.'

'I think your housekeeper is already frowning on my being here with you alone, it not being proper, you understand, so I doubt you offering to apply salve to my...sore bits, would go down at all well.'

'And why not?' Simon questioned curtly. When he had no other purpose in mind but to help her, he could find little sympathy for her views on propriety. 'You need somewhere to stay and be looked after. Being here with a houseful of servants isn't going to jeopardise your virtue and I'm not about to throw your skirts up and have my way with you. Believe me, Henrietta, you'll know it if I ever set my mind to compromising your modesty, because I won't start with your sore bits.' His eyes drifted to her bosom, as if pointedly denoting the place he'd begin and then just as quickly rose to meet her astonished stare.

Henrietta's jaw dropped open and then she closed it quickly. It certainly didn't help her composure to feel scalding heat creeping into her cheeks. Self-consciously she crossed her arms over her breasts. 'I assure you, Simon, that concern for my virtue was the furthest thing from my mind—and I'll keep my *sore bits* to myself, if you don't mind.'

A brief twitch served as a substitute for a smile. 'If you decide otherwise, Henrietta, I'll be happy to accommodate you—without compromising your virtue.'

'No, thank you. Now go away. I am sure you have seen enough to appease your ardour.'

Simon's teeth flashed like a pirate's in his swarthy face. Settling his hands on his hips, he slowly advanced towards her, the torment of wanting to see more of her almost unbearable. 'Indeed, you are extremely fair to look upon. My eyes have not seen nearly enough and ache to see more.'

Something in his expression made Henrietta shrink back. She was conscious of his height and how his mere presence seemed to fill the confined space. Because he was fully dressed, she was extremely conscious of her own nakedness and was also conscious and alarmed that she was stirred by his masculinity. But she refused to surrender to the call of her blood and crushed these treacherous feelings that threatened to weaken her. Glaring at him, her eyes were vibrant and burning with ire and indignation.

'Don't you dare lay a hand on me, Simon Tremain. Come any closer and I swear I shall scream the house down.'

Simon's bold gaze continued to openly rake her body but, recognising the merits of restraint, he checked himself and advanced no further. His eyes passed over her with warm admiration. She sat low in the tub like a limp rag doll. Her arms were crossed over her chest to hide her breasts from him, even though they were submerged beneath the suds. His experience with the fair sex could not truthfully be termed lacking, yet it was hard in his mind that this delectable creature he had thought was a precocious lad, whom he now scrutinised so carefully, far exceeded anything he could call to mind, whether here or across the water in France. There was a graceful *naiveté* about her that totally intrigued him.

Bending down to her, he reached out his hand

and gently cupped her chin, turning her face up to his. Now the grime had been washed away he studied her with fresh eyes. Feeling compelled and at liberty to look his fill, he felt his heart contract, not having grasped the full reality of her loveliness until that moment. The cropped, red-gold hair framed a creamy-skinned visage. The lips were soft and sensuous. She was remarkably lovely. Her beauty was at once wild and delicate—as dainty as sculpted porcelain, her expression full of caprice. But as he watched her, what struck him most was her innocence. Though her slanting, sparkling green eyes fringed by thick, black lashes hinted at untapped wantonness, he could feel the freshness of her spirit—a tangible force as golden as the highlights in her hair. She was the kind of woman who made a man want to fall on his knees at her feet or run like the devil.

His scorching perusal suddenly became too much for Henrietta. Hot, embarrassed colour stained her cheeks as he met her gaze with a querying, uplifted brow.

'I would be obliged if you would please stop looking at me in that way. Anyone would think you hadn't seen a woman before. Your critical eye pares and inspects me as if I was a body on a dissecting slab.'

'Does it?' Simon murmured absently, continuing to look at her, at the soft lips and glorious eyes.

Her flush deepened. 'I have imperfections enough without you looking for more. Please stop it,' she demanded quietly. 'You are being rude.'

'Am I?' he said, his attention momentarily diverted from her enchanting face.

'Yes. And if you persist I shall be forced to shout for Annie.'

Her words brought a slow, teasing smile to his lips and his strongly marked brows were slightly raised, his eyes suddenly glowing with humour. 'I apologise. But I cannot help looking at you when for the past nine days I believed we were of the same gender.'

Hot-faced and perplexed, Henrietta almost retorted that she was not a rabbit in the sights of his gun, but she halted herself in time. She had never known a man to be so provoking. She was suddenly shy of him. There was something in his eyes that made her feel it was impossible to look at him. There was also something in his voice that brought so many new and conflicting themes in her heart and mind that she did not know how to speak to him.

The effect was a combination of fright and excitement and she must put an end to it. She was in danger of becoming hypnotised by that silken voice and those mesmerising blue eyes.

'Are you quite sure I can't assist you with your bath?'

'Quite sure,' she stated. 'Now go away.'

A chuckle started low in his chest. 'I should have given you a bath when I first met you.' Releasing her chin, he straightened up. 'Come, enough wallowing in the suds. I've brought you a toddy. Drink it and I'll send Annie in to help you get dressed.'

'I've a mind to wallow a while longer,' she answered in a voice dull with fatigue. 'Could you pour that pitcher of warm water into my bath, please?' she asked, indicating the receptacle on the floor where Annie had left it. She squinted up at him as tiny runnels trickled through her lashes. 'I would like to give my hair another wash.'

Simon did as she bade and poured the water into the tub, catching a glimpse of slender white limbs beneath the suds.

'Be careful you don't burn yourself,' Henrietta patronisingly retorted when some of the water splashed his dry breeches.

'I must learn to be cautious of wayward lads and pitchers of hot water,' he answered, his eyes twinkling with amusement at her remark.

He watched her rub an eye with bunched fingers, much like a child who found it hard to stay awake. 'Are you quite certain I can't be of some assistance?' he persisted, his voice as soft as silk.

Henrietta felt a sudden quiver run through her, a sudden quickening within as if something came to life, something that had been asleep before. 'No—thank you,' she replied quickly. 'I think I can manage. Now go away and leave me alone. I will not get out until you have left the room.'

'I'll not be far away.' A wicked smile crept over his lips. 'Don't disappoint me, Henrietta,' he murmured, his eyes agleam with a very personal sort of challenge. 'Don't tell me you're going to start behaving sensibly now.'

Henrietta stiffened at Simon's smooth taunting, but she could hardly take offence at his mild accusation after duping him into believing she was a youth.

As he was about to slip behind the screen he turned and looked at her once more. 'If I don't see you again tonight, I must warn you that the old timbers creak and groan, so don't be alarmed if you hear anything untoward during the night. The house is called Barradine, by the way, and it belongs to me.'

With his gaze looking into her large, liquid, bright eyes, she was oblivious to the sight she presented to him. The pure, sweet bliss of her spurred his heart. She was too damned lovely to be true and he could not believe that he had not seen through her masquerade. Her cheeks were rosy from the heat of the bath, and her hair—all the wonderful shades of red and gold formed a cap of brilliant silk curls, with adorable damp tendrils clinging and curling around her face. The very sight of her wrenched his vitals in a painful knot, and the urge to go to her and pull her into his arms savaged his restraint. If she knew the full force of that emotion he held in check, she would tremble and take to the road on the morrow without him.

'Sleep well, Henrietta. We have much to discuss in the morning.'

Henrietta's eyelids fluttered slowly open as the morning light intruded and roused her to awareness. The dark blue velvet bed hangings had been drawn back, allowing the light to penetrate her world. A cheerful fire crackled and danced in the hearth.

Henrietta elbowed herself up the bed and tucked the pillows behind her. A rattle of dishes came from outside the door, and she clutched the sheets beneath her chin as Annie entered the chamber, carrying a covered tray. Her face broke into a smile when she found the occupant of the bed awake and sitting up.

'Oh, you're awake, I see.' The friendliness in her voice was as noticeable as the warmth in her eyes and smile. 'His lordship said you would be tired after the journey and your ordeal in the storm yesterday and to leave you to sleep in.'

'His lordship being Lord Tremain.'

'Aye, miss. That's right.' Annie brought the tray to the bed and removed the cover to reveal a pot of tea and an appetising plate of ham and eggs and freshly baked bread and creamy butter. 'You look like a young lady who could do with a hearty breakfast. You ate nothing when you arrived, so tuck in and enjoy it.'

'I will. It looks delicious, Annie. I have to say I'm quite ravenous.'

'Eat up then. I'll see to it that hot water is brought for you to wash and I've already laid out the clothes the master has provided.'

'But—what has happened to the clothes I was wearing when I arrived?'

'They're in the laundry, miss.'

'I see,' Henrietta murmured cautiously, casting a dubious eye over the female clothes draped over a chair. 'I—I would prefer to wear my own clothes if you don't mind, Annie.'

'Oh, no, miss. The master was most firm about you dressing as a lady. When you're ready I'll come and help you.'

'Thank you,' Henrietta conceded, reconciling herself to the *master's* orders. 'Then until my own clothes are fit to wear, I shall be happy to wear them.'

'That's good,' Annie said, still smiling as she went out.

When she had eaten, hearing the clatter of horses' hooves on the cobbles in the yard below her window, Henrietta went to look. There were half a dozen gentlemen, all finely garbed, all on horseback and wearing expressions of intent. Where they came from Henrietta did not know, but they entered Barradine with a purpose. It was all very mysterious and as usual Henrietta's curiosity got the better of her.

She turned her attention to the clothes laid out, surprised to find them remarkably grand. The undergarments were very fine, the gown apple-green damask trimmed at the hem with gold embroidery. A light grey shawl and a pair of dark green slippers completed the outfit.

Her pleasure as she donned the dress was truly feminine. Before leaving the room she looked in the mirror and contemplated herself with some satisfaction. The dress might have been made for her. The bodice sat well on her slender waist and the colour emphasised the gold highlights in her hair. Draping the shawl about her shoulders, she pirouetted lightly and made for the door.

She moved silently along the passageway to the top of the stairs, where she paused, standing in the shadows and looking down. The men were huddled together near the huge stone hearth, their worried looks and urgent conversation presaging some bad news. It had been declared that Charles Stuart, the son of the man James Stuart, who had named him Regent, giving him permission to act in his name, had been declared a rebel, a traitor, and a public enemy to the Commonwealth and of England, along with the abettors, agents and accomplices and public enemies.

'What do you make of it?' Simon asked from within their midst. 'Tell me what you know. Will it come to a battle?'

'Aye, I reckon it will,' was one answer. 'Against long odds and with the support of Donald Cameron of Lochiel, an army has been raised which numbers almost two thousand Scots. Sir John Cope, the general commanding the government forces in Scotland, commands less than four thousand in two regiments. He's beset with problems.'

'Which are?'

'His senior cavalry officer has taken sick and he has a lack of gunners to man his artillery. Acting on advice from the government, Cope marched with his infantry to Fort Augustus in an attempt to overawe the Highland clans and nip any rebellion in the bud.'

'And how have the clans reacted?' Henrietta heard Simon ask.

'Many are evading calls to take up arms on behalf of the government. Our agents have reported that on hearing Charles Stuart is preparing to oppose Cope at Corryarrack, Cope's turned about and is now marching on Inverness.'

'And the prince?'

'He considered pursuing Cope, but instead he's decided to march into the Lowlands, which Cope has left almost undefended. The last I heard was that he's reached Perth.'

'Then I'll know where to find him when I ride north.' He looked around at the faces of the men. 'What will you do if it comes to conflict? Will you take up arms against King George?'

'It's not that I mind risking my life,' said the man who had done most of the talking. 'But if we fail and are captured, they will take my house and land, and I'll not be there to protect my family.'

'It's the same for all of us,' came a gruff reply. 'But if we don't do it now, the opportunity to bring the Bonnie Prince to his rightful place may never come again.'

'Then let's pray the conflict ends with Charles on the throne and it doesn't come to such a pass.'

Henrietta stood in the shadows as the men began to disperse. She felt numb and then consumed by panic, as her mind went over what had been said. If, as she intended, she continued on her journey to Inverness, then it was inevitable that she would come into contact with the government army.

The big case clock in the great hall was striking ten o'clock when she went down the curved oak stairs. Glancing at the windows, she saw the heavy clouds loitering overhead heralded more rain. Simon stood close to the hearth where a fire blazed, taking off the dank chill. In repose his expression was tense as he considered the information brought to him earlier.

Displaying a calm she did not feel, Henrietta studied him surreptitiously as he watched her walk across the hall towards him. A world of feelings flashed for an instant across his set features when their eyes locked, but it was the expression of immense concern Henrietta saw that touched her the most, replaced at once by one of polite enquiry. His long, muscular frame was attired in the clothes he had been wearing the night before. He had the look of an adventurer and appeared most worldly, yet his whole body was tensed into a rigid line, as if he fought some private battle within himself.

Despite the days they had spent on the road together, it was like coming face to face with a stranger. Now her masquerade had been stripped away their attitudes towards each other had changed completely and it concerned her, especially when those thoroughly blue eyes searched her own. She had not realised how brilliant and clear they were. In some mystical way they seemed capable of stripping the lies from whatever had passed before. It was all she could do to face his unspoken challenge and not retreat to the safety of her room.

Chapter Four

Simon watched Henrietta approach. Ever since he had left her he had tried not to think of her and to concentrate on the arrival of the men he had arranged to liaise with here at Barradine, but now he became consumed with anxiety and was unable to think of anything other than what he was to do with this young woman who had insinuated herself into his life and threatened to disrupt it.

Last night when she had revealed her true sex he had been taken unawares and his sudden passion for her had been torn asunder by guilt and his conscience. He had lain awake almost the entire night. He could not stop thinking about her. When he shut his eyes she was there and when he opened them she stayed with him. Such sleeplessness was unusual for him. He rather hoped that in daylight she might not be as he remembered.

He was mildly irritated with himself. He certainly did not need his life complicated by a woman. Perhaps the half light of the moment of her bathing had helped create a fantasy—but it wasn't so. In daylight her charm seemed all the greater.

Nothing was more obvious to Henrietta at that moment than those eyes that immediately took in every detail of her appearance. The clothes he had instructed Annie to pick out for her to wear belonged to his mother. The dress was a perfect fit and, as slender as she was, Henrietta was not without womanly curves. She was a sight that caused his heart to lurch in admiration and something else that appealed to his baser instincts.

He must stop now, before things went too far for him to draw back. Because she was not the kind of sophisticated, worldly woman he usually sought it made her more alluring, more desirable. She was nothing like the glamorous, experienced women who knew how to please him, women who were mercenary and hell-bent on self-gratification, whose beds he sought only to leave the moment his ardour was spent.

It could not continue. In the past hard logic and cold reason had always conquered his lust—with Henrietta he knew it would be different. He had to purge her out of his mind before he was completely beaten—and if he continued to have her near him he would lose the battle. He was in danger of becoming enamoured of her and he would not permit that. The stakes were too high.

He tried to concentrate on the next stage of his journey, but in his state of relaxed ease he was more inclined to dwell on the amazing—and perverse—quirk of fate that had caused this girl to be ensconced in his house. It would have been far better if he were alone, but now that she was here he couldn't just ignore her and pretend she wasn't there.

'Thank you for the clothes,' Henrietta said. 'Who do they belong to?'

'My mother, but don't concern yourself. I know she would be happy for you to wear them.' He pulled two chairs close to the hearth. 'Come and sit down. We need to talk.' Silently she did as he bade, sitting awkwardly on the edge of her seat. He raised one brow in enquiry. 'How are you feeling this morning? Better, I hope?' he said, sitting across from her and lounging with one booted foot resting casually atop the opposite knee.

'Yes—much better.' He nodded, which left Henrietta wondering why he was adopting this cool, remote attitude to her. Was it possible he was ashamed of the way he had behaved towards her when he had intruded on her bathing, or was his desire for her so great that he couldn't bear to be close to her? Despite the complications it would bring, she secretly hoped it was the latter, but the way he was looking at her made her discount it. Her eyes met his.

'You said you want to talk, Simon? I think I know what it's about. I suspect you want me off your hands and deeply regret encumbering yourself with me in the first place.'

Henrietta expected the words to get a reaction, but except for a hardening of his eyes and a muscle that began to twitch in his jaw, there was none.

'What is done is done and I have to consider what sensible action to take. One thing is certain—you cannot continue on your journey alone and where I am going I cannot take you with me.'

'So you are to dismiss me as though I am an untouchable.'

Untouchable, Simon thought wretchedly. She was certainly that and must remain that way. While ever they remained in the same house she was too much of a threat to his sanity. Everywhere he turned she would be there to ensnare him and when she was absent his need to see her would make him seek her out. He was furious with himself for feeling like this—for wanting her. He'd never realised that sexual desire for a woman would become a complication. Better that they were apart altogether, before she disrupted his whole life.

'Not at all. Despite not knowing anything about you, I feel a deep sense of responsibility which cannot be easily dismissed. Which is why I think the sensible thing would be for you to remain at Barradine for the time being.'

Henrietta could hear the determination in his voice that told her he had already decided what to do with her. But she would have none of it. She stared at him for a long, indecisive moment, then she said, 'I will do no such thing. You may have given me your protection on the journey and I am indeed grateful—in fact, you just might have saved my life. But that does not give you the right to have a say in what I shall do next. I do not wish to be kept by you, or by any other man. I am fairly self-sufficient and I prefer it that way.'

'Good Lord, Henrietta, I'm not asking you to become my mistress. I just feel obligated—'

'You needn't,' she interrupted coolly. 'You owe me nothing, and I will take nothing from you, Simon, and you need not feel any responsibility towards me. I embarked on this journey knowing what I was taking on. What happens next is up to me, not you. I thank you for your protection since we met—and your hospitality,' she said with the polite cordiality of a guest who was about to depart. 'I have enjoyed your company and now I must continue on my journey north.'

Suddenly Simon looked at her with unexpected softness. Surprised by the change in his expression, Henrietta opened her mouth to speak, but he stopped her and, taking a deep breath, continued speaking. 'You cannot go alone, Henrietta. You must stop and think of the hazards that may arise. At this time there are government soldiers all over the place. You will never make it on your own.'

Henrietta's face was a pale, emotionless mask as she tore her eyes from his face and watched the dancing flames in the hearth. Her heart and mind felt empty and she was chilled to the marrow. Even now, when she was desperate with the thought of leaving him, she had to ask herself why it should hurt so much and to question what was in her heart.

'Yes, I will. I must.'

'You were set upon by ruffians at your first stop, you little fool. Did you not realise what they might do? Look at you.' He swept a gesture from her feet to her head, scowling crossly. 'By all intents and purposes you were a lad—on a fine horse, I might add. They could have gutted you like a fish if they'd a mind and stolen your horse. And good God, Henrietta—do you know what would have happened to you had they discovered your true gender? Have I not enough to contend with already without having to protect and coddle a young woman?'

Henrietta bristled at the insult. 'I haven't held you back so far and I'm hardly likely to do so now that you've found out I'm a woman. But if you find the influence of my gender and so much beauty and femininity elevating to your moral sense, then accept that we must go our separate ways and I will make my own way from here on.'

'Damn it, Henrietta!' he said fiercely, springing to his feet with frustration and combing his fingers through his hair. 'Your change from youth to capricious female is the greatest stumbling block I have ever encountered.'

'You may blame it on my Scottish blood, Simon. 'Tis strong-willed and usually gets the upper hand despite my very best efforts to cool it.'

He glared down at her. 'That I can believe, but I feel most deeply the burden of your present distress and accept that it is in the greater part my fault. I brought you with me only with the kindest intent and because I thought you were well in need of my attention and protection. I am hardly likely to abandon you now. If the rising and ensuing battle become a reality, if things go badly for us and the English come looking, do you think that I value my own miserable hide so much that I'd leave you to be slaughtered like the Holy Lamb?' His voice softened and hurt darkened his blue eyes. 'Do you not know me better than that?'

He looked at her sitting stiff and proud, her fine-boned profile tilted obstinately to betray her mutinous thoughts. Not for the first time he wondered at her life that she had been forced to take to the road. Turning her head, she met his gaze. He saw youthful guile in those beautiful green eyes, like the colour of a tropical sea. He could sit and look into them and drown himself, going ever deeper and deeper. With a jerk he pulled himself back and looked away. He could not help but wonder at the grit of this young woman. He had known no other quite like her and the disturbing fact was that she seemed capable of disrupting his whole life.

Contritely the young girl hung her head. 'I know you well enough, Simon, but I thought... perhaps...you'd want rid of me now we've reached Scotland.'

Simon drew up his chair and sat across from her once more. A frisson of excitement was like a plucked lute string in the silence between them. The great hall seemed smaller, the firelight more richly golden as it played over his wary face, sculpting its hard planes and sharp contours.

'I failed to offer you commiserations on the death of your guardians,' he said suddenly. 'Forgive my lack of manners.'

'Think nothing of it,' she said graciously. 'I'm sure they would be most obliged to you for offering me your protection on my journey north.'

He sighed, steepling his fingers in front of his face, watching her. 'I know now that you are a girl dressed as a boy. I know not your reasons, nor do I particularly wish to know. Suffice it to say that it is your business, not mine. But I sense you are in trouble and perceive you need to talk to someone. If I can be of assistance in any way, I would like you to tell me why you're running away.'

Henrietta met his gaze, tension in the angle of her shoulders. 'Why should you care? You have troubles enough of your own with the arrival of the Bonnie Prince to concern yourself with mine.'

'True, but it so happens I have experience with these things.' He paused. 'Generally, I've found that running away is a very bad idea.'

She stared at him in surprise. 'Did you run away from home?'

He grinned and nodded. 'When I was a lad—five years old, to be precise—one day I packed a bag with clothes and food and set off for Edinburgh. I'd been told what a big town it was with a grand castle on a rock. I wanted to see it for myself. I didn't get far before my father caught up with me. By that time I was very cold and very scared—and regretting my foolishness. So trust me. I wouldn't recommend it.'

Henrietta glanced at him, uncertain about what to say.

Simon could sense the suppressed agitation in her, noted her clenched hands. 'You can speak freely. It will go no further. It may not resolve anything, but it will make you feel a damn sight better.'

Conscious of his scrutiny, suddenly agitated, Henrietta got to her feet. 'How can you be so sure of that?'

'I'm not, but it can't do any harm.'

Henrietta looked at him long and hard before turning away, wrapping her arms about her waist as if to contain the horrors of what she knew Jeremy to be guilty of. Simon was right. It would be a relief to reduce her overburdened mind, for no matter how she tried to push the memories and the danger Jeremy posed to her away, they returned. Still she hesitated, but she was beginning to realise that it was important to unburden herself to Simon, who would listen and maybe offer a solution to her problem. In the end she turned to confront him, and a flicker of sanity lit the chaos of her thoughts.

'I know you are right, Simon. I should tell you. I owe you that, at least.' Henrietta held his eyes a moment, then her gaze slid away. Drawing a deep breath, she let it out harshly. 'It's difficult to know where to begin.'

Simon settled himself in his chair, crossing his legs, watching her calmly, his heart going out to her. 'When your guardians died would be as good a place as any,' he suggested quietly.

She paused, and, although Simon appeared calm, he waited in a state of nervous tension for her to go on, relieved when she did, but she wasn't looking at him, she was looking into the flames, as if the images of the past were marching with each dancing flame. She recounted everything that had occurred on the night Jeremy had come to the house—the misunderstanding about the wills, his bullying and the threats he had made.

Wringing her hands in front of her, she turned away and hugged herself again. Watching her, Simon listened with avid interest, clenching his hands into fists, having to struggle to stop himself going to her and cradling her in his arms. When she told him of the tragedy which had robbed her of her guardians, that it had not been an accident as everyone surmised and that Jeremy was responsible, her voice tore through him. Her face was ravaged, but he couldn't make it easier for her. He had to let her go on. But how alone she must have felt, how terrified when faced with the daunting journey ahead of her.

As the full implication of what she was telling him began to sink in, he saw the truth at last, along with all the fear and horror locked away inside her since that night.

'At that time neither Jeremy nor Mr Braithwaite were cognizant of the fact that his uncle had drafted a new will. Mr Braithwaite was abroad at the time and had only recently returned to London when the tragedy occurred. I discovered the truth about what happened when I overheard Jeremy discussing with his wife how he had killed his aunt and uncle. Fearing for my own life, I knew I had to get away. It was a matter of personal survival. By now Jeremy will have discovered the truth and he will plan to kill me as soon as it's convenient.'

'You say you took the copy of the newly drafted will.'

'Yes. I have it with me.'

'Have you read it?'

She nodded, looking down at her hands. 'I looked at it before I left. I truly believed Baron Lucas had left everything to Jeremy. He was the sole heir, you see. That was the case in the first will the baron drafted before I became his ward, but when he changed his solicitor it was altered in the second. Apart from a few paintings and things, he left everything to me. I couldn't believe it. I didn't want it. Fearing reprisals from Jeremy, I was quite desperate. That was when I thought of my uncle. I know he will provide me with sage advice about the best course of action to take.'

'It's a long way to come for that. Couldn't Mr Goodwin have advised you? After all, that is what Baron Lucas paid him for.'

'I thought of that, but I know Jeremy. He's clever and has the cunning of a fox. He was relying on the money from his uncle's estate to keep him out of debtors' prison and he would find some way of getting rid of me to get his hands on the money as soon as it became convenient. I have no doubt he would assume legal guardianship over me, render me feeble and incapable of communication with strong potions and force me to sign a will which would leave him everything in the event of my death.'

'Does he know you have come to Scotland?'

'No. I imagine he'll make enquiries among his aunt and uncle's friends. When he fails to locate me he'll begin ferreting out any connections I might have. Given time, he'll discover I have an uncle in Scotland. He'll also realise I've taken my horse. I can only hope he will think I haven't the courage to travel all that way on my own.'

'Do you believe he would follow you?'

'I think he might. He's going to have to find me to resolve the matter of the will. I expect he's feeling pretty desperate by now. I really did consider the full depth of my predicament before I fled. Jeremy has gained enough stature in society to be dangerous to me and I know him to be most persistent when it comes to something he wants. He will not leave me be. He will bide his time until the moment is ripe and then I will find myself in dire straits.'

'In the event that he does journey to Scotland we must keep you safe. You have need of some convincing protection.'

'What do you suggest?' she asked with growing alarm.

'That you remain here. It is the only thing I can offer towards your safety. Since no one knows of our connection, he's hardly likely to come here. You will be safe, Henrietta. I can promise you that.'

'Safe, but restrained like a prisoner.' Her alarm turned to anger and she shot him a mutinous look. 'And what am I supposed to do?'

'Be sensible, Henrietta,' he said sternly. 'I've talked it over with Annie and she's more than happy to have you stay at Barradine.'

Henrietta had become so angry it almost choked her. It could not be true. How dared he think of leaving her here in this desolate place for what could turn out to be weeks? 'I will not stay here. You have no authority over me, Simon. I do as I please. I have to go on.'

'Forget it. I will not permit it,' he said arrogantly.

'I do not remember *asking* for your permission,' Henrietta retorted defiantly, stiffening her spine.

Caught off guard, Simon stared hard at her. Grown men rarely dared to challenge him, yet here was this slip of a girl doing exactly that. If his annoyance hadn't matched his surprise, he would have chucked her under the chin and grinned at her courage. 'You're right. You didn't,' he snapped.

'I must go to my uncle. If you refuse to take me with you part of the way, then I shall leave of my own accord, I promise you.'

'And so you shall, but I have plans of my own and they do not include you.'

'I know that. But I mean it, Simon. I will go on my way with or without you.'

Simon sat quite still, watching her. She was furious with him, he knew, for trying to order her life, and she was dying to loose a tirade at his head—he could see it in those flashing eyes of hers. What a proud, spirited beauty she was, he thought impartially. She had seemed such an odd little thing before, dressed in her boy's clothes, but he hadn't expected her to blossom into a full-fledged beauty simply by shedding that unflattering garb.

And therein lay his problem—despite her alluring curves and that intoxicating face, he was rapidly becoming convinced she was an inexperienced innocent. An inexperienced innocent who had landed at his feet and for whom he was now unwillingly responsible. The thought of this naive girl travelling alone to Inverness filled him with genuine alarm. She had no idea what she was getting into. And yet the image of himself as her protector was so ludicrous that he nearly laughed aloud, yet that was the role he was going to be forced to play.

His features relaxed and a spark of amusement lit his eyes. 'You're one of the few rays of light I've seen in a long time, Henrietta. Though you're stubborn to the point of recklessness and that concerns me.'

'I'd never wittingly concern you, Simon, and I thank you for your offer for me to remain in your house. But I do not wish to be a burden to you.' She had her pride and her reasons—Jeremy was indeed a threat, but Simon posed a threat in an entirely different way. 'I shall do as I originally intended and go to Inverness. I'm not afraid.'

Simon sat forward, his expression hardening. 'Listen to me, Henrietta. What you—'

'*Don't* try talking me out of it, Simo—'

'By God,' he growled, 'you will listen.' He sighed heavily. 'You are a wilful woman, Henrietta, but I will not abandon you now.'

'If you are to go to Perth, I could ride with you as far as there.'

Simon threw her a sharp look. 'Perth? How did you…?' He nodded, understanding. 'Some of my neighbours called on me earlier. You must have heard us talking.'

'Yes—but I didn't mean to.'

'No doubt you said that when your curiosity got the better of you on Hampstead Heath. One day that curiosity of yours is going to get you into trouble. When did you last see your uncle?'

'When I was seven years old.'

'Then he's probably been labouring under the misconception that you are still a child. He'll no doubt be amazed when he sees you.'

'So you will take me with you to Perth? You won't change your mind?'

Simon sighed, knowing his limitations too well. Having failed during the previous night to banish Henrietta from his mind, he knew he'd have to face days of acute torture if he allowed this lovely, gracious and utterly tempting girl to accompany him on his journey. Yet if he left her at Barradine, he knew she'd be on his tail the minute he'd ridden out of the yard. 'I fear not.'

That was all he said and that was all he needed to say for her to accept his answer as final.

'If I am to take you with me to Perth, will you not at least tell me your name?'

'You know who I am. I told you.'

'I know your given name is Henrietta. I would have your family name.'

Henrietta stared at him. Uneasily she warned herself that she would have to be careful. But surely no harm could come from him knowing her name. Brody was not an uncommon name.

'It is Brody. My full name is Henrietta Maria Brody.' Simon eyed her as though weighing each one of her words. 'Why do you look at me like that?'

'The name is familiar to me—but I cannot think…' He fell silent, considering. 'Unless…' His face suddenly went quite white. He looked at her hard. 'Brody? It is a Scottish name.'

'Yes.'

His eyes locked on hers. 'Are you a Roman Catholic?'

'I am of that persuasion,' she admitted, prepared for his reaction. If he was surprised, he did not allow it to show on his face.

'Yet—like your sex, you concealed it.'

'Yes,' she replied slowly, 'for it's a dangerous time to be a Roman Catholic.'

'That is true. Well—this is a turn-up. Although after what you overheard on the heath that night, I cannot for the life of me understand why you chose to keep it from me. I did not think you were a defender of the Jacobites.'

A savage gleam entered her eyes and her tone was just as savage when she quickly replied, 'I'm not. I hate the Jacobites and the harm they do in support of the cause—what the cause did to my family—to my father.'

'Who was...?' His eyes were suddenly hard and penetrating as he awaited her answer—as if he already knew what that answer would be.

'Andrew Brody—who was a long and ardent and active supporter of the Jacobites.' She shuddered as she remembered the brutality of her father's death.

'Why did you not tell me this before?'

'I had no reason to tell you. Why should I?'

Simon was stunned by Henrietta's disclosure. The truth and the enormity of the dangers this posed to her finally dawned on him. 'I remember Andrew Brody. I also remember Andrew Brody was executed for his involvement in a plot to help King James regain his throne. Was he your father?'

'The same.'

'And you chose to keep this startling piece of information to yourself.'

She shrugged. 'It was my concern, not yours. I never talk about it—I choose not to, but, yes, my father was a Jacobite. He confessed it openly. In fact, he more than confessed it. He went to Rome where King James has his court. He was undoubtedly involved in plans to bring James back to the throne.'

'Which was a foolhardy thing to do considering the failure of the rising back in fifteen.'

'Yes,' she said quietly. 'But whatever my father may have done, my mother suffered terribly. When he was executed, she never got over his death. It hit her hard. She…lost her mind afterwards. But this was nothing I did not expect—how could anyone keep one's wits in her circumstances?' She found she was unable to speak of her mother's suicide. It was too painful. 'I was a child when they came to arrest him. I knew something wasn't right and I was devastated when I was told he wouldn't be coming back—although I didn't know the whole of it until later. The stigma of his execution will not go away, which was the reason I did not turn to my guardian's friends for help. They are all of the same opinion—that I was not worthy of their care. The accusations of conspiracy against my father were based on a good deal of evidence.

His captivity was short-lived. Which, following the suffering his torturers inflicted on him, I can only look on as a mercy. When I was still a child and feeling as though my father had been stolen from me, there were times when I swore that were I a man I would avenge his death.'

'I knew you had courage, Henrietta, but I failed to notice your wits are addled.'

Henrietta's body became rigid and she glowered at him. 'I'm sure if it came to it, I could fight as well as any man, but if I were to do so to avenge my father, then I would be inadvertently supporting the Jacobite cause. I would never do that.'

She saw his blue eyes darken to indigo, but not even an eyelash flickered to betray his alarm. He raised his eyebrow with an amused admiration which exasperated Henrietta.

'What a bloodthirsty wench you are!' he said softly. 'It has not escaped my mind that when we met you threatened me by drawing a knife on me.'

'Don't mock me—and don't underestimate me either. And you are mistaken, Simon. When I drew my knife on you that was no threat. Just proof that I can take care of myself.'

Simon's eyes narrowed, studying her with unnerving intensity. 'Don't underestimate me either, Henrietta. I am well trained in the arts of combat. Surprise tactics and cunning are my strongest weapons. But are you aware of the danger to yourself at this time? If there is to be another rising and it fails, if you are apprehended, because of who you are you will suffer the same fate as your father. Let there be no doubt about that.'

Henrietta blanched. 'I—I did not think... When I ran away I was running for my life. I had no thoughts of plots and Jacobites until my encounter with you on the heath.'

'Then you had better give it some thought, Henrietta Brody, because your life is in danger—from two sides apparently. But the danger Jeremy poses will be as nothing compared to the full might of the English. If you are to remain with me for the time being, I shall make rules for your behaviour. The first is that you will accompany me as my servant and continue to dress as a youth.'

'Can I get away with it, do you think?'

'I see no reason why not,' he replied drily. 'You fooled me well enough and if you can do that you can fool anybody.'

'Annie wasn't deceived.'

'Annie's different.' He chuckled. 'She's been the housekeeper at Barradine since I was a lad.

Never underestimate her. Always in command of herself is Annie. You must never think of her as anything less than a warship under full sail, gun ports raised and cannon at the ready.'

'Oh, dear. As bad as that?' Henrietta uttered with a smile.

'Absolutely.'

'Then she is a woman after my own heart.'

'The second condition that I ask of you is that you keep out of sight as much as possible—some of the scurvy lot who call themselves soldiers can't be trusted with a lady—much less a comely lad who looks like one. 'Twill be lucky if any of them are fit to fight the way they would be wont to ogle you.'

Henrietta's eyes opened wide and she had to stifle a smile. 'Why, Simon! I would take that as a compliment if I didn't feel it wasn't meant to be one.'

'You're right. It wasn't. The next condition is even more important.'

Henrietta waited.

'You'll speak of your past to no one,' he said bluntly. 'What you have told me just now concerning your father you will tell no one else. Do you understand?'

She nodded. 'Anything else?'

'Yes,' he said, shoving himself out of the chair. 'For God's sake keep your hat on. That hair of yours is like a beacon on a dark night.'

* * *

They were to remain at Barradine for a few days before leaving for Perth. Not fully recovered from the gruelling ride to Scotland, Henrietta welcomed the respite. Simon had many things to occupy his time and was away for most of the time, so Henrietta took the opportunity to explore the house.

It was a fine, square-set, stone-built house, its imposing front three storeys high. A broad terrace dropped down to a beautiful garden with carefully clipped hedges overlooking the River Tweed. It was also opulent, with beautiful artefacts reposing on gleaming tables, and on the walls were portraits of long-dead family members in gilded frames. The house exuded indefinable qualities—a sense of order, centuries of happiness and disappointments, memories of men and women who had lived and breathed within these walls.

This was a time for her to idle the time away. She often found herself wandering along the banks of the Tweed and stopping to dangle her feet in the cool, swift flowing shallow water. It was as if the whole world existed at Barradine. Nothing outside it—not Jeremy or the Bonnie Prince—existed. She couldn't think of anything else. There was nothing else.

Only Simon.

She was no more immune to Simon than he was to her, for the longer she was a guest in his house she could not prevent her eyes from searching him out or prevent her eyes from straying in disquieting directions. Nothing in her limited experience had prepared her for such a man as Simon Tremain. If she had found him impressive before, to see him at Barradine, surrounded by the men and women who depended on him, made him grow, in her estimation, to an almost invincibility.

The effect he produced was not merely the result of his incomparable handsome looks—it was more than that. The monumental energy he seemed to possess was volcanic, and the discipline and courtesy of his manner, and his occasional sardonic humour, made him distinct from any other man she had ever known.

She would watch him from the window in her chamber talking with the men who worked on his estate, and even when he was absent she felt his dominating presence everywhere. She told herself that nothing he could do could tempt her, but she always looked for him, as if the sight of him was reassuring, quelling her fear and anxiety of the future.

It was Simon's custom to be up at daybreak and about his business. On the fourth day of her stay at Barradine, as she descended the stairs later, she heard voices coming from the dining room. It was certainly not out of the ordinary for him to receive callers this early and Prince Charles was generally the topic. But somewhat wary of who visited, Henrietta made her way more cautiously.

'Good morning, Miss Henrietta,' the house-keeper greeted her cheerily, coming out of the room carrying a tray. 'Another bright morning.'

Henrietta glanced inside the room. Five men sat at the large rectangular table where Annie had dispensed steaming bowls of porridge and freshly baked bannocks spread with honey and they were all looking at her.

'Henrietta—please, come in.' A chair creaked and a moment later Simon filled the doorway as he came to greet her.

He had hoped to keep her tucked away from prying eyes, but now she was here he could hardly ignore her. His heart began to hammer in deep, aching beats as his eyes glided over her from head to toe in a lingering appreciation of everything they touched. With her hair brushed in a glorious cap of short curls and attired in a deep rose-pink gown, she looked stunning. Despite the crushing chain of circumstances that had bedevilled her since her guardians had died, it was plain to him that she was undaunted and of no weak spirit.

'I'm so sorry,' she murmured. 'I would not have come down had I known you had visitors.'

'It's too late now. Allow me to introduce you. I had hoped to avoid this happening, but there's nothing for it but to brave it out.'

Henrietta's instinct was to protest and return to her chamber, but too many curious gazes were watching them.

'Come.' Taking her arm and squeezing it reassuringly, Simon led her towards the fresh airy room where the open windows allowed breezes to flow through.

The gentlemen all rose simultaneously and nodded graciously. Henrietta could feel their curious glances. All of them were dressed in serviceable shades of grey and brown, and one in the soft blue-and-green tartan of a hunting kilt.

'Miss Lucas, these gentlemen are neighbours of mine. They have come to discuss with me the matter that is on everyone's lips at this time and, since I've been away for some time, I must consider their advice on some local matters. This is Miss Lucas, gentlemen, come to visit my mother, Lady Mary—who we all know is in Paris at this time staying with friends and visiting my young brothers. Unfortunately, Miss Lucas was not aware of the fact. If there is to be any kind of conflict due to Prince Charles's arrival in Scotland, it will affect us all—Miss Lucas included, since she is to visit a relative in the north.'

'Is that so?' a sturdy-looking individual in leather trews remarked grimly. 'And do you think it wise for a young lady to go visiting in this time of unrest?'

'I will take my chance,' Henrietta replied lightly, praying she was not about to be drawn into a discussion as to her destination.

'Miss Lucas, I am indeed honoured to make your acquaintance,' a tall, good-looking, auburn-haired gentleman by the name of Iain Frobisher said. He cast his host an amused glance. 'Simon, did you intend to keep this ravishing creature to yourself?'

Simon laughed good-heartedly. 'That is for Miss Lucas to decide. She is welcome to stay at Barradine for as long as she wishes and I am not averse to feminine company, as you know, Iain. However, since the recent addition to your brood of offspring—Alice, I believe you have named her, who will no doubt turn out to be as wild as her brothers—I imagine you will have a good deal to occupy your time without concerning yourself with my—ravishing guest.'

Henrietta smiled, happy to go along with Simon's subterfuge. 'Do not mistake my friendship with Lord Tremain,' she was quick to point out.

'He is a friend of my family and a man of impeccable honour. I will not deprive him of my company just yet.'

Simon grinned. 'Do I look deprived?'

His casual remark caused much laughter. 'Have a care, Miss Lucas,' Iain warned. 'Simon loves and leaves his ladies with frequent ease. But *I* would be your most devoted slave,' he said, affecting a courtly bow.

'Tell that to your wife,' one of the others quipped, giving him a good-humoured slap on the back.

'You will eat with us, Miss Lucas?' Simon offered.

'No—I thank you. I have already eaten.'

'Then some tea, perhaps.'

'Yes—yes, that would be nice. But I have no wish to intrude on your conversation. I am sure you and these gentlemen have much to discuss.'

'Nothing that you cannot be privy to.'

'Then I will sit over here,' she said, moving towards a small table close to the window.'

Annie set a cup of tea before her and went out, leaving her to listen to the conversation. While their voices drifted across to her, she sipped her tea, listening quietly as Simon expressed himself in bold opinion in response to his neighbours' questions, quickly taking up a quill and making sketches of the Highlands and Lowlands of Scotland when needed, acting as a valued peer. He discussed all matters concerning Charles Stuart's arrival in Scotland and the support he was getting from the Highland clans. Henrietta was anything but bored as she listened. She realised he was as clever and keen minded as her father had been. In fact, as the conversation progressed, it became evident he could have taught her father much.

He really was the most impressive man Henrietta had ever met. There was an indomitable pride chiselled into his handsome face, determination in the jut of his chin, arrogance in his jaw and intelligence in every feature of his face. There was an aloof strength and a powerful charisma about him that had nothing to do with his tall, broad-shouldered physique. He was also an experienced man of the world and all those experiences were locked away behind a lazy charm and piercing blue eyes.

And therein lay his appeal. The challenge.

Stealing another look at his profile her heart turned over. She gave herself a mental shake. What did all that matter? Simon Tremain was nothing to her and never could be. All that mattered was that she reached her uncle with her heart, her mind and body intact. She must not allow herself to succumb to Simon's charm. He was a Jacobite, like her father, and only misery and suffering could result from knowing him. He would rend her heart in two—as her mother's had been broken by her father, which had sent her to her grave.

Henrietta would not ignore what her common sense was telling her. She would not allow that to happen to her. Not again. Not ever!

Having no notion of the paths along which Henrietta's mind wandered, from where he sat Simon couldn't help but admire the depth of her composure and the delicate, almost ethereal beauty in the young face. She had been gently reared in a well-to-do household. He could see it in the way she walked and carried herself. She had the confident, refined elegance of one who has been well tutored and instructed in the social graces. In repose she was the quintessence of the beautiful female animal, her face and body as perfectly formed as they could be. Her sensuality was so beguiling that the gentlemen's eyes seemed to burn with unconcealed pleasure as they sought and lingered on her.

He gritted his teeth in what might have been jealousy as he watched these men covet her. He watched the appreciation in their eyes as they regarded the creaminess of her skin and the simple elegance of her gown, the scooped neckline offering a tantalising view of smooth flesh. He wondered how they would have reacted had they come upon her as the unkempt youth.

He was not sorry when his guests got up to leave. Excusing himself to Henrietta he went with them, but he was impatient for the time when he would return.

It was nightfall when Simon arrived back at the house. Having eaten, Henrietta was on the terrace, about to take a stroll before retiring to her chamber for the night. The air was chilly and she drew her shawl tighter around her.

Simon emerged quietly from the house. Henrietta had one arm draped loosely round a stone urn brimming with flowers. He paused to watch her for several moments, the moonlight playing over the planes of her face as she stared off into the distance with a melancholy look.

'Here you are,' Simon remarked at length, joining her.

Henrietta lifted her face and smiled at him. For Simon it was as if a shutter had been flung open and the sunlight had rushed in. Her smile was compounded of a luminous gentleness in her eyes. Her fine-boned face, framed by a halo of red and gold stirring in the flower-scented breeze, was a dainty image of fragility as she stood before a man who dwarfed her. Tenderness washed over him and he wanted to pull her into his arms.

Henrietta's pulse rate quickened when she met his dark blue gaze. Her gaze shifted and took in the whole of him. The muscles of his body rippled beneath his coat as he moved, and the sense of his physical power struck her like a blow. She noted the swell of his powerful shoulders concealed by the cloth with a fascination that was disturbing, a little frightening. His body seemed so honed to be perfect—tough and hard as his mind. Standing close, he was looking at her intently. The effect of that look was physical. At that very moment it was as though her heart expanded.

'I was about to walk to the river before retiring. Will you accompany me?'

'I would like that.'

He took her arm as they descended a flight of narrow stone steps to the garden below. His was such an easy, graceful strength, lazy as a big cat stretching in the sun, alert as a cat to spring and strike. His touch and the clean, masculine smell of him, all combined to form a warm, thoroughly intriguing essence that quickened Henrietta's awareness of the man. She realised she was affected in ways she had never dreamt possible, for her womanly senses responded to his gentle touch.

Preoccupied with his thoughts, Simon didn't speak as they walked. On a sigh Henrietta gazed up at the clear expanse of sky.

'It's a full moon,' she murmured, looking up at the huge yellow orb. When Simon didn't reply, she cast about for something else to say. 'I can't quite believe I'm really back in Scotland.'

'Whatever happens, Henrietta, whatever you decide, you do realise that you must go back.'

'Home,' she murmured. 'How can it be home when I am a stranger there? There was a time not so very long ago when I believed I could make my own destiny. Suddenly I feel that I am at the mercy of fate.'

'Maybe it's a bit of both. Sometimes, when we're forced out of the protective walls of the homes we grew up in, we have an opportunity to become instrumental in determining our own fate. We are born with things that define us—personality, humour, resilience—but we can make our own future, too.'

'What you say might be true, but now that I have been thrust out, I have no greater ambition than to return.'

'What is he like, your uncle?'

She thought for a moment, then she said, 'Uncle Matthew is tough—like my father—eccentric, a scholar, perhaps unorthodox. When my father was executed he went away. I don't think he could bear it. I wish he hadn't.'

'And your mother?'

She averted her eyes. 'Mother needed someone very badly after... She bore it as best she could. Before the tragedy, I never knew anyone who had so much self-discipline, such control over herself as my mother. Afterwards she—she lost her mind. There was a lot I couldn't understand when my understanding was that of a child. I learned that what couldn't be cured had to be endured and to endure was unrelenting and doomed from the start.'

Shifting her gaze to the river ahead of them, she became quiet, so quiet and so still that a white moth drifted close, but she continued to stare at the water, deep in her own thoughts. Simon watched her, filled with compassion, for she spoke in a tone of unutterable sadness. He sensed there was more she wasn't telling him, but he wouldn't ask.

After a moment she spoke again, her voice sorrowful, almost vague. 'There was some kind of fatalism about my mother. One thing I learned about her was that something deeper and more complex was involved, that it was the hardiness of her spirit that drew sustenance from her memories of my father. I didn't understand her. I felt so inadequate.'

'Why? Because you were afraid of letting her down?'

'I don't know. But I never aroused in her the same kind of feelings she had for my father.'

Simon thought he had never heard such desolation, or felt it. He felt a surge of admiration for what she had achieved, for what she had overcome, and his admiration was enforced by the pain and loneliness she had endured as a child.

'Do you regret coming back to Scotland?' he asked in an attempt to draw her back to the present.

They were approaching the river's edge and behind them the lights from the house faded and then vanished completely.

'No. I had no choice.'

Suddenly there was nowhere else they could walk, nothing in front of them but the river. They stopped and Simon shoved his hands into his pockets, staring at the river where it meandered into the distance.

Chapter Five

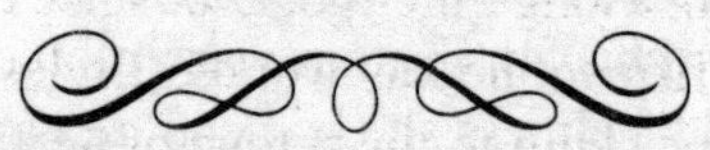

Uncertain of Simon's mood, Henrietta wandered a few paces away from him. It seemed colder here by the water and she pulled her shawl closer about her shoulders, stealing a surreptitious look at him. In the moonlight his profile was harsh and he lifted a hand, rubbing the muscles in the back of his neck as if he was tense.

'I suppose we ought to go back,' she said after a long minute's silence and his silence became unsettling.

In answer Simon tipped his head back and closed his eyes, looking like a man in the throes of some deep, internal battle. 'Why?'

'Because we've reached the river and there's nowhere else to go.'

'If only that were true,' he murmured.

She gave him a questioning look. 'What is it, Simon? Have those men you were with earlier upset you in some way?'

He turned his head towards her and his relentless gaze locked with hers. 'No. We are all of the same mind.'

'You will offer your support to Charles Stuart?'

'I offered my support to his father James Stuart's claim a long time ago. Ever since the rising back in fifteen, he has worked tirelessly, reiterating his claim to the throne of Scotland and England, and the position of his son Charles as heir to that throne. I was in France with Prince Charles for many months—to smooth his path as much as may be with those men who will be of use to him should he head an army of restoration. Restoring kings takes money and he was biding his time in Paris while awaiting King Louis and the French bankers' generosity. But Louis couldn't afford to fight the wars in Brussels and finance invasions in England.'

Simon looked at Henrietta with darkly troubled eyes. He hated conflict of any kind, for though he was confident in his skill with the sword, had trained with it most of his life, he hated the thought of plunging that sharp steel into another man's flesh. 'Don't judge me, Henrietta,' he said quietly.

'I don't. You will do what you feel is right—where your conscience leads you. It's not for me to say whether what you do is right or wrong, only to ask you to think carefully of the consequences should you fail. Because should you fail, the English will give you no quarter. You will be arrested and executed for treason. It seems a dangerous thing you do to me.'

'Aye, but if I die in the process, I'll die knowing I did my best for the cause.'

Suddenly angry at the pressure Charles Stuart was inflicting on men like Simon all over Scotland, Henrietta turned from him, her shoulders tense. 'I hate this. I wish Charles Stuart would take ship back to France. If you must know, the glimpse you and your friends gave me on the heath that night of secret communications and clandestine meetings repelled me. To me it was another world—one that I had supposed to be long gone.'

'But it isn't, is it, Henrietta?'

Her eyes lit with anger. 'No. There will be conflict—it is inevitable, but I want no part of it. I cannot forget the misfortunes that fell upon my family because of Jacobites and my father's treasonable activities. The circumstances have blighted my whole life. I would be mad to associate with them—with you.'

'But you did and you are. I am no traitor, Henrietta.'

'Tell that to King George. If this business is to come to a head, let it burst and be done with it.'

'Which is why I would persuade you to remain at Barradine if I could. I would like to know that you are safe.'

'I can't do that. I have issues of my own to take care of that have nothing to do with your prince. When do we leave for Perth?'

'In the morning.' He put his hands on her shoulders and looked deep into her eyes. 'What if I said that I *wanted* you to stay here?' His voice was husky and there was such intensity in his gaze that Henrietta felt her heartbeat slow. He was a handsome man and in the days they had been together she had become extremely fond of him, more than she was prepared to admit.

She shook her head. 'I can't. I shall miss you when we part,' she whispered.

'Then stay.'

'No, Simon.' She was startled at how difficult it was for her to form the words. The regret in his eyes was sincere. She pressed a hand to her lips, her eyes closing at a renewed sense of loss.

On a sigh he stepped back, but his eyes remained fastened on hers. 'You will forgive me if, for the time we have left at Barradine, I use my powers of persuasion to get you to change your mind.'

'As you like, but my own powers of persuasion are often to be reckoned with.'

Simon grinned. 'You certainly appear to

have worked wonders on my neighbours earlier. They scarcely removed their eyes from your face throughout the repast. It's amazing what effect a beautiful and talented woman can have on men—even men such as they, whose heads are filled with conflict. Before too long you'll have every one of them eating out of your hands—and may well break several hearts—as you did mine, when I witnessed you in your bath.'

'That night there was only one particular heart I would truly have liked to render into little pieces for your audacity,' she said quietly, a hint of savagery in her tone.

Simon laughed softly, chucking her under the chin. 'I fear you are going to need to keep your wits sharp and all your courage in future dealings with me. So take heed. You might find yourself out of your depth—and you will not be the first woman to do so.'

Henrietta's eyebrows flicked upwards. 'I think I have made an accurate assessment of your character, my lord,' she said, speaking with confidence, for it did not occur to her that she was already falling under the spell of a practised seducer, such men being beyond the realms of her experience.

'You are proving to be the most charming diversion, Henrietta. I'd be willing to wait a while longer before joining the prince if it allowed us to become better acquainted.'

Simon looked at her, his eyes softening at the tantalising picture she presented in her pale green dress, the fabric shaking like a leaf in the breeze blowing off the river. Her cropped hair made her face look naked, giving it the appearance of fragility and wantonness, a striking contrast that touched him. The tender pink flesh of her lips looked so appealing that he was tempted to savour them.

The colour on Henrietta's cheeks was gloriously high. Her eyes were sparkling like twin orbs. They were the most brilliant eyes Simon had ever seen, of a green so bright they seemed lit from within. He was not a man of such iron control that he could resist looking down at her feminine form. Noticing things such as how her gown clung to her round curves so provocatively, concealing the sweet treasures beneath, gave him a clear sense of pleasurable torture. Now she was so close he could feel her warmth, smell the sweet scent of her body, all in such close proximity. The explosion of passion that erupted in his body surprised him and sent heat searing into his loins.

Wary of the look she saw in his eyes, Henrietta stepped past him, but he caught her arm and pulled her back. She stood close to him, momentarily stunned by the force of his assault. He stood poised above her, blocking out the night sky, her surroundings, so that she felt a rush of helplessness and was aware of nothing else but his overwhelming presence. His eyes held a burning glow of intent, but deep in their depths there was something else she had never seen before, something that defied analysis and made her afraid.

'Let go of me, Simon,' she whispered. 'I think we should go back.'

'Why? Do not turn from me.' His voice had softened to the timbre of rough velvet and made Henrietta's senses jolt almost as much as the strange way he was looking at her. 'I've known many women, Henrietta, and ventured far and wide, but no maid has provoked my imagination to such a degree as you do. You are a temptress, dangerous and destructive in your innocence. 'Tis hard for me seeing you day after day, knowing you are almost within my arm's reach night after night, and not touching you as I want to. I want to kiss you now—which I am sure you will find pleasurable,' he murmured, his eyes fastened on her trembling lips.

With her heart pounding in swift beats, she swallowed audibly. 'I don't think I will.'

'How can you be sure—until you've sampled it?'

Panic seized her but she was powerless to escape. 'Please, Simon. Let me go.'

'Not a chance,' he murmured huskily, his face lowering to hers, the subtle fragrance emanating from her body firing his desire.

Simon's face was poised above hers, close, looking deep into her eyes, his warm breath caressing her face. Lowering his head, he covered her mouth with his own, his lips insistent, parting her own and kissing her slowly, long and deep. She strained to resist the feel of his hands on her body, his mouth on hers, but her weak flesh began to respond and at last she yielded, her lips answering his in mindless rapture.

She became languid and relaxed with sensuality, uttering a moan and a sigh of pleasure. Sensations like tight buds were opened and exploded into flowers of splendour, growing stronger and sweeter. She felt the hardness of his body pressed close to her own and a melting softness flowed through her veins, evoking feelings she had never experienced before or thought herself capable of feeling.

Simon lifted his head and looked down at her with burning eyes before his mouth claimed hers once more. There was nothing gentle about this kiss, not like the first. This time it was hard and brutal, making her realise the tender kiss had been but a ploy to what would inevitably follow if she remained.

Henrietta struggled in the circle of his arms to get away, but she was filled with a like need, wanton and shameless and, closing her eyes, her treacherous woman's body cleaved to his. Her fear was gone and she was devoid of will as she threw her head back so that he could bury his lips, warm and soft, in the creamy hollow of her throat, trailing them down to the partly naked, gentle swell of her breasts above the bodice of her gown before finding her lips once more, sending her soaring into a void of violent pleasure. Time ceased to exist and nothing that had gone before mattered to her then. Her body glowed and throbbed with delicious need and she was drowning in a sea of pleasure.

When Simon raised his head and pulled back she was not aware of it at first, but her disappointment was real when she realised he was no longer kissing her. She was shocked with its strength and intensity. This, her first kiss, was an embrace that surged through her body, mind and soul. The length of the kiss had no relevance. It was powerful enough to feel, even though her life now divided to two parts—before and after the feel of his lips on hers.

She opened her eyes to see him looking down at her and he watched as she struggled to return to the conscious world. Gently he kissed her again, a kiss unrelated to time or space, past or future, a kiss that was neither a beginning nor an end, but something mystically complete. Neither of them had any idea how long it lasted, but after a moment Simon had to find the strength to put a stop to what he had so dangerously begun, because the only alternative to going on was to go nowhere, because there seemed to be between them a mystical alchemy that could only lead to disaster.

'You are wanton, Henrietta,' he murmured smoothly, his lips against hers. 'Wanton and unable to protect yourself from your own desires. You are young and inexperienced in matters of love—and yet your body seems to know how to respond perfectly.'

His soft words and quiet smile brought Henrietta quickly to her senses—angry with him as much as she was with herself for yielding to his will so readily, shamelessly, telling herself she should have known better. She stilled beneath the spotlight of his gaze, trying to hold her breath for fear of what he might say next, which made her feel as though she might burst.

'Well,' she said when his words were not forthcoming, 'was that what you wanted?'

Her question was not what Simon had anticipated, but he had to answer. 'It was more than I hoped for. You must forgive me, Henrietta. I got quite carried away by your charms. I had to stop lest I forgot myself altogether and tumbled you here and now—which would never do.'

Horror at her own reaction brought Henrietta moving away from him. His seductive eyes met hers and she realised her body had provided the information as to its willingness to comply with his needs as he had wanted. She stood looking at him with her cheeks burning, trembling, unable to conceal her feelings, the gentle amusement he did not attempt to hide in his eyes making her blood boil.

'How dare you do that!' she cried in an attempt to conceal her confusion and mixed-up emotions with a show of outrage. 'How dare you take advantage of me when I am at my most defenceless! I am no common trollop to be tumbled at will—unless, of course, molesting respectable females is the usual thing with you. Why—if—if I were a man I would call you out and have you horsewhipped.'

Simon sighed, a smile curving his handsome mouth. 'And there was I thinking you wanted me to kiss you.'

'I most certainly did not.'

'Perhaps you should try harder at being a lady then,' he admonished. 'A gentlewoman should try harder resisting a gentleman's kiss.'

'And do you accept that a gentleman should handle a lady so rudely?' Henrietta scoffed with rancour. 'I declare that, in spite of the many threats against his person, Henry was treated more gently than this. Perhaps I chose the wrong disguise. You would no doubt have been more at ease with the lad.'

'Maybe so,' Simon murmured distantly. 'But I favour your present form above that of an unkempt lad.'

His face was so close, Henrietta had no difficulty discerning its every detail, and the soft lazy smile it bore awoke burning memories of the kiss that, while thrilling, were most disturbing. The shivery warmth that ran through her completely disturbed her composure. She turned her face away and thus betrayed the sudden blush that was discernible in the misty darkness.

Pivoting around, no longer able to look upon his handsome face without reaching out and slapping the insolent smile from his lips, hearing him laugh softly behind her, she hurriedly strode towards the house, the memory of his burning kiss, of his hands as they had caressed her body, and all the dark and secret pleasures they had aroused in her, filling her with fresh paroxysms of anger. It was necessary to kill what had happened between them, now, and finally. The risks were too great.

Not even when she reached the sanctuary of her bedchamber did the humiliating sickness leave her.

The smile left Simon's lips as his gaze followed her and he was puzzled by his own reaction to her. She was a curious mix of child and woman, an adolescent on the brink of adulthood, naive and yet worldly. She exuded a sensuality, the memory of which would keep him awake at night. He could still feel the lingering, warm, beguiling sweetness of her. His smouldering stare took in her retreating figure. She was so lovely, so innocent, so ripe for seduction.

But the girl was vulnerable, traumatised. He could not take advantage of such an innocent creature. He knew that what she needed right now was someone she could trust, not some stranger seducing her. He turned away, suddenly furious with himself for having succumbed so easily and foolishly to her charm. He had let himself be mindlessly borne away on a rush of passion. Was she some kind of sorceress who had cast a spell on him?

But never had he met a female who possessed so much freedom of spirit and courage, who was so open and direct. He knew she would never be anything other than honest, and the brightness in that steady, often disconcerting gaze was an intelligent brightness that proclaimed the agility of an independent mind. There was an untamed quality about her that found a counterpart in his own hot-blooded, impetuous nature.

Unfortunately, the realisation of what was about to happen on the political scene and that he had no time for affairs of the heart banished his pleasure. But he could not escape the fact that from the moment she had shed her masquerade she had fascinated and intrigued him.

Henrietta's stomach tensed at the memory of what had occurred in the garden. Having breakfasted in her room and dressed in the clothes of a youth once more, ready to begin the journey and waiting for Simon, she was seated in a window recess in the hall, watching the servants as they bustled about. Wearily she rolled her head against the pane. She knew with certainty that she would never be free of Simon Tremain. With each day he grew bolder. It was a good thing they were leaving Barradine for Edinburgh and then on to Perth, where they would part company and she would go on her way alone to Inverness.

Aware of someone walking towards her, she opened her eyes and lifted her head. It was Simon. His masterful face was set in taut, unreadable lines. As he approached her she looked into his eyes, which were startling and distracting. So many conflicting and unfamiliar emotions were at war within her—anger, humiliation, hurt pride—but also frightening and exciting emotions that were bewildering, weakening her resolve to remain detached from him to the point where restraint ended and submission to his will began. No longer could she maintain her indifference towards him, or ignore the strange forces that were at work between them, drawing them together.

What had he done to her? What had happened to her? Was she wanton and shameless for wanting him to repeat the kiss—and more? They were not romantically attached and yet she was not so naive as not to recognise that his kiss had been given out of passion. His behaviour towards her had been both playful and serious, and he seemed to delight in her confusion.

As Simon approached her, her look of nervous apprehension took him aback. Her smile was turned inward to a sweet, imploring look of appeal. How different she suddenly appeared from the young woman who had revealed herself to him on the night they had arrived at the house—that proud, controlled creature whose beauty and self-possession filled him with longing. He thought that perhaps she was feeling unwell—but then he realised that what had happened between them the previous night had affected her in a way he had not realised.

To lighten the mood between them he said teasingly, 'Coward.'

Immediately her eyes widened. 'Are you calling me a coward?'

He nodded, looming over her and challenging her with a direct stare.

Indignation flared in Henrietta's eyes at the slur. 'Please explain to me why you accuse me of such. I have done nothing deserving of the insult.'

Simon shrugged slightly, a gleam of humour in his eyes. 'Last night when we kissed, you obviously assumed the worst—that I was bent on seducing you into further submission. Rather than wait and see, you ran from the garden as if your petticoats were on fire.'

A rush of colour brightened her cheeks. 'At the time it didn't seem advisable to stay. Now please forget what happened between us and concentrate on today.'

Not wanting her to see that he was concerned, he poured her a glass of wine, hoping it would fortify her for the journey and help her to compose herself. He was glad to see the return of her proud smile, but though her assurance and confidence returned, that glimpse of her vulnerability drew forth emotions that he had never known before. He felt the desire to protect her, to keep her from harm, but how was he to do that when she was hell-bent on going to Inverness?

Standing up, Henrietta set the empty glass down. 'Are we ready to leave?'

He nodded. 'I'm relieved to see the clothes fit you.'

'Yes, thank you. They are surprisingly comfortable, although the breeches are a little tight in places.'

Simon's gaze travelled with satisfaction over her boyish garb. She had looked so appealing and accessible in her feminine dress and in her boy's clothes he had thought he'd be able to ignore her better. But the lad's breeches had deftly conspired to make her look all the more feminine and desirable. They showed every detail, cleaving to her legs and buttocks like a second skin. When she bent over to stroke the silky ears of a small dog running about the hall, he found himself viewing a very fetching *derrière* stuck up in the air like a flag of truce. He could gladly have accepted Henrietta's surrender almost on any terms, yet he was prone to wonder if he was having another lewd fantasy involving her.

'They belong to my brother Edward.'

'I hope he won't mind you giving them to me.'

'He has no need of the clothes. By the time he returns to Barradine, he'll have outgrown them.'

When she made to walk past him to collect her bag he took her arm, halting her. His relentless gaze locked with hers. 'Will you not reconsider remaining here, Henrietta? My home is at your disposal and you will be quite safe.'

'No. I've told you,' she said, finding it difficult to continue looking into his eyes, 'I must go on. You won't stop me, will you?'

'I won't, despite my own selfish reasons for wanting to keep you here. Neither of us has anything to gain by pretending the other doesn't exist—that the kiss we shared in the garden never happened. I remember it, and I know damn well you remember it, too.'

Henrietta wanted to deny it, but she couldn't lie to him. He was right. The burning memory of that kiss lay between them, which had become a source of hideous anguish to her now. 'I haven't forgotten. How could I?' she added defensively.

'I do realise that you must go to your uncle—and I have the serious business of joining Prince Charles. But you could stay here as long as you need to.'

He spoke in that cajoling tone that charmed Henrietta. She shivered when she recalled the touch of his lips, which she was consciously yearning for. Glancing up at him, she found him gazing at her with a look that was questioning and much too personal, almost possessive. It disturbed her greatly for she could not ignore it. She could feel the power within him and sensations of unexpected pleasure flowed through her. However, she had too many complications in her life just now and had no intention of becoming emotionally entangled with him. At this time of uncertainty she could not afford to.

'No, Simon. Your offer is indeed generous, but I cannot accept it. I must be cautious, lest I forget who you are and why I am here in Scotland.' She became thoughtful, observing him with earnest attention. 'I don't want to fall in love with you.'

His expression became grave. 'I have no intention of making you.'

'I am relieved.'

'Why?'

'Because that would never do. I admit I am attracted to you and it's the hardest thing trying to resist you—you can be extremely persuasive. But I trust you understand why I must go. I don't want you to feel rejected, spurned—anything like that. You are very special to me. I like and respect you too much. You do understand, don't you?'

'I'm trying.'

'You are also a Jacobite, about to rise in arms against the Protestants, against the king. You remind me of my father—and the misery the cause he worked for brought to the lives of my mother and me. I will not go through that again. I don't think I could bear it. You must forgive me if I seem ungrateful, but please understand that I would feel uncomfortable staying here. I am beholden to you enough as it is for letting me accompany you to Scotland and stay here—and the clothes you have so generously given me.'

'Beholden? What a strange woman you are, Henrietta Brody. However, I have no wish for you to feel beholden to me—for anything,' Simon said, clearly at pains to control his mirth.

'Good. And don't mock me,' Henrietta reproached, glaring at the wicked humour she saw dancing in his bright blue eyes. 'But I really must thank you for allowing me to accompany you to Scotland.'

Simon looked at her, his smiling face setting in grave lines. 'It was my pleasure.' He meant what he said. Beneath the heavy fringe of dark lashes her eyes were mesmerising in their lack of guile and her smooth cheeks were flushed a becoming pink. 'You are refreshingly open and honest, with a gentle pride I admire. I want to kiss you again—very badly, in fact—to hold you in my arms. But you are right. You are wise to resist me and I understand your reasons perfectly. What do I have to offer you? Only myself and a life that is at best precarious.'

His reply had a deep, hypnotic quality. Henrietta gave a wistful, almost shy smile. 'There you are, then. We are agreed on that.' His handsome face was sombre. She was acutely aware of his powerful male body looming over her, tall and strong—of a man who had gallantly taken care of her and shouldered all her burdens for the past two weeks. The combination of that was becoming dangerously appealing. When a lump of emotion rose in her throat and tears threatened, helplessly she met the probing gaze of the man. Considering how resolutely she had defied Jeremy's attempts to see her humiliated and destroyed, she could hardly believe that she could lose control just because someone was showing a bit of kindness.

Henrietta didn't know how explicit her expression was—like an open book, exposing what was in her heart. Simon saw it and was immediately wary and in that moment he realised that eliminating her from his life when they reached Perth was going to be harder than he'd imagined. He looked at her hard, tracing every line of her face, every warm, beating part of her. He breathed in the essence of what lay between them, as if to imprison her image into his memory.

The words she had spoken were sincere and heartfelt. She was right. She couldn't waste one moment of her life believing she was in love with him and he had done well, not letting her know how much he had come to care for her, how much she belonged in his heart. There was no time or place for love in his life, he asserted to himself. No room for it as long as Charles Stuart called the faithful to arms. But it was hard, no matter how he tried, to still his emotional rebellion against the rational reason of his mind.

'Now come along,' Henrietta said, picking up her bag and hoisting it to her shoulder. 'If we dally much longer we'll be hard-pressed to reach Edinburgh before nightfall.'

Simon followed her out of the house. At the door she turned and looked back at him. It was a special look just for him. It seemed to beckon with strange energies. It seduced him absolutely and left him bewildered in the most sensual way. He was intrigued by the enigma of this young woman, whose naive personality concealed a mysterious core of which Henrietta herself was perhaps not aware of.

He followed her, heeding her words and forcing himself with an effort to shift his thoughts to who she was and why she was here, but somewhere in the caverns of his mind, he knew there would come a day when he would possess her completely.

* * *

The sky was clear and blue as Simon and Henrietta continued on their journey. On Simon's advice Henrietta left her horse at Barradine. Mounted on a sturdy, short-legged, shaggy Highland garron—essential for the route they were to take, for they were admirable for travelling over distance and rough ground, but not so fast—she was less conspicuous.

The countryside was wild and desolate, just as Henrietta remembered. She tipped her head back to catch the warmth of the midday sun on her face and breathed deeply of the cool, fresh breezes that brought the tang of the heather to her from across the moors. There were two buzzards soaring high in the blue sky, while far below them the martins dashed about in droves, hunting their dinner.

Henrietta had left Scotland as a child, but seeing the gently undulating Cheviots in the north and seeing the familiar shaggy cattle and black-faced sheep was like balm to her soul.

They followed drovers' and packhorse tracks, tracks that had been followed for centuries. Henrietta felt secure in the presence of her companion. Having lived there all his life, Simon knew the area well and, looking fearsome astride his huge horse, with a pistol at his belt and a sword hanging from his saddle, he would instil caution in the meanest robber. He pointed out places of interest, enthusing at length about each and every one of them. It was clear to Henrietta how much he loved this country, that it was as familiar to him as his own heartbeat.

They finally reached Edinburgh, Scotland's capital city, the glowering presence of the castle on its rock dominating the town with its massive structure. The long days of summer were drawing in and lamps had been lit in windows. They found themselves on the Royal Mile with its wynds and closes, the cobbled street climbing from Holyrood House to the castle.

The town was crowded to suffocation point and reeked of humanity. All but nauseated by both what her eyes and her nose told her, Henrietta was astonished that Simon seemed not at all affected.

'You shall grow accustomed to it,' he remarked, noting her discomfort, his lips curved into a slight smile.

'I doubt that very much,' Henrietta said, shaking her head. 'I feel as though I cannot breathe.'

'It takes some getting used to for the first few days. But I assure you that in a day or so you won't notice. There's so much going on in Edinburgh, so one stops worrying about the stench.'

Henrietta was not convinced of that. Continuing to hold the handkerchief to her nose as they rode, she glanced at the buildings that soared on either side of them with a feeling of being boxed in. The whole town was thronged with the Highland army and men gathered and talked in earnest, stirring the embers of rebellion. Others had their heads bent as they went about their business and women watched their men and kept their children close. There was a general air of excitement and speculation, and in many homes weapons hoarded since the rising in '15 were excavated from hiding places and burnished and sharpened. Scottish chieftains—Glengarry, Clan Ranald and McDonalds to name but a few—had all declared their loyalty and staked their lives and reputations on the success of Charles Stuart.

Impatient to join the main body of the army, Simon lost no time in renting rooms above an alleyway in Canongate. Fortunately they were spacious and relatively comfortable.

'Get some rest,' he said to Henrietta. 'You look exhausted.'

'What about you?' she asked, shoving her hand through her hair.

'I'm going to the army's headquarters to find out what's happening. But with things as they are and the town full of Highlanders, I am cautious for your safety. The owner of the rooms will see that someone sees to your needs, but make sure that you lock the door when I've gone.'

* * *

When Simon returned, the hour was close to midnight. He found the welcoming warmth of a well-banked fire awaiting him and a goodly supply of wood had been laid up on the hearth. Pulling a chair close to the flames, he slowly worked his boots from his feet. Adding another log to the fire, he strode about the room, removing his jacket and loosening his shirt. Knowing he would have to leave Edinburgh before dawn and reluctant to leave Henrietta, with nothing to occupy his roaming mind he was restless to a fault.

He went to stand beside Henrietta's door, there to listen for a long moment. He could not hear even the faintest breath of a whisper or movement. Curiously he reached out to test the door, pushing it open, and in his stocking feet, crossed the room with noiseless tread. In the light from the open door he looked down upon Henrietta's sleeping face. Her long lashes lay like dark shadows on her fair cheeks and her soft lips were slightly parted as she breathed long and slowly in deepest slumber. Her hair curled on the pillow in deep golden hues while her arm rested in a flawless ivory curve above her head, leaving her shoulder and the higher swelling curves of her bosom naked to his gaze.

He allowed his gaze to linger on her face and

the tempting fullness of her breasts, as one who had chosen to savour a special treat. In sleep she seemed indeed most innocent with her delicate features and creamy skin and yet, when awake, she seemed to exude the very essence of life. Though the sight inflamed his passions and started the blood coursing through his veins, Simon reminded himself that he was not there for a lover's tryst.

As if in response to his musings, the long lashes fluttered open and, when she turned her head on the pillow, he found himself gazing down into the green depths. She stared at him calmly, as if her thoughts were readily at her disposal and not dazed by the confusion of sleep.

'Simon?'

'I did not mean to wake you. Go back to sleep.'

Her gaze passed slowly over his naked chest to the breeches that clung boldly to the manliness of him. He made no attempt to hide evidence of his arousal, which prompted Henrietta to lower her gaze. 'You are leaving, aren't you? When must you go?' Her voice was small and timid.

'Soon.'

'Would you have wakened me?'

He nodded. 'I would not have left without talking with you first.'

'Thank you.' Protecting her modesty with the sheets and sitting up, she reached for her shirt and dragged it over her head. 'What is happening?' she asked, shoving back the covers and getting out of bed, pulling down the shirt to cover her nakedness.

'The Highland army is ready to stand against the English.'

'Where?'

'At Prestonpans to the east—near the coast. The main bulk of the Highland army occupy the surrounding hills.'

'Does that mean you won't be going to Perth?'

'Yes. I must leave to join up with the men from Barradine. They are here in Edinburgh. I must ride with them to Charles Stuart—whom duty and honour call me to follow—while wishing there were some way I could pervert his cause that I am sworn to uphold.'

'Such gallant foolishness could get you killed,' Henrietta whispered, but she knew that she could not turn him from the course he had decided on.

'I know that, but I will not turn back—I cannot,' he added quietly. 'I have come too far. I have no choice but to help Charles Stuart win. And to that end, as many men and arms as can possibly be summoned at Barradine will be summoned to the cause.'

Henrietta shivered beneath the steely glint in

his eyes. Setting her mouth in a stubborn line and holding her arms across her breasts, she turned her profile to him with her nose lifted in the air. 'Even though you might fail and your life and property will be forfeit to the Crown?'

'I have taken care of that. I have conveyed the estate to my brother Edward. The property will be held in trust and administered by my mother and her brother, who has proved his loyalty to King George on numerous occasions. The document is signed by me and witnessed. It is dated the first of March, 1745, before Charles Stuart launched his rebellion in Scotland and made me a traitor to the Crown.'

'I congratulate you on your foresight, but should you not be killed in battle, you will be rightly branded a traitor to the king and sought, and when you are caught you will be led straight to the gallows.'

'I know all that.'

'And—and so you should,' she chided.

Hearing the catch in her voice and seeing that her eyes brimmed bright with tears, Simon caught her shoulder and turned her to face him. A strange look of reluctant sadness showed through the otherwise determined mien he always assumed.

Unable to bear the thought of him dying, Henrietta swallowed down the lump that suddenly rose in her throat. 'God willing there will be no battle, and if there is you will come through unscathed.'

Chafing over his difficulty to forge ahead into the bare facts of their predicament and thereby strip Henrietta of all hope of him accompanying her to Perth, he looked away and combed his fingers through his hair in frustration. Tentatively he approached the subject. 'Believe me when I tell you that my intentions were to see you taken to Perth and then to secure you an escort to take you to the safety of your uncle.'

'An escort to take me?' Henrietta grasped hold of his words, and when she spoke her tone was thick with emotion. 'You should not have made plans for me. I make my own way, Simon. I thought that was understood.' Her voice betrayed her crumbling composure. 'I have stressed time and again that I will not become embroiled in what is happening. I have my own problems to sort out without taking on Charles Stuart. But what will happen? Will you win the day?'

'This time, maybe. Though my provisions were to see you safely away by now, it cannot be done, for the threat from the English is too great. 'Tis a long and dangerous trek to Inverness for a woman alone at the best of times. Now, in the violent, self-seeking climate of the times, it would not be wise. I can neither take you to your uncle nor allow you to take yourself. There are enough raw Highlanders about to give a virtuous maid cause to worry.'

'But by all intents and purposes I am a youth. Are you saying my disguise can be seen through?'

'Not at all, but you make a bonny lad, Henrietta, and will stir the basest inclinations of some. You must be sensible and stay here until I return.'

Henrietta stared at him in wonder, beginning to understand that he was afraid for her and was strangely ashamed that events had not worked out to allow for her to leave. 'Is this the thing that eats at you, my staying, or the battle?'

'I thought I had planned well enough to see you safely on your way by now,' he confessed in a hushed whisper. 'It pains me much to know that I've failed you.'

Henrietta stared at him in disbelief. '*Failed me?* How can you say that? Without you I would not have come so far. I stand much in awe of what you have done for me. And what of Charles Stuart? You were not to know that his army was gathering at Prestonpans. There was nothing you could do.'

'Yes, there was. I should have left you at Barradine—under lock and key if necessary.'

Henrietta would have protested, but he pressed his fingers gently against her mouth to still her arguments. She blinked at the sudden wetness in her eyes as he leaned down to press his lips to her brow. His mouth found its way to hers, and a long moment passed as he kissed her, then, raising his head he clasped her close to him, as if he would draw her into himself.

'We cannot remain together now. Please understand.' The muscles flexed in his cheeks as he fought for command. 'I'll come to you later. I promise. You will be here, won't you, Henrietta?' he asked at length, watching her intently.

She lowered her eyes for a moment, then sighed. 'Yes. Yes, I will be here.'

'I do sorrow for our parting, Henrietta.'

'So do I,' she confessed. Weak from the turbulence of her emotions, she thought her heart would break. Holding her away from him, he stepped back. She looked at him, holding her breath for what was to come. His face was as still as his body, expressionless, except for his eyes searching hers. She felt those eyes, felt them as a physical force, as powerful as a physical force, probing deep within her.

'I think it is time we reached a clear understanding about what is happening between us.'

His words confused her. This man was everything her father had been. The dangers he posed to her senses and emotions were immense, yet the physical desire she felt for him continued to ache inside her. A small insidious voice whispered a caution, reminding her that any liaison with Simon would bring her nothing but heartbreak, but another voice was whispering something else, telling her not to let the moment pass, to catch it and hold on to it. The intensity of feeling between them was evident, but not easily understood. What she did know was that now, on the eve of a battle that could remove him from her life altogether, this might be the last time they could be together like this.

But still she hesitated, for what she was contemplating went beyond anything she had ever contemplated before. She was more frightened than she had ever been in her life and was both appalled and ashamed that she could even consider doing such a monstrous thing. But wasn't this what she had wanted, what she had thought about ever since he had kissed her at Barradine? All she wanted was for him to hold her like that again and to kiss her into insensibility.

As if her need had communicated itself to Simon with his eyes fastened to her lips, he said, 'When I kissed you just now, your lips tasted as sweet on mine as I remembered.'

'It's strange that I have come so far from home to find you.'

His eyes searched hers for evidence of her meaning, and almost hesitantly he enquired,

'Should I take encouragement from your statement, Henrietta?'

Gathering together all her strength, she thrust away her fears, her anguish and all thoughts of farewell. 'I grant you leave to think what you might,' she murmured softly. 'Must you leave so soon?'

Simon looked into her eyes with frightening intensity, and a long moment passed before he frowned and shook his head. 'It's for the best. We both know what would happen if I stayed. I don't want you to be hurt.'

'I—I won't be—but I will if you go.'

Her voice trembled and she looked at him. He stood there, silent, frowning still, the frown digging a deep groove above the bridge of his nose. The air between them was charged with a new kind of tension and anticipation. Those blue eyes studied her, darkening to almost black. Henrietta knew what he was thinking. It frightened her just a little, but she did not lower her eyes. Her silence, her level gaze, said more than words. The decision was hers, she knew that, and she knew that she should let him go, now, while there was time, while there was still a choice—but she could not do that. After tonight she might never see him again. There really wasn't any choice. She looked at him.

He knew.

Chapter Six

Henrietta was nervous now, trembling inside, longing to be safe somewhere else, longing not to know the meaning of these new emotions that held her in thrall, but her step didn't falter as she moved towards her destiny. She was destined to love this man and knew it would be futile to try to resist. She shouldn't love him—common sense told her this was dangerous folly, but what she felt for him was too strong, too compelling, and she refused to listen. And yet, inexperienced as she was, she felt helpless, filled with longing, filled with love, not knowing how to express it.

Simon took a deep breath and saw what was in her eyes. Tentatively she reached out and touched his hand. His chest rose as he took another deep breath, and his mouth tightened, his eyes full of indecision. She reached up and brushed a V-shaped wave from his brow. It was heavy, like silk to the touch, the hair spilling through her fingers and tumbling back into place immediately.

She dragged her hand away, in the course of which she heightened a multitude of sensations that had already been stimulated in Simon when he had lightly kissed her. The hot blood had surged through him with all the swift and fiery intensity at the very instant his lips made contact with hers, making him achingly aware of his ravaging desire. Now, a moment after her hand was removed from his forehead, the ravenous flames still pulsed with excruciating vigour through his loins. With every fibre of his being, he was acutely aware of the elusive fragrance of Henrietta filling his head, that same fragrance which he breathed with intoxicating pleasure every time he was near her.

Her soft bosom drew his sweeping perusal, and when he finally lifted his gaze to meet hers, he found himself staring into widened eyes filled with need. That simple act proved his undoing. Whatever noble intentions he had meant to manifest in her presence, no matter how scant they might have been, were hacked asunder as his male instincts rose up. He was a man famished for want of a woman and his hungering eyes devoured the delicious sights as if he contemplated his first meal after a lengthy fast.

He hesitated a moment longer, then his eyes

filled with tenderness, and Henrietta knew he was feeling as she did, fight it though he might. With a sudden move he slid an arm about her narrow waist and pulled her close. The faltering limits of his will were sorely strained. He knew well enough what her scantily clad form was doing to him. Yet for the life of him, he could not abandon the tantalising situation he now found himself in.

His boldness knew no bounds as he spread a hand over the curve of her buttock and pressed her hips tightly against his loins and sought her lips. His heart was hammering so hard that Henrietta seemed to feel it beating in her own breast. She felt the shuddering of his whole body and she knew that his desires had grown beyond his power to master them.

A knowledge only confirmed when, lifting his head briefly from the lips which he had been crushing under her own, he whispered softly, 'A man cannot always control how his body responds to a beautiful woman. Being with you arouses longings I've struggled hard to suppress for a long time. I'm a man, Henrietta, subject to all the feelings and flaws of my gender. As a man I greatly enjoy having you near me. You're soft and alluring and you graced my home like a delicate, fragrant flower that bestirs the senses. I do desire you as a woman and yet I would never force you or knowingly hurt you.'

A soft, quavering sigh passed Henrietta's lips. 'I do not want us to part,' she admitted diffidently. 'I have the same feelings as you.'

'Then don't be ashamed of them. They are honest feelings and all part of being human. My love, I entreat you not to…'

She placed a finger to his lips, stopping his words. 'Don't say it. I know there is no future for us together and I do not know what you expect from me, but this may be our only chance.'

Losing the battle, Simon reached a hand beneath her chin, lifting her face as his own lowered. His kiss was gentle and loving, but as it lingered, their emotions turned on a different path. A slow warming began to spread through their minds and bodies, and all thoughts of Charles Stuart and what was to come were swept away as Simon lifted her in his arms and carried her to the bed. He drew in a ragged breath. It was a momentous task for him to hold her naked form in his arms and remain tender and patient when his hunger for her had brought him to the brink of starvation.

'Teach me how to make love to you, Simon,' she whispered. 'Let me know what is so pleasurable to a man. For this one night I want to be your lover, replacing all thoughts of any other you might have once cherished.' What she was doing suddenly halted her, her breath stopping for barely a pause as she raised her gaze to the slight, questioning curve that traced the handsome lips.

'Are you not afraid?' he asked.

Thoughtful for a moment, in the soft light Henrietta considered the question. She saw the desire gleam darkly in his eyes—she shivered. It was her first time. Never before had she wanted to do this, to make love to a man. She was so ignorant—she did not want him to despise her timidity. It was the rivulets of excitement that pulsed through her body as she stared at him that brought a soft, challenging glow to her eyes. 'Not afraid. Curious, perhaps.'

'I will be gentle,' he said, drawing her close.

With a beguiling smile she placed her lips softly on his, sliding both hands slowly over the wide chest, marvelling as she caressed the rugged firmness of the muscular expanse.

Since the moment her deception had been uncovered Simon had never ceased to be amazed and fascinated by the enticing blend of innocence and boldness he had seen in the woman he now held in his arms. Each trait was wonderfully intriguing and he was never more aware of his infatuation than at this present moment, when they were about to enter the world of intimacy. Warmed and intrigued by her and accepting her touch and the warming heat in her eyes, enjoying the moment he leisurely caressed her lips with his own, eventually abandoning them for the tantalising fullness of her breasts. He caressed them with his mouth, pressing wanton kisses over their warmth.

Henrietta's head fell back as fires raged in the depths of her body. His hands, powerful and devilish, ran down her sides, down her legs, inciting fires in her. She moaned aloud as his hands caressed her firm breasts, tweaking the proudly jutting nipples, then proceeded with agonising slowness, to explore her body. Down past her flat stomach his hands roamed, down to the juncture of her slender legs. A pulsing heat began to throb in her loins, spreading upwards and outwards as his deft hands sought the centre of her passion.

Fires that she had never known existed, had never before felt, flamed within her body. She thrust out her breasts to luxuriate in the hot, flicking strokes of his tongue. Her breath was wont to catch in ecstatic gasps, interrupting the quickening, shallow rhythm. She felt consumed by a pleasure that threatened to melt every fibre of her body. Never in her wildest imaginings had she guessed the height to which a lover's touch could send her.

Simon rolled her onto her back, leaning over

her, at the same time settling her beneath him. His mouth blended with hers as his hands continued to move leisurely over her body. The sensations aroused with his kisses and the touch of his hands on her body, combined with the subtle pressure of his maleness, set Henrietta's heart beating to a new, frantic rhythm that suffused her with an expanding warmth. A strange frenzy seized her and she cried out in fear and surprise as his manhood made its first foray against her virginity. But the pain of penetration was but a brief discomfort that she forced back as she became aware of a driving need to appease an insatiable hunger.

Simon touched her lips, drinking in the glory of her, his hands cupping her buttocks, bringing her closer as he began to move. Amazement etched her flushed face as he met her stroke for stroke with vigour and the budding, blossoming pleasure in Henrietta's loins intensified and swept her on with the promise of still greater heights to reach.

More passion erupted within Henrietta and she arched her back to meet Simon. Their bodies, slick with sweat, adhered one to the other, and for a lingering moment, a perfect moment, she thought, a moment without end, they were one. Flinging her head back, she let him love her with all her heart, mind and body. Nothing existed for her outside this man and their love. Then he growled deep in his throat as his large surge of ardour was released.

For a moment Henrietta seemed to glide and then her world reeled out of control as a ravishing, rapturous splendour burst upon her as a myriad of scintillating flashes of ecstasy rippled over her. For ever joined as one, they remained fused by the heat of their loins, joined by the love in their hearts.

Limp and exhausted, a long, ragged sigh slipped from Simon's lips as he slowly withdrew and relaxed his body against her. He kissed her soft shoulder as he felt her fingers play in his hair. He was so breathless he waited a long moment before he could speak. His head rested on her breast, and he could hear her heart beating.

'Henrietta—' he began.

Her fingers pressed against his lips and he kissed them. 'No,' she said softly. 'Don't speak.'

He nodded, feeling the smoothness of her ivory breast under his cheek. Rolling to the side of her, he gathered her to him, holding her close, kissing her and stroking her body as if he would never let her go. As he released her lips, his eyes gleamed into hers. Though recently sated, he could feel again an awakening deep within his loins.

'Is your curiosity appeased, my love?' he murmured at length.

Feeling the returning heat, Henrietta moved against him, deliberately arousing him as she slid her arms around his waist and breathed softly. What they had done had been so beautiful, she wanted to cry. Never had she felt so alive, so aware of the world around her. Her entire body felt charged, as though she had been struck by lightning. And when she thought of what they had done, her face flushed with pleasure. It had been glorious, this making love. So wonderful with this man.

'Not quite. I think you've much more to teach me.'

'And you feel no pain?' he whispered with a brow raised questioningly.

Henrietta smiled up at him with sweet seduction. 'Pain? What pain?' Her smile widened as she breathed deeply with the sheer luxuriousness of the moment. 'I feel almost wanton.' She shivered, repeating the word once more. 'Wanton.'

'You are not wanton, my love,' Simon murmured, nuzzling her hair. 'A wanton is a loose woman, a woman who will bed with many men, as often as not for payment. You have not. You are beautiful, Henrietta,' he whispered, his breath catching at her incredible loveliness. No woman had ever made him feel this way.

'Then I am completely at your mercy, my lord.'

'In which case prepare yourself, my love,' he murmured as he covered her once more, and for a time, as they again shared a rapturous journey to the stars that seemed to last for an eternity, they did not care at that moment what transpired in the world beyond.

But as the night drew on, Henrietta crept close to him and her eyes looked at him. They bespoke a sadness—no doubt afraid for what was to come. Simon saw in her eyes, in the red-gold hair, in the delicate shape of her chin and the soft expressive lips, a hint of the woman she was, the woman he could have. He swept her into his arms and held her close, breathing deeply to quell the fear in his heart. He kissed the soft curls. Again their eyes met, and in that long moment was born between them a bond that nothing could sever.

When dawn came, sending a glimmer of grey light into the room, Simon considered his slumbering companion. Her tousled head rested against his shoulder, and she was curled into his side as if she sought his warmth. A soft breast seemed to brand his flesh and it was all he could do to keep his hand from encompassing its fullness lest he wake her. Her nearness filled his senses with the delicate essence of her. It was pleasurable to watch her sleeping in the gentle light of dawn, to scrutinise every detail about her and to fix her image in his mind.

A sigh escaped her parted lips, caressing his face as he leaned down and gently placed a kiss on the soft fullness, careful not to wake her. For the first time since taking her to bed, he was overcome with a feeling of remorse. He should not have bedded her, ignoring the consequences she might reap if some fatal blow struck him down and she was found to be with child.

When Henrietta awoke with a pleasant feeling of well-being and contentment, she was disappointed to discover that Simon gad gone. The last dregs of sleep vanished abruptly. Only the familiar scent of his body lingered on the sheets, drugging her senses.

Memories of the night that had held a thousand unexceptionable and unexpected pleasures came rushing back and a rosy hue mantled her cheeks when she remembered the incredibly wanton things they had done. Her body still tingled with their lovemaking. There wasn't an inch of her that he hadn't touched or tasted as he had aroused her body with such skilful tenderness and shattered every barrier of her reserve.

Quickly she slipped out of bed and stood at

the window, hoping for a last glimpse of him before he rode off to join Prince Charles with the men from Barradine. Looking down into the alleyway which was already thronged with Highlanders heading out of town for Prestonpans, she dissected each moment they had shared with meticulous deliberation in an attempt to put some semblance of order to her emotions.

Simon had the infuriating ability to pluck at the worst of her nature, to see what no man had ever seen before and drive her to passionate fury. But, she thought, on a warm tide of feelings, he also had the ability to tease, to cajole, to delight her senses in a way no other man had succeeded in doing before. He had created yearnings inside her she was a stranger to, yearnings she wanted to satisfy, and only Simon could do that. He had been gentle with her, tender, considerate. Her experience with him had been so unlike those she had heard of from other women, who had whispered of pain and little pleasure.

So how could she even think of breaking away from him now, for go she must. She closed her eyes. Why, *why* had she said she would wait for him here in these rooms? She could not. It was impossible. Tears formed in her eyes, blurring her vision. Their love had no future. She could not marry him and she could not stay and pursue their present course. But after what they had done, she would be unworthy of any other man, since she had sinned both in the flesh and in the mind. For even as she felt guilt seize her, she knew she would go to Simon again and again, that no warning voice in the back of her mind could stop her overwhelming need for Simon Tremain.

After a while she turned away from the window, her eyes dry and her face set in determined lines. Now was not the time for senseless reflections. Conscious of a growing, insidious fear, she did her best to thrust it away. She must not think about the increasing danger to Simon if there was to be a battle. She had to keep a clear head and a cool brain if she was to leave Edinburgh and continue on her journey north.

Later that day when Simon returned to the rooms, expecting to find Henrietta waiting for him, she had been on the road for some hours. At first he was surprised to find her gone, then his surprise quickly disappeared. He was enraged. His face blanched and a muscle leapt in his clenched jaw. Something shattered inside him, splintering his emotions from all rational control. A million thoughts and feelings spun in a chaotic turbulence and he was scarcely able to contemplate this enormous debacle.

Eventually he flayed his thoughts into obedience. He had known and made love to countless women, but he had never wanted any of them as he wanted Henrietta. What was it about her that he found so appealing? Her innocence? Her sincerity? Her smile that set his heart pounding like that of an inexperienced youth in the first throes of love?

He frowned. No, not love. Love had always passed him by and he had assumed it was for others, not for him. And yet Henrietta affected him deeply. He remembered when he had kissed her and wondered if he would ever go back to Barradine without remembering the time he'd spent when she had been there. He could still hear her musical laughter, see her glowing eyes and jaunty, heartrending smile. He closed his eyes to shut out her image, but he could still smell the scent of her in the air. He told himself that what he felt was the ache of frustrated desire, but he could not deny that whenever he thought of her his mind was beginning to dwell more and more often on love.

If circumstances had been different, if she had simply gone riding in the park for pleasure, he would not have worried. But these were troubled times with all manner of desperate and brutal humanity roaming the hills. He was overwhelmed by the impulse to go after her, but he couldn't abandon his duty on the eve of battle.

And so he lived from day to day in a silent, barely controlled rage, rage at himself for having emotions he could not control. He cursed Henrietta and yet he missed her, and wondered at the cruel removal from his life. But what was done was done. It was better this way. Hopefully she would soon be with her uncle—back where she belonged. He would take care of her.

From Edinburgh Henrietta headed north to Queensferry and crossed the Firth of Forth. She took the back roads rather than the main route, thinking she would meet fewer people that way. She'd had the presence of mind to purchase bannocks and cheese before leaving Edinburgh so she didn't have to stop until nightfall, when she acquired rooms at hostelries along the way. It was September and the weather was warm, but she covered herself with her cloak and kept her hat pulled well down. It was a relief that the Highlanders she encountered going south paid her scant attention. Their minds were set on joining the Bonnie Prince, but she did her best to evade and hide from them whenever possible.

Pushing herself hard, the last part of the journey was the most trying of all. With her head down against the buffeting wind, her cloak tight about her, mud-spattered, stiff with fatigue, she rode on into the emptiness, following a track made by generations of Highland sheep and shepherds on their migration to and from the summer pastures. She drank from streams, the water clear, cold and pure. At one point when she was quite alone except for the rabbits and deer that inhabited the heath and woodlands, the circumstances and the injustices that had driven her from London swept through her mind in bitter recall, sparking her resentment anew until she longed to shout her rancour to the sky. But experience had been a harsh taskmaster on her journey north, brutally convincing her that cool-headed compliance was the only way she could ever hope to survive this last leg of her journey.

Closing her eyes, she let the horse take her. Against the dark screen of her eyelids, an image of Simon appeared. He was as she had seen him in the garden the night before they left Bar-radine. In her imagination, she felt the warmth of his breath and daydreamed that he was only a few yards away, waiting for her. Remembering the moments they had spent together in Edinburgh, of the fierce pleasure, halfway between ecstasy and pain, which she had felt in his arms and he in hers, the sweetness of their kisses when their first desire was slaked, only to return again with renewed fervour, the temptation to step into the dream began to seduce her. But she knew that with each passing hour she was going further away from the man she had come to love beyond measure.

Would she ever see him again? The thought that she might not tore at her heart. Never again would they be so intimate. They could not be and she was engulfed by a deep sadness for what she had gained, for what she had lost. For the first time in her life she had fallen for a man—a man she could not be with. Her unhappiness folded around her like a cloak and she wished with all her heart she had not laid eyes on Simon Tremain. Then she would have come straight to Scotland and her uncle.

But as her mind continued to wander, she wondered what Simon was doing now, this minute. Did he think of her, as she thought of him? And Jeremy, she thought with a slight shudder, did he also think of her? That, too, she did not doubt, and the thought provided little comfort to her.

Opening her eyes, she urged her mount to a faster pace. All of a sudden, the scudding breezes strengthened and swept across the moor, snatching her from a morass of morbid uncertainty as her eyes lighted on a building crouched low to the land. It dawned on her that she had much to be grateful for, for she had proven herself capable of existing under the most intolerable conditions Jeremy had created. It was strange, but the memory of the terrible circumstances that had driven her from her home seemed strangely detached from the reality of the present. Yet for all the injustice she still endured, she knew without a doubt that she was still wonderfully, desperately alive. Please God Simon was, too.

The cottage—a long single-storey building of stone and thatch—stood amongst the whins and large outcrops of glowering rocks. It was remote, in as savage a situation as can be imagined. No other house or haunt of man crouched within sight of it.

She hadn't known what to expect on arriving at the cottage. Her mind was braced on her meeting with her uncle. Would he be happy to see her, or would he be angry with her?

A small Highland pony with its head poking over the half-door of the stable whickered softly as she made for the house. After knocking lightly on the door, when there was no answer she pushed it open and went inside. She was pleasantly surprised. Facing south, the house was sun filled, polished and scented. It was larger than she had expected and well furnished. Everywhere she looked there were books carefully arranged on shelves or strewn on tabletops. She looked around, wondering where her uncle could be when a voice spoke behind her from the doorway.

'My dear Henrietta—for it is you, is it not?

Well, here is a delight. On my soul, it is good to see you! But have I taken leave of my senses? Henrietta? Here? What are you doing in Scotland? I hope all is well—but alone and far from home, I suspect it is not.'

Henrietta swung round. She had been prepared for and anticipated the impact of her uncle, remembering so well the quality of the man. Yet even so, she was somehow taken by surprise. It was partly the complete contrast of the man with his surroundings, the so-obvious unsuitability of everything about this remarkable place as a background for him. She could see his face was weathered with the elements and age, but even so it bore a strong resemblance to her father's. His eyes were still sharp and intelligent and showing no film of age. The feelings that welled up in Henrietta drew her towards him.

Smiling, hands out, he stepped forward to embrace his niece, to kiss her on both cheeks French-fashion, for as a youth and then as a young man he had spent a good deal of his time in France. 'I am not dreaming! It is really you! Good heavens, child, how lovely you have grown! Over ten years it has been, Henrietta. Too long. Too long to be separated from family.'

'It was you who chose to isolate yourself,' Henrietta pointed out.

'Aye—well—that business with your father…'

He shook his head sorrowfully. 'I never did understand why he involved himself with those damned Jacobites.'

Henrietta smiled. 'You always were a militant Catholic. Have you recanted your faith altogether, Uncle?'

'Sanctimonious hocus-pocus doesn't interest me.' He took in every inch of the young woman before him before he spoke again. 'Dear child, how often I have thought of you in London and wished you well. Your letters were a delight, to be sure, but I cannot tell you how your arrival has lifted my spirits. I had begun to despair that I'd never see you again. You're the only family I have now.'

With those simple words, Henrietta felt the wall she had erected in fear crumbling away. 'Well, I'm here now,' she murmured, wishing she had known him better before he'd disappeared from her life. Yet she had every hope that would soon change. 'Are you ever lonely?'

Shaking his head, he smiled. 'I like being alone. I often sit in the dark and meditate—which may sound odd to you, but that is what I do. I have friends in and around Inverness, and when I'm in the mood I visit them. From time to time they arrive with their hounds and I am whirled into the fine company of the hunting scene. But for much of each year I am alone.'

'Why did you never marry, Uncle Matthew?'

'Never wanted to. I was too busy travelling and…'

'Reading your philosophy and history books,' Henrietta finished for him quietly.

'Aye, and that. Then, too, I found myself at odds with women. I'm sure those with whom I came into contact with thought I was a crusty old so-and-so and not worth the bother.'

'I find that hard to believe,' Henrietta said affectionately. 'My mother always said you were pleasing company. Indeed, you have a way about you that reminds me of my father—when he wasn't trying to incite rebellion in his fellow Jacobites.'

'And we all know where that got him.' Shaking his head dejectedly as memories of his dead brother assailed him, at length he said, 'I don't know why you are here, attired as you are, but I imagine you have good reason and will get round to explaining in due time.'

'There are some things you should know, Uncle, and I think we should talk about them at length.'

Matthew glanced curiously at his niece's face, deciding it was a matter of some urgency. 'Of course, and so we shall. But come.' He waved her to a settle before the fire. 'What kind of host am I? You look quite done in. Sit down and I'll make you some tea—so you see I am quite civilised. Indeed, I have a woman, Moira, whose son brings her over from Inverness in the cart once every week to cook and clean the house and bring whatever provisions I need—although of late she's become rather hard of hearing and doesn't see too well, but she declares she's fit enough to carry on.'

'I'm glad to hear it. The cottage is so isolated I should hate to think of you here alone day after day. From the neatness of the house I can ascertain that in spite of her limitations Moira is fully capable of doing the chores.'

'Be seated and get comfortable and you can tell me what it is that has brought you all this way. Something tells me I will not be liking the sound of it.'

Over tea and muffins Henrietta told her uncle everything that had befallen her. Handing him the copy of the will, he read it carefully. His appalled face was a study. 'But this is the work of the devil. It must not be. The man's a first-rate crook—and a murderer, if what you have told me about your guardians' death is to be believed,' Matthew stated sharply.

'It is, Uncle Matthew. You don't know Jeremy and the lengths to which he will go to get what he wants. I did not seek to inherit my guardians' wealth. Indeed, I did not want it.'

'Will Jeremy Lucas come here?'

'I very much think he might. He will hound me until he catches me unawares. Now he knows my guardians left everything to me, he'll be more adamant about killing me.'

'I can understand now why you were so anxious about the man. He certainly seems intent upon doing you some harm. You were right to come to me, even though you put yourself in some amount of danger. But now you are here I will do all I can to ensure that you are not harmed. Of course you must return to London at some point. It is necessary. I will go with you—but I think we should wait a while until the unrest in Scotland caused by the arrival of Charles Stuart settles down.'

'I must confess that I'm weary of travelling for now.'

'Then if you can tolerate the seclusion of my humble home, my dear, we shall wait until the spring. But in the meantime I shall write to Baron Lucas's lawyer, Mr Goodwin, and explain the situation.'

'Thank you, Uncle Matthew. I would be grateful if you would. I know I should have spoken to him myself, but I was afraid of Jeremy and what he might do. When I left London I was quite desperate. I didn't know who to turn to—there was no one—only you, and you were hundreds of miles away.'

'But you came. And you rode from London alone—all that way?'

'No—I—I met someone who was also bound for Scotland. His home is in the Borders, south of Edinburgh.'

'And does he have a name?'

'Lord Simon Tremain of Barradine,' she answered, lowering her eyes lest he read in them what was in her heart.

'And is he honourable?'

'Yes, yes, he is.'

'May I ask where he is now?'

'When we parted company he was going to join Prince Charles at Prestonpans. I have heard nothing since leaving Edinburgh, but I believe there was to be a battle.'

Matthew nodded. 'The Battle of Gladsmuir. I heard reports of the fighting when I was in Inverness yesterday. The government army loyal to King George was defeated. The Highland army suffered few casualties.'

Henrietta's relief was so overwhelming that tears started to her eyes.

Matthew glanced curiously at her and, after noting the sudden welling of emotion in her face, decided there was more to his niece's relationship with this fellow Scot than she had admitted to.

'And what does he mean to you, this Jacobite lord? Is he special to you, Henrietta?'

Her eyes jerked to his and she shook her head. 'Oh, no, Uncle. Lord Tremain is a Jacobite. Do you see?'

Matthew considered her for a moment, then he nodded, understanding. 'Yes, my dear, I see. I really do.'

The following weeks were filled with assorted activities, for Matthew would not allow his niece to be idle. When he wasn't engrossed in his books she saw little of him during the day. Sometimes he was off riding or hunting with his neighbours—the closest being two miles away—for Matthew was a vigorous man, despite his age.

News reached them that Charles Stuart and his supporting Highlanders, buoyed by their success at Prestonpans, were preparing to march into England—even to going as far as London, to reclaim all his father's lands. Scottish chieftains were not so enthusiastic and tried to dissuade him, for while men poured to his side from the north, there seemed little support from the south. The prince was contemptuous of the weakness of the Jacobite lords and chieftains and turned a deaf ear. He invaded England in the latter part of that year.

* * *

Simon had no intention of accompanying Prince Charles south. Charles was disgruntled, but after drawing a promise from him that he would ride north and rally further support from the Highlanders, and after wishing the prince good fortune, with a small party of men Simon headed north for Inverness.

Try as he might, he had been unable to stop thinking of Henrietta. He was tortured by the thought that something might have happened to her, preventing her from reaching her uncle. Was she safe? He had to know. Dourly he wondered if she'd left for London. Sadness settled on him as he thought of that. He wanted to kiss her again, hold her in his arms, look upon her face.

What would have happened, he mused, had he met Henrietta Brody some years earlier? Would he have fallen in love with her? Perhaps not, for that Simon Tremain was different from the one who existed now. He had been hardened, physically and mentally, by the years spent as a soldier and pandering to Prince Charles in France. Still, to look at her beautiful face, her wonderful green eyes, her cropped golden hair…

He shook his head. There was no use conjecturing about the past. What was done was done and the past could not be changed. But he might be able to change the future….

This woman, whom he knew he wanted to make his wife, was beginning to seep into his very soul. She had branded him, burned him with a fire that had made him for ever her slave. Never again would he be free of her. He loved her with a fierceness that was new to him and knew that if that love was not returned then he would be condemned to live in hell itself.

'Something is wrong,' Matthew stated with conviction one day. 'You're as pale as a daisy and the way you've been moping around here lately, you've undoubtedly become bored after the excitement of the journey north. A young girl like you should be out with friends and going to balls and such. Perhaps a visit to Inverness would improve your frame of mind. I have to go there to see my solicitor and you will accompany me.'

'I would like that,' Henrietta acquiesced, enthusiastic about a change of scene.

'Perhaps you would like to do a little shopping,' he suggested, eyeing her boy's clothes with distaste. 'I confess I would feel better with you attired in a more feminine fashion. Women always enjoy such things and I understand there are some excellent dressmakers there.'

His suggestion brought a smile to Henrietta's lips. Her sweet, scholarly uncle was so concerned about her lack of feminine clothes that he imagined a new gown would be effective in cheering her. She was in no mood to fret over fashions just now, but he was offering to spend his own money and time escorting her to dress-makers in the hope that it would make her feel better, so she would humour him.

'I'd love to go with you to Inverness, Uncle Matthew, and I suppose you would like to visit some bookstores while we're there.' The sudden sparkle that lit his eyes told her she had hit the right note.

Henrietta enjoyed the outing to Inverness in Uncle Matthew's small cart pulled by his shaggy old Highland pony. The scenery was spellbinding, the mountain slopes thick with the growth of larch and alder and birch. Set on the banks of the sparkling River Ness, which was less turbulent than the sea into which it merged and from which a freshening wind blew, it was like no town she had ever seen, with dwellings cluttered on a spacious estuary. Despite a change in the weather of late, with rain never far away, the day fairly sparkled beneath a clear sky, while the air was imbued with the scent of the moor.

They shopped for clothes—plain, serviceable garments that would serve Henrietta well for the time she was in Scotland. Matthew visited his favourite book shop, taking pride in introducing her to the proprietor, and escorting her to a meal at his favourite tavern smelling of roasting meat, damp wool, whisky and ale, before setting off for home. The light failed early at this time of year and Matthew had no wish to be on the road after dark.

The following afternoon while the weather held, Henrietta left her uncle engrossed in his books and went on to the moor, sidestepping the little glittering streams that threaded through the heather and myrtle and springy moorland grass. The silence and the freshness of the air acted on her like a tonic. There were mountains to the north and west, mountains that were a miracle of shade and shadow.

The sudden appearance of a horse and rider ahead of her dragged her from her melancholy thoughts. She ceased walking and, hugging her shawl about her shoulders, stood and watched the rider come closer. He dismounted when he was just a few yards away and her heart turned over. He was tall, broad-shouldered and blue-eyed, with a proud face and unruly black hair beneath his broad-brimmed hat.

'Simon!'

How could she have thought he wouldn't come to her? Too late she realised that she ought to have known he would—that it would come down to this moment. She needed to think and to endeavour to gather her wits about her—she needed to steady her pulse—steel her heart.

She breathed, quietly wild with joy, and silently uttered thanks to God. In an instant, her heart had made its choice between fear and happiness. Everything but the glow of that happiness had been swept aside. Her whole being was irradiated. But no sooner had she allowed her happiness to overcome her fears than she was regretting it. She had not been able to resist the impulse which had made her heart soar as soon as she set eyes on him. Too much so, perhaps, and even as he stepped closer she was suffering a return of all the clear-headedness which had flown so deliciously to the winds a moment before.

Yet there was something inside her she had not been aware of until now, and that something was the depth of her love for Simon. She loved him enough to crush down her own fiercely urgent desire for him. In a lightning flash of understanding, she knew that she could not, must not, be his while the bloody conflict that tore through Scotland and his own strong commitment to the Jacobite cause remained unresolved.

Chapter Seven

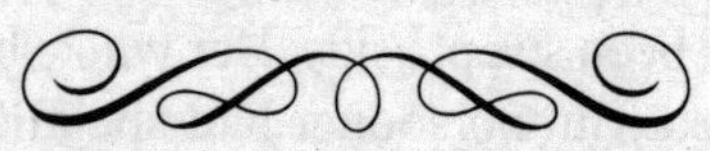

One look at Simon's face convinced Henrietta that he was angry with her. Not only were his eyes glinting with icy shards, but the muscles in his cheeks were tensing and vibrating to a degree that she had never seen before. Immediately she was on the defensive.

'You take me by surprise, Simon. I thought you would be occupied aiding Prince Charles in his rebellion.'

Completely alone on the moor, they stood and looked at one another with some amazement—she on account of the hard, stubborn line which had settled disquietingly between Simon's black brows—he because he had encountered resistance from that soft, graceful creature with her deceptive air of fragility. Beneath her cloak she wore a deep-turquoise wool gown. Her short cropped hair was partly concealed by a lace cap.

Wispy curls escaped around her face, lending an enchanting softness to her features.

'Are we to view each other with such formality now, Henrietta? Just tell me one thing. Was it too much for you to wait until after the battle at Prestonpans before leaving Edinburgh? Or were you so impatient to leave me you couldn't wait?'

Simon's impatience was supreme, yet he couldn't entirely decipher where it was centred. After all she had made it perfectly clear that she intended going to her uncle. The fact that she had, had cut through his heart like a knife, leaving him with a dark sense of having been betrayed. In spite of his past qualms about becoming involved with her, he was reluctant to let her go and see it all end without making some effort to hold her to him. 'Was it really your design to provoke every contrary emotion I'm capable of feeling?'

Stunned with an unwilling fascination at Simon's fury, Henrietta stared at him in amazement. In the face of such flaring emotions emanating from this man who towered over her, all reason had fled.

The dubious scowl that Simon slanted down upon her suggested that he had serious doubts about her sanity. 'You left Edinburgh without even so much as a whisper to anyone,' he accused. 'You didn't even say goodbye. Nor did you even hint of your intentions to leave. You told me you would wait until I returned.'

'My main reason for leaving Edinburgh was to go to my uncle. Another reason was because my feelings for you are of a kind that no woman should have for a man who has broken the laws of this land. And what if you had been killed in battle, Simon?' Henrietta replied in a soft, quavering voice. 'It seemed an appropriate time to leave.'

'Appropriate!' he snarled. 'Inappropriate would be more like it. I left the prince to come after you.'

'Why would you do that?' she asked without revealing her feelings, though she was deeply moved and touched by his confession.

'I had to come. Good God, woman! I might have got you with child. Did it not occur to you?'

'It did and I'm not, so you can return to the prince. I have heard he is marching into England. I am surprised you have not gone with him,' she uttered quietly. 'Why have you come here? What do you want from me? Thinking I might be carrying your child is only the half of it. If you are hoping to convert me to your cause I would advise against it. I haven't come all this way to be drawn into something that was lost before it began.'

'I came to find you because I wanted to see

you. The conflict goes on, Henrietta, and there will be no let up until Prince Charles is successful. But it will not always be so. Prince Charles will—'

'The prince! Always the prince!' she chided angrily. 'You are a traitor to the English Crown, well and truly launched on the seas of rebellion along with your precious prince. You and men like my father talk about the cause as besottedly as though it were your mistress. Have you forgotten that I've rather less reason to love the cause? You may cherish understandable nostalgia for a Scotland ruled by the Jacobite prince. My own memories are far less alluring, I assure you.'

'You are wrong in assuming I want any of this. Yes, I am a Jacobite and I admit in the beginning I was drawn in by illusions of a Scotland ruled by James Stuart. But Scotland is my home and I have no intention of becoming any further involved in its politics. It is enough that my country should be risking her peace at the whim of a prince. I believed it was foolish to embark on this campaign without the support of King Louis—or at least of his bankers—but I have committed my resources to the cause and there is no going back.'

On a sigh he took hold of her hand. The deep-blue eyes were hooded in thought as his gentle fingers stroked the soft palm. 'Henrietta! Oh,

Henrietta! Forget all that—everything but us. There's a part of me that would like nothing better than to take you back to Barradine as my wife, to hunt and work the land and come home in the evenings to you. But if I did there's a part of my soul that would feel as though I had perjured myself and would for ever hear the voices of the people I had betrayed.'

'I'm sure you would feel that way.' She paused, looking for words. As so often before, the sheer enormity of what was happening in Scotland staggered her and left her speechless. Who was she to ask him to abandon the cause he had fought so long to uphold? But no matter how much he tried to explain the whys and wherefores, she wanted no part of it.

'I'm sorry I angered you and I certainly didn't expect you to come after me,' she murmured contritely, prudently changing the subject. 'I really didn't think it would matter.'

'It did matter. A lot, in fact. One moment you were there, where I could see you, and the next, you had fled. I couldn't believe that you'd leave without a word. As difficult as it was to accept, I should have known. You've proven yourself quite adept at escaping. What were you afraid of, Henrietta? If I didn't know better, I'd be inclined to think you were afraid to face up to what happened between us that night.'

Taking offence, Henrietta raised her chin a notch at his insinuation. 'I'm no coward, Simon.'

He snorted in disagreement. 'Right now, I'd say that isn't exactly the truth. But then, I'm the one from whom you fled.'

'I saw no need in delaying our separation,' she explained mutedly.

'That was obvious,' he retorted cuttingly. Her simple statement only heightened his irritation. 'I can only thank God that you reached your uncle without molestation.'

'You knew where I was heading,' she said, somewhat heartened by the fact that the muscles in his cheeks were no long tensing beneath his skin. 'I am to return to London. Uncle Matthew is to accompany me.'

'And when Jeremy Lucas is charged with murder and you are ensconced in your house, you will soon be relentlessly bombarded with marriage proposals from every unattached male in London. How long will it be before you find yourself a husband?'

She gave a laugh and he glared at her.

'I hardly think this is a laughing matter, Henrietta.'

'Why, you are jealous, Simon.' Silence met her words and she knew she was right. 'There is no need to be,' she said softly. 'I have lain with you.'

'Yet you will marry someone else.'

Her temper flared. 'And shall I marry you? A man who has no future—as we both know? I cannot be your wife, so what would you have me do? What could you give me except a life as a fugitive? I do not know what you expect of me.'

For answer Simon took hold of her and pulled her into his arms. Sweeping off his hat, he began covering her face with kisses, tugging at her clothes.

'This is what I expect from you,' he whispered, his mouth against her lips as he gently pulled her down into the heather sheltered by alder. His hand was beneath her cloak now, stroking her hardening nipples with his deft fingers.

Henrietta gasped, knowing that she should not encourage him, that she should pull away and have nothing further to do with him. Once had been madness enough, but twice…twice was a mistake, unthinkable. And yet to experience once again the things he had done to her that night in Edinburgh—twice was wonderful.

She treacherously forgot all he was as the warmth of his touch began to reassure her and the pressure of his lips became more eloquent. Carried away by the touch and the scent of him as he enveloped her again in his disturbing caresses, Henrietta was too weak and much too enslaved to fight against it. With a little moan far down in her throat, she began to respond. Returning his kisses, she wrapped her arms around him, yielding to passion.

His hands were racing down her body, touching her breasts, caressing her thighs, her flat stomach. He found her waiting for him and effortlessly slid inside her. She bit her lip, pressing back a small cry, and then she murmured, half moaning beneath him. Her body arched to meet his as he drove deeper and deeper into her. The waves of passion eventually ebbed, and their united bodies lay quietly within the circle of each other's arms. Both trembled, and the only sound on the moor was the occasional cry of a bird somewhere in the undergrowth or high in the sky.

'Henrietta,' Simon said, touching her cheek with his fingertips. She stared at him and fright was reflected in her green eyes, but her fear was second to her passion.

Quickly she scrambled to her feet and adjusted her clothes. She was trembling and wondered if she was chilled—or if it was nerves. He had been gentle with her, tender, considerate, and there was love in those blue eyes, love even in his deep, magnetic voice.

Their union had brought pleasure—and guilt. Guilt always seeped in after the pleasure receded. She was an unmarried woman and if, as she strongly suspected, Charles Stuart's attempt to roust King George from his throne failed, then Simon would be a fugitive from the law. Their love had no future. She could not marry him and, if they pursued their present course, they would both die upon the hangman's tree. She closed her eyes tightly in an effort to blot out the gruesome image this conjured up. To die in such circumstances was hardly the vision of eternal bliss that marriage was supposed to be.

'Please don't say a word. I must return to the house. Come, and I will introduce you to Uncle Matthew. He knows how you protected me on my journey to Scotland. I know he would like to thank you.'

'Uncle Matthew,' Henrietta said on entering the cottage, closely followed by Simon. 'This is Lord Simon Tremain, the gentleman I told you about. 'We—met on the moor just now.'

Matthew put down the book he was reading and stood up. With great dignity he directed his attention to the tall stranger. The implacable authority in the man's bearing caused him to step back apace. When Henrietta had told Matthew about journeying from London alone with this man, he had been fearful of making any comment lest he betray his concern. The matter had been preying on his mind, but it was his fear of what had been on Lord Tremain's mind that had created his greatest anxiety. As much as he had sought information about him, Henrietta hadn't been able to talk about him, only to say that he was a Jacobite who supported King James's claim to the English and Scottish throne.

'I am happy to make your acquaintance, Lord Tremain. I gather I have you to thank for my niece's safe journey into Scotland,' he said, shaking Simon's hand.

Simon took note of Matthew Brody's unease. It was important to him that this man should know he meant Henrietta no harm. 'I was glad to be of assistance, sir. Although she had me fooled for a time. It wasn't until we reached my home that her masquerade slipped and I realised she was not a lad, but a lass.'

'And a bonny lass at that.' Matthew chuckled, glancing affectionately at his niece. 'What brings you to Inverness, Lord Tremain? We know little of the battle at Prestonpans, only that it was defeat for King George's army, and that offers of armed support and money are pouring in from the north in support of Prince Charles.'

Simon nodded. 'That is so, but there is not enough money. The promised gold from France and Spain has failed to materialise. The Lowlands remain unwilling to send men to support him. The army is composed of Highlanders and likely to remain so.'

'And yet in spite of this, he is carrying his father's standard south.'

'I am of the opinion that he will not get much support from England and will soon turn tail and head back to Scotland.'

'So he is unlikely to take London by storm.'

'I doubt he will do that.'

'So do I. But what brings you to Inverness? Why did you not accompany the prince?'

'Accompanied by a small party of men, who await me in Inverness, I've ridden north to rally further support in the Highlands. I do have an understanding of the Highlanders. There will be no peace in the glens until a Stuart is restored to the throne—and the majority of the clans strive towards that end.'

'So you are a formal emissary of the Stuarts?'

Simon grinned wryly. 'You might say that. I also wanted to check on your niece,' he said, glancing with unconcealed tenderness at Henrietta who had not left his side since they had entered the cottage. 'She left Edinburgh without a word. I had to find her—to make sure she had reached Inverness without mishap. This is not the best of times for a lone female to take to the road.'

'I couldn't agree more. In these troubled

times, one never knows who will knock on the door. What is the overall mood among the men who have rallied to the prince's side?'

'Many of the Scottish chieftains are not enthusiastic about marching on England at this time. They are of the opinion that the prince should pull back into the Highlands for the winter months. Prince Charles seems to forget that while the Highlanders may be fierce fighting men, they are also farmers. Cattle need to be provisioned for the winter, fields got ready for spring planting, which is why many have resisted going south. As for myself, at this present time I must return to my men.'

'Will you not stay and eat with us?' Matthew offered.

'Thank you, but I must decline your invitation.'

'A whisky before you go?'

Simon shook his head. 'I really must be on my way.'

'I understand,' Matthew said, looking at him with a keen eye. 'Is there a Lady Tremain, sir, who will be missing you at home?'

'Beyond my mother and two young brothers, who are in Paris at this time, I'm without a wife,' Simon answered, glancing meaningfully at Henrietta, whose resulting blush lent him a small measure of satisfaction and brought an understanding gleam to Matthew's eyes.

Matthew noted that Lord Tremain had elected to stand close beside his niece. The two truly made a handsome couple. A vivid hue darkened Henrietta's cheeks and her eyes glowed softly—he could only wonder at what had transpired between the two of them when they had met on the moor. He escorted the visitor to the door while Henrietta divested herself of her cloak.

'I see my niece has grown up into a woman and has a mind of her own,' he said quietly, careful not to let Henrietta overhear their conversation.

'I had not been in her company long, sir, when it became apparent to me. However, my concern for her cannot be dismissed. She has told you of the circumstances surrounding her hasty departure from London?'

Matthew nodded gravely. 'She has. She was under great duress at the time. I, too, am concerned. The possibility of this Lucas fellow appearing to exact his revenge is troubling and cannot be ignored.'

'I share your concern. I have become extremely fond of Henrietta, sir—in fact, she has come to mean a great deal to me. Be confident of my good intentions where she is concerned. I should hate to see harm come to her over this.'

'Be assured that I shall guard her well.'

'I know you will, but it is with regret that I shall not be with her to protect her. I would never forgive myself if something happened to her which I could have taken measures to avert. I have done my best, but unfortunately she seems to find it especially difficult coming to terms with my loyalty to King James and his son.'

'That is understandable. She—has told you about her father and the tragic circumstances of his death?' Simon nodded. 'It was unfortunate. It was a dreadful time for both Henrietta and her mother. It affected her rather badly, I'm afraid—and her mother…' He fell silent, reluctant to reveal the full tragedy of that time. 'Henrietta tends to be intolerant of all those with Jacobite sympathies.'

Simon nodded gravely. 'It is understandable.' His gaze settled on Matthew. 'At this time it might be safer for her to return to London—both of you. There is no telling what might happen when Prince Charles returns to Scotland. One thing I do know is that he is determined. He will continue the fight whatever the cost.'

Matthew stepped back and retreated into the room when Henrietta came to bid Simon farewell. Stroking his chin reflectively, he watched the couple. It was rare indeed for a man and woman to complement each other to such a degree, causing his heart to swell with spiralling hope, but then, Matthew was of a mind to think Henrietta could have fallen for a man who, despite his Jacobite sympathies, was far worse. No one could rightly judge the manner of a man on first meeting, but he had made a good assessment of Lord Tremain's character, and it was evident he cared for Henrietta. As for the future, that was anyone's guess.

Simon glanced over to Matthew as he turned away and shoved a log into the fire. He had the feeling that the man would prove a formidable foe should anyone offend or hurt his niece. At the same time he accepted the fact that if he seriously intended making Henrietta his wife, then he would have an ally in Matthew Brody.

Henrietta and Simon stood and stared at each other, not knowing when they would meet again—if they ever would, even.

At last Henrietta murmured, 'Are you sure you would not like something to eat before you go?' It was commonplace enough, but it was something that mattered. Hunger could be very debilitating and very distracting.

'Thank you, no. Take care of yourself, Henrietta. I only want to make you happy, in spite of yourself. When you journey to London, you are welcome to avail yourself of my home. Remember that.'

Gently, but firmly, she shook her head. 'I thank you, Simon,' she said quietly. 'But, no, I can't do that.'

She gave a sad little flicker of a smile as once again her memories came rushing back to torment her, memories which were becoming a great deal more inconvenient than she would ever have thought possible. So much stood between them, but she knew the main obstacles came from herself. Couldn't she subdue her aversion to the cause for the sake of her love? Once again there came the temptation, so powerful as to be almost irresistible, the temptation to give in, to cast herself into this man's arms and allow herself to be carried away, without further thought. She needed him so much, his strength and his protective and so very tender arms. Yet, because she had suffered so much already, her pride restrained her on the very verge of yielding.

The worst of it was that she could not really blame Simon. From his point of view, he was right. But neither could she retract. She raised her head and met her lover's gaze squarely.

'I have given you my reasons many times why this rebellion is anathema to me. Nothing has changed. The question of your involvement in the rebellion remains my primary concern. It is a matter that will remain a sharp wedge between us, dividing us—one from the other.'

It was said quite simply. A statement of fact.

'Be fair,' he reproved gently. 'It seems to me that you made your point in an emotional gesture which, though understandable, I implore you to reconsider.'

An expression of pained sadness entered her eyes. 'You may know the body, Simon, but you have much to learn about the person.' Her voice was quiet and oddly strained.

'I know you as a lover and as a woman. I'm not going to give up, Henrietta,' he said forthrightly. 'No matter what your feelings are for me, I want you for my wife. I accept there is still the matter of my allegiance to Prince Charles to deal with first. But be assured it is your life and your welfare that concern me—and, of course, your happiness. I have a care for the future and I will not rest until I am assured of that.'

As she looked up at him her emotions were torn asunder and she could find no peace in the depths of her thoughts. What her heart yearned for went against everything she deemed honourable. 'Do not think of me being your wife, Simon. It cannot be. I will not. I cannot.'

His dark blue eyes seemed to withdraw more deeply beneath the black brows and Henrietta's heart was wrung as she read the vast disappointment in them. He made as if to go to her, but checked himself and bowed slightly, without a word. Then, crossing the room in a few swift strides, he opened the door and went out.

With her heart breaking, Henrietta followed and stood in the doorway as he mounted his horse. 'Goodbye, Simon. May God go with you and keep you safe.'

A muscle contracted near the corner of his mouth and he looked straight ahead. The chasm between them, so perilously bridged on the moor, gaped yawning and impassable once more.

Henrietta stood and watched him ride away. The moments they had been together earlier had held a million and exceptional pleasures for them both. She had known full well what he was doing to her and that he was capable of annihilating her will, her mind and her soul, and how she would hunger for ever for that same devastating ecstasy she had experienced in Edinburgh. But she would not allow herself to be caught up in some romantic dream. She had told him they could not be together. She would have it no other way. It was instilled into her heart. Soon she would return to London, where she would take up the thread of her broken life.

She went back inside. Her uncle noted the sadness in her eyes and the dejected droop of her shoulders.

'Lord Tremain must have been extremely concerned about you to come all this way to assure himself of your safety, rather than ride into England with Prince Charles.'

'You read too much into it, Uncle. You heard what he said. He came north to rally support for the cause.'

'Think that if you must, but he must care for you a great deal, Henrietta—and I suspect his feelings are reciprocated, even though you will not allow yourself to admit it.'

'But I do,' she confessed quietly. 'The worry of it is that I do care for Simon—so much that it hurts. I believe I always shall. I cannot fight it, you see. Feelings are not things to command.'

'Well, then. When this is over—'

'No, Uncle Matthew.' Henrietta lifted her chin as if to oppose him, and Matthew saw she was in full possession of herself. 'We cannot be together. The die is cast,' she reminded him forcibly, her voice steady, 'and there are certain things one cannot undo.'

'Aye,' he murmured, shaking his head at her stubbornness and taking his seat before the fire, 'more's the pity.'

'Please try to understand,' she pleaded, falling to her knees in front of him. Taking his hand, she looked up into his face for understanding. 'The loss of a loved one is common to us all, and under normal circumstances we have been given the means of overcoming it. But I can neither forgive nor forget the manner of my father's death and what it drove my mother to do. When he was brought home and laid to rest, it was as if he entombed a major portion of my heart with him. I cannot and I will not endure that again.' She sighed. 'I did not come to Scotland to have my heart ensnared by a Jacobite. With everything else that is going on in my life and my thoughts on returning to London, this is not the time for senseless reflections.'

'I am sorry, my dear. How I wish things could have been different.'

'So do I,' she whispered. 'You'll never know how much.'

Simon awoke in the semi-darkness of the tent, surrounded by Highlanders gathered for the fight that was to come. The air was cold yet his skin was damp, almost feverish, and he drew a deep breath. He'd had a dream, a dream of intense passion, and a woman.

The woman had been Henrietta.

He could vividly recall all of it. They had been making love. He had caressed her. He could almost feel the softness of her skin, her breath, soft and warm, the line of her cheek, the grace of her neck and shoulders. He had kissed her lips, her thighs, stroked her until she was aching with pleasure, and she had moaned and writhed and called his name. She had clutched his shoulders and they had melded into one.... Afterwards he had kissed her gently awake, and she had opened her glorious green eyes and smiled up at him, happy to be with him. He remembered her soft touch, her pliable mouth, her—

Then it had gone, vanished. And he had awakened abruptly, out of breath, hot to the touch, his desire unquenched. Somewhat unsteadily, he rose and poured himself a drink before going to the opening in the tent and staring out at the encampment.

It had been so real, the sounds, the caresses, the heat. So real. He turned back to the crumpled bed and massaged his shoulders. They ached as they had in the dream. His memories of her were all too vivid.

He set his drink down heavily on the small table with a crash and watched impassively as the glass shattered into a thousand glittering shards. Shattered like his life. All those memories of Henrietta were of before she had told him not to think of her as his wife.

When he had left her he believed his world had ended.

Prince William, the Duke of Cumberland and younger son of King George II, was appointed to put down the Jacobite rebellion. This caused morale to soar amongst the public and troops loyal to King George.

Recalled from Flanders, when the Jacobites received limited support from the English Jacobites and Prince Charles decided to withdraw to Scotland, the Duke of Cumberland went in pursuit. When the Highlanders took Carlisle in December, the Duke returned to London where preparations were in hand to meet a suspected invasion from the French. His replacement in Scotland, Henry Hawley, was defeated at Falkirk in January.

When the French invasion failed to materialise, the Duke of Cumberland returned to Scotland and decided to wait out the winter in Aberdeen, where he trained well-equipped forces under his command for the next stage of the conflict. In April he set out from Aberdeen for Inverness.

Matthew and Henrietta remained in the cottage. The cold, wet weather had turned the roads south to squelching mud and groups of men, walking doggedly, their heads down against the wind, roamed the land. They had no choice but to delay setting out for London, especially at the turn of the year when the sun skimmed the mountain tops for no more than a couple of hours, and some days when the sky was heavy with sleet, not even that, and when they were snow bound, they were as cut off from the outside world as if the cottage were some island in an unknown sea.

They knew the Battle of Falkirk had been a success for the Scots, but there was no knowing where the Scottish army was now. It was rumoured to be somewhere in the north, but the condition of the army was not encouraging. The weather had been bad, rations had been short for weeks, desertions rife, and now the men were staggering with exhaustion and starvation.

And then word reached them that the Scottish army was moving towards Drummossie Moor—a stretch of open moorland enclosed between the walled Culloden, five miles north-east of Inverness.

And so they waited.

On the sixteenth of April there was noise to the east—thunder, Henrietta thought, but then she realised the noise was more sinister than that. The faraway gunfire was like the crack of doom. She hadn't heard from Simon since he had left the cottage in December—but then she didn't expect to. Her heart was heavy as she listened to the far-off battle. Simon would be in the thick of it, she had no doubt. Please God, she prayed, let him live.

The Jacobite army was outnumbered and Culloden lent itself to Cumberland's strength in heavy artillery and cavalry. The artillery decimated the clans. The battle was quick and bloody, lasting less than one hour. Following an unsuccessful Highland charge against government lines, the Hanoverians blasted the Jacobite army into a miserable retreat.

Simon dragged himself through the darkness and leaned weakly against the rocks, sucking deep breaths of clean, fresh air into his lungs. Everything had been confusion since the Jacobites had been routed and driven from Culloden Field, with the keening of men and horses moving to and fro among overturned wagons and abandoned equipment. For the best part of an hour the cannons had roared their fury, hiding the fear and revulsion that turned men's guts to water. On that field of battle leading his men, he'd felt as vulnerable as though he were naked. His skin crawled at the thought of pike blades gouging into his flesh. And when the battle was lost, wounded and bleeding, he'd left the churning, killing quagmire as though Satan were at his back.

The English were thick on the ground. Gunshots could be heard long after the battle had ended, as English officers administered the *coups de grâce* to the wounded Jacobites before tossing them onto a pyre to be burned. Many Jacobites heading for Inverness were hunted down and killed without mercy by Cumberland's Dragoons. Others, who headed for the mountains, stood a better chance of survival, but the Government troops were thorough in their retribution.

With his body pain-racked and bone-weary, more and more Simon felt the disorientation, the fragmenting of himself as his injury began to take its toll. He knew the seriousness of his wound and, if he didn't get help soon, he would die. Driven by hunger, pain, freezing rain and moonlight, he'd wandered the land like a wounded beast from its lair, and by some miracle he'd found his way to the cottage—to Henrietta. The name knifed through him with a pain that was more racking than anything his body had ever had to endure.

Ever since they had parted she had never been far from his thoughts. The memory of their parting haunted him. He'd tortured himself constantly, hoping to God she was all right. There were so many things he wanted to tell her, so many things he needed desperately to say to her—one of them being that the time he had spent with her had been the most exquisitely beautiful days and nights of his life.

* * *

Henrietta could not sleep. She was aware of the faintest trembling deep in her limbs. Not because she was cold or fearful as such, but rather because a feeling of unease gripped her. She lay cocooned beneath a heavy quilted coverlet, listening to the mice scratching in the rafters above her bed and the wind softly moaning as it went searching across the land. Moonlight bathed the room in an unworldly hue that revealed the room's contents—the washstand on which sat a washbasin and pitcher, a chair strewn with her clothes.

In the early hours she kicked off the covers and went over to the window. Her breath misted the pane and she shivered now as she stared out at the moon-washed landscape and the dark mountains in the distance. But then something in the near distance caught her eye, some movement that made her start, a sudden intake of breath catching in her throat where it stayed as her senses prickled. She was aware of her own heartbeat throbbing against the windowpane as her eyes strained to see better the moving shape from the outcrop of boulders some way from the cottage. It was a man, she realised, but whoever it was was trying to keep to the shadow of the rocks.

A creeping dread raised tiny bumps on her

arms and stiffened the hairs on the nape of her neck. Part of her was tempted to go and wake her uncle. To warn him. Another part of her preferred to watch a while longer. This was the stronger instinct and so she waited. Watching.

A man stood there shrouded in a mud-soaked cloak. He was swaying and holding the rocks for support. But then the figure suddenly moved and looked up, as if sensing her eyes on him. And then the moonlight revealed his face as his eyes locked with hers.

'Simon!'

She stared at him a moment longer, wondering why the sight of him did not disperse the feeling of dread. Then she turned and, throwing a cloak over her nightdress, shivering with a sense of trepidation, she opened her bedchamber door and descended the stairs and across the parlour and opened the door. He was crossing the open ground to the door, breathing hard, as though he had been running. Shock hit her like a blow in the stomach.

'Simon!' she called softly. He didn't raise his head or answer her and she felt a thrill of fear. 'Simon.'

He looked up then—his face was white, unshaven and sheened with a cold sweat.

'Henrietta!' he gasped, speaking hoarsely

through lips cracked with dryness. 'I won't stay long—don't want to put you in danger.'

'Don't be ridiculous.' Seeing his legs were about to give way beneath him, she ran to him and pulled him inside, closing the door. 'What has happened to you?'

'Shot. I've been shot. A damn pistol ball got me.'

Bracing him up with her own body, she eased him to the sofa. The sound of the door opening brought her around with a start. Her breath came out in a long sigh of relief when she saw her uncle.

Totally astounded, he looked at his niece bending over the wounded man whose eyes were closed. 'What happened?'

'It's Simon,' she replied anxiously. 'He's wounded.'

'How badly?'

'I don't know,' she replied, looking at Simon. 'I think he's passed out.'

A debilitating coldness swept through Henrietta, but she gritted her teeth in sudden determination and refused to yield to her pervading fear. The situation demanded action. Her confidence quickly returned.

Matthew took a couple of candles from the mantel over the hearth and with the poker stirred the embers of the fire which he had banked before retiring to bed. When a flame licked up the chimney back he lit the candles and carefully placed some kindling on the embers, hoping to dispel the night chill that filled the parlour.

'I'll see how badly wounded he is,' Matthew said, standing over the wounded man. 'I cannot lay such a task on you. You have no experience of tending such wounds—and I cannot allow you to be so familiar with a man who is not your husband. However, I know the bounds of my limitation and will rely on your assistance. I'm going to need plenty of hot water, fresh linens and a knife.'

Henrietta nodded and Matthew turned his attention to Simon. He had thrown off his cloak and his shirt was stained with an ever-increasing redness. Ripping the neck of the shirt, Matthew felt his stomach tighten precariously as the gaping wound was exposed. Dread shivered through him with a coldness that was oppressing. The raw red hole welled blood with every heartbeat. He wondered with dismay if he would ever manage to staunch its flow.

Taking the fresh linens Henrietta handed to him, he pressed the cloth over the wound. Carefully, so he would not disturb him more than necessary, he slid his hand under Simon's back to measure the extent of the damage and felt a sticky wetness. He sighed with relief.

'There will be no need of the knife, Henrietta. I will not have to dig the musket ball out of his body so he will be less likely to die of blood poisoning.' He examined the wound more closely. 'Another fortunate aspect of his wound is that the ball has penetrated the left side of his chest, not so close as to threaten his heart. My only worry now is that he might die from loss of blood.'

Henrietta hung back, cringing as now and then the pain of the probing fingers penetrated Simon's oblivion. A moan came from his pale lips as he writhed in agony and she muffled a frightened sob beneath her hand. She had not known how deeply she cared for Simon until this moment when she saw him helpless and in need. He had always been so strong, so capable. It was her torment that she could not touch him in a loving manner and tell him that she cared.

Tearing the linen into strips, Matthew put one behind the injured man to apply pressure to the chest wound. Soaking more linen in warm water, he then placed it on the open wound. Simon groaned in his unnatural sleep. Matthew glanced with concern at him. His face was slick with sweat and pain twisted his features. He sighed with relief, deciding the pain was probably a blessing, for it was so unbearable, it kept him from waking and feeling the full onslaught of his ministering.

* * *

'He cannot remain in the house,' Matthew said when the wound was clean and bound and he had managed to get him into one of his clean nightshirts. 'The Dragoons are probably searching for those who escaped the battle. They will come this way soon. We have to move him.'

'But what can we do?' Henrietta cried frantically. 'Where can he go?'

'The cave.'

She stared at him with astonishment. 'Cave? What cave?'

'In the outcrop of rocks beyond the back of the house.'

'I know nothing about a cave. Is it large?'

'Not very, but large enough to conceal a wounded man. It was last used for such purpose after Cromwell defeated the Royalists at Dunbar. I believe several Royalists made use of it when hiding from the Roundheads. No one will think of looking for him there. Leave it to me. I'll go and make it habitable.'

Half an hour later, between the two of them, they carried Simon out to the low cart, which was drawn by the horse to the cave's entrance. Henrietta couldn't believe she had walked past the rocks almost every day since she had arrived at the cottage and not been aware of its existence.

But the entrance was small and well hidden and no one would think the accumulation of boulders concealed a hidden chamber. She was also surprised how dry and warm it was. A single lamp placed on a rocky ledge lit the interior.

They placed the wounded man on the makeshift bed, which was comfortably made up with a mattress and pillows. Simon seemed to rest easier now, having entered into a deeper sleep that even her ministering could not disrupt.

Henrietta gently shaved the dark stubble from his face, and with his cheeks devoid of the prickly growth, he looked more like himself, making her suddenly and acutely conscious of his naked chest wrapped round with strips of linen. In the dim lamplight, his bronze-hued skin showed dark against the sheet. The long, muscular form was so superbly proportioned, with broad shoulders tapering to narrow hips and lean thighs, that Henrietta felt her cheeks grow hot as she realised that her gaze was lingering overlong and she hastily pulled the covers over him.

'You sit with him for a while, Uncle. I think we should change the bandages every hour.'

'I agree, and we'll take it in turns to watch over him.'

'Yes,' Henrietta said, smiling gratefully at him.

'I'll also get word to Moira, telling her not to

come out here until things have settled down. It could prove difficult should she suspect we are harbouring a rebel from Culloden.'

Henrietta agreed. She passed a hand over her face, unmindful that she was stained with Simon's blood. 'I'll go and tidy up in the house and change my clothes, then I'll relieve you. Until Simon comes round we'll have to be with him.'

She excused herself quickly and left without waiting for her uncle to reply. She sought the night air to cool her flaming cheeks, and it was a long time before the trembling in her body ceased.

In her chamber she quickly stripped off the bloodied clothing, washing until all the blood was removed from her and dressing in clean clothes. Lying on the bed, she closed her eyes to snatch a moment's rest. But rest eluded her. The events of the past few hours had simply happened too speedily, and she needed to review them in her mind.

She thought how happy she had been to see him when he had entered the cottage—at least until she had noticed his ashen face and how he had struggled to remain upright. And now he lay very ill in the cave, and perhaps, she thought, tears stinging her eyes, perhaps he would not live to open his eyes again.

She released the tears to flow freely now, turned her head into the pillows and wept.

For the next two days Simon tossed in a fevered slumber as Henrietta and her uncle alternated watching over him. As she listened to his moans and watched him twist and turn in the sweat-drenched sheets, it wrung her heart. How she wished she could call a doctor to take a look at his wound. But these were not normal times and she dared not take the risk. The doctor would insist on knowing his identity and word might reach the Dragoons. They would come and take him away, and she would no doubt be taken with him, along with her uncle.

Alone with Simon, she stared sadly into his face. Dark circles lay under his eyes and when he opened them from time to time he saw nothing. Yet his blue eyes were bright with fever. His face had become pinched and his skin hot to touch. Picking up his hand, she held it in her own cool ones. When he groaned she released it and, wringing out a cloth that had been soaking in cool water, sponged off his face and neck, hoping it would bring his fever down.

'What can we do?' she asked her uncle despairingly when he came to relieve her. 'The fever shows no sign of abating.'

'I believe it is in God's hands,' Matthew replied quietly.

'Yes, I believe you are right.'

Henrietta continued to watch over him, tortured as she watched him wrestle with his unseen demons. Time passed her by. In this, his most crucial hour, she wanted her full attention focused on him. She was willing him to live, to fight the fever, for his eyes to open and look at her, and for his beautiful mouth to smile. She prayed, she talked to him, occasionally weeping over him, and when exhaustion took over, she fell asleep still sitting beside him.

Chapter Eight

Simon lay still for a moment. A small sound from somewhere close by convinced him he was awake. Slowly he opened his eyes and his amazement was complete as he took in the place he was in. It was some kind of small cave, lit by a lamp, and from the comfort of the mattress beneath him and the clean sheet over him, he guessed that he was in a bed. There was a dull, throbbing pain in his chest, but when his finger touched it, he found it snugly wrapped in a neat bandage.

The slender form of a woman moved in the cave, and though he had no idea who she was, when she looked towards the bed, he'd have known that pert profile anywhere. He tried to wet his dry, parched lips with the tip of his tongue and called out to her.

'Henrietta?' His best effort was a hoarse croak.

Henrietta came quickly to his bedside, her

eyes questioning as they searched his face in anxious concern. Touching his brow, she was relieved that his temperature was normal and his cheeks were no longer ashen. With his eyelids opened she found herself drowning in his vivid blue stare.

'Welcome back to the land of consciousness,' she said. 'You gave us quite a scare. How do you feel?'

'Can you get me a drink?' His voice was little more that a rasping whisper.

She moved away from the bed, then returned. He opened his eyes to find her watching him closely. Accepting her assistance, he rose slightly and drank deeply to satisfy his burning thirst. The fever was gone, but every muscle in his body was on fire and there seemed to be no ease from the pain that ebbed and flowed through his chest.

Henrietta's face mirrored his grimace. 'Does it hurt very much?'

Simon lightly kneaded the bandage over the wound. 'Like hell.' His eyes crinkled at the corners. His stare was so tender that her heart contracted. 'I had forgotten how beautiful you are, Henrietta,' he managed to say, finding it easier to speak. 'Where am I?'

'In a cave close to the house. You're quite safe, but you'll have to stay here if you want to remain so. English soldiers are looking for those they rousted from Culloden Field. You must not be found in the house if they come.'

'I apologise if I put you in danger. It was not my intention.'

'You would have died had you not come here. You were shot—you do remember that, don't you, Simon?'

He nodded, his eyes suddenly bleak as memories of the battle came flooding back. 'I was not the only one wounded that day. How long has it been?'

'Three days.'

'And now? What time of day is it?'

'Early evening.'

Closing his eyes, he let his head fall back onto the pillow. 'Those who fled the field will not get far, weakened as they were by cold, hunger and fatigue. It was a slaughter. As far as I am aware all the men under my command from Barradine were wiped out. Cumberland authorised the immediate execution of any man found to have engaged in the rebellion. His troops will ravage the Highlands in their thirst for revenge.'

'Charles Stuart is a fugitive,' Henrietta told him quietly. 'You are also a fugitive. For now your cause is lost. You have to save yourself, Simon.'

'I will—when I am recovered. I will make

my way to the Western Isles. From there I will try to take ship for France. It will not be easy.'

'It is best to wait until the furore has died down. You are still very weak. Don't speak any more. You lost a great deal of blood.'

A spasm of pain clouded his eyes. He closed them for a moment while it passed. When he opened them again they focused on her face bent to his. Raising his arm, he attempted to touch her hair, which curled about her cheeks and almost to her shoulders, but the effort proved too much.

'What is it?' she queried softly.

'Your hair…'

'What about my hair?'

'It's grown in the time we've been apart.'

'Yes.'

'You look…'

'Yes?'

'Very feminine and very lovely, Henrietta.'

He smiled and his eyes at last fluttered closed. She sat with him and watched him sleep.

The hammering on the door was urgent. With a glance at her uncle, Henrietta put down her sewing and went to open it. A tall man stood there. His boots were muddy and his clothes wet with rain.

'Yes?' she asked.

'I beg your pardon, miss, but I am Captain Garnet of His Royal Highness's Dragoons.'

'Dragoons!' Henrietta said, feigning surprise. Fortunately her uncle had seen the Redcoats on the moor and had had time to warn Simon. They'd left him in darkness and gone to the house to wait.

'Yes, miss,' the captain said politely.

'Whatever do you want? Are there others with you?' she asked.

'Yes. My men are waiting.'

'Waiting?'

'We're looking for escaping Jacobites—those who left the field after Culloden. We believe some have come this way.'

'Jacobites!' she exclaimed.

'There are no Jacobites in this house,' Matthew said, coming to stand beside his niece. 'I am Matthew Brody, Captain, a loyal subject of King George, and this young lady is my niece. We have seen the odd rebel on the moor, but I assure you there is none in this house.'

The captain nodded. It was not unknown to him that Matthew Brody was a Glaswegian—a learned man and something of an eccentric with a strong dislike of all Jacobites. In the main he had been left alone, but many crofters with Jacobite sympathies were not so lucky. Their homes had been burned in the search of the rebels.

'That may be, sir, but we are ordered to search all households where we believe a rebel might hide. I must therefore demand that my men be allowed to enter and search this house.'

Henrietta's mind raced. If they refused, the captain would be suspicious. Worse, they could force their way in and destroy her uncle's home as they searched. For a moment she panicked, thinking that the Dragoons might suspect something, might know that they were harbouring a rebel. But had they not prepared for this very situation? They had no choice. The ruse would have to be tested.

'Very well, Captain. Tell your men to come in.' She stepped back. 'But please have them wipe their feet first.'

'Yes, miss.' The man smiled at her and touched his hand to the brim of his black hat. She looked at her uncle, who nodded encouragingly. They waited for the captain's troops to enter.

Henrietta stood aside, outwardly calm as the men came through the door. The cottage was small so it did not take them long to search the few downstairs rooms. As they mounted the narrow stairs to her small chamber, it seemed to Henrietta that she had stopped breathing. Even though she knew there was nothing to be found, the tightness increased in her chest.

When the troops came down, shaking their

heads, the captain looked at Matthew. 'Are there any other rooms here?'

'No, Captain. There is a stable and storehouse attached to the house—a couple of mounts, that is all.'

'We'll take a look before we leave.' Once he was satisfied that no rebels hid in the outside buildings, he returned to the house. 'I do not think we need tarry any longer, sir. Just a word of advice before we go. Keep an eye on those horses. They might attract unwanted attention from scavenging rebels. I am sorry we have inconvenienced you.'

'Not at all, Captain. You are doing what you have to do.'

Matthew went out to see them on their way.

To make quite sure they were not under surveillance, it was another hour before Henrietta returned to the cave to change Simon's dressing.

'They've gone,' she told him as she lit the lamp. 'They didn't suspect a thing. Hopefully they won't come back. I'll change your bandages and then you can eat. You must be hungry.'

He was propped up against the pillows, a worried frown on his brow. A week had gone by since he'd arrived at the cottage and, though his wound still pained him and his body was weak, he was a little improved—although it would be some time before he was strong enough to embark on the long and perilous trek west.

After seeing to his dressing, Henrietta sat and began spooning the nourishing broth into his mouth. He could probably feed himself, but his hands still trembled and he was likely to spill more than he ate. He studied her as she fed him. She was so lovely. With such a soft, kissable mouth. He remembered that night in Edinburgh—so long ago now, it seemed, and for the first time since he'd been injured he felt the stirrings of passion.

His eyes glowed with warmth as he gazed at her. 'You spoil me, Henrietta.'

Her lips curved upwards in a gentle smile. 'Is it not gratifying to be spoiled once in a while?'

'Your very presence spoils me to distraction,' he replied with sudden candour. His eyes swept boldly down the line of her bosom, respectably concealed by a plain blue woollen dress. As if she sensed his less-than-pious thoughts, her hand jerked, spilling the liquid on to him.

'Please forgive me,' she said, distress showing on her face as she dabbed at the stain. 'I hope I have not burned you.'

'It was nothing,' he replied, unable to keep his eyes from her face.

'I am sorry—' she began.

'Henrietta,' he said, setting the bowl aside and

taking her hand in his. Her eyes, so large and startled, widened. 'Please. It is nothing. I assure you.'

'Very well.' For a moment she did nothing, then she looked deliberately at his hand. Gently his fingers relaxed and she withdrew hers.

His meal was completed in silence. She rose to leave.

'Don't go,' Simon said in a soft voice. 'Could you not stay and talk to me? My world,' he said, gesturing the cave with one hand, 'is severely limited.' He watched as several emotions warred on her lovely face.

'I apologise for neglecting you as I have.' She looked at him then, an honest and pained expression in her green eyes.

Simon could find nothing to say to this pronouncement, so he continued watching her. He wondered why she seemed so cool to him, so reserved. What had he done? It was as though they had never shared moments of intimacy. He felt an intruder—an intruder into what? Her life? Her heart? There was so much he wanted to say to her, but he could not find the words to express his feelings properly.

'I want to say thank you for taking me in and saving my life in the face of so much danger to yourself. It is a great risk you and your uncle take letting me remain.'

For a moment he sensed a softening in her attitude and then the mask was back in place once more.

'You are most welcome, Simon.'

At length, he said in a low voice, 'I have missed you.'

'Have you?' she asked, her tone a little aloof.

'I thought you enjoyed my company—if what happened between us in Edinburgh and again on the moor is to be remembered.'

'That is past,' she murmured, lowering her gaze.

'And you are sure about that, are you, Henrietta? What is it?' he asked gently.

She started at his question as if it burned. Silence deepened between them—then she looked at him, meeting his eyes watching her intently. 'I thought you had been killed at Culloden.' She paused. 'I did not expect to see you again.'

He ached to hold her, to reassure her. But how could he, when he did not know what tomorrow would bring? 'I am sorry if I've caused you pain. Do you believe me?'

'Yes.'

'Your eyes are red. Have you been crying, Henrietta? Why?'

'I cried for us,' she answered simply. 'For what could have been, but will never be.'

Simon felt a constriction in his throat.

She rose to her feet, picking up the empty bowl. 'I shall come to you later—perhaps you would like me to read to you.'

'I want…' he began to say, then stopped.

'Yes?'

He wanted to say that he desired her to stay longer. She seemed so different, so formal now, not the woman he had loved in Edinburgh. What had happened to her since then? Did she now hate him? He had known many reluctant virgins, who grew quite heated with the flaming of their passions and then chilled afterwards, as if they had almost forgotten their appetites. But Henrietta wasn't one of these women. This was no unwilling maiden, who had kissed and given herself to him with such fervour, with such abandonment.

Reluctantly he agreed that she was right to keep him at arm's length. Soon he would have to leave her. The longer he stayed, the harder it was going to be when the time came. It was not going to be easy making his way to the Western Isles, but keeping Henrietta and her uncle free from suspicion was worth the added risk. Any further searches by the Dragoons might not prove so lucky the next time.

'We've been parted a long time, Henrietta. Did you ever think of me?' he asked on a change of subject.

'Yes, of course I did. Sometimes.'

He lifted a brow. 'Only sometimes?' His voice was marked with humour.

'Every week.'

'That's brutally honest, but not very flattering. Only once a week?'

The intensity of his gaze ploughed through her composure. 'Did I say only once a week?' She could not resist teasing, relieved to feel the tension easing between them.

'Twice a week?'

'Maybe, but I'll not pander to your ego. It's already overinflated.'

He grinned, satisfied. 'Still the same old Henrietta, giving nothing away.'

She smiled back at him. 'I can't afford to—not where you are concerned, my lord.'

When she turned to leave he reached out and caught her hand. 'Come back if you have the time.'

'I will. I promise.'

Having discovered a sensuality within herself that she had been ignorant of before Simon had awakened it, Henrietta found it difficult to keep her thoughts well aligned to that which a virtuous young woman might ponder. Her sudden propensity for wayward thoughts became even more apparent when she was with him. His very presence evoked an unfamiliar tumult within her, making her fearful of what he might discern if he looked into her flushed face or took note of her trembling fingers as she tended his wound.

Even though she focused all her concentration on her task, her eyes were wont to covertly caress the manly torso, and it shocked her unduly when she found herself closely eyeing the sheets that settled softly over his loins. The torpid fullness led her mind swiftly astray to visions of his long, nude body glistening with droplets of sweat after he had made love to her in Edinburgh. The kindling warmth that swept through her in ever-strengthening surges affected her until she became a bit ambiguous about her own reserve.

Glancing at him now, the trace of an amused smile on his lips told her he was obviously much better than on the previous day, and there was a hunger in his eyes that had nothing to do with putting food in his stomach. It triggered a quickness in her heartbeat, one she strived hard to hide with a scolding.

'If you wish me to attend you, Simon, I insist that you exercise a finer degree of self-control.'

Unmoved by her gentle chiding, he plucked at the bandage. 'I am surprised you have a stomach for this.'

Henrietta seated herself on the edge of the bed, facing him. 'I'm not squeamish, if that's what you think. Besides, the wound is looking much healthier.' A rueful smile brought up the corners of her lips. 'However, I should warn you to hold yourself still, or I might be tempted to remove some portion of your hide as recompense.'

'I am yours to command.' He spread his arms, completely surrendering himself to her ministering, and let his hand fall casually upon her knee as she leaned forward and began to snip at the bandage that criss-crossed his shoulder and chest. She paused and purposefully lifted his hand by the wrist, moving it to where it could rest harmlessly on the covers.

'I will not stand your tomfoolery either, Simon,' she admonished.

A slow, seductive smile curved his lips. 'You're being terribly formal, my love. Have you grown averse to me all of a sudden?'

'I wish to change your dressing as quickly as possible and I have no wish to encourage you in your blatant disregard of my status as an unmarried woman, that is all,' she explained pertly.

'Do you think denying what is between us will stop me from wanting you?' he asked as his eyes caressed her. 'You know very little about me if you think mere words can quench what I feel for you. It is no simple lust that torments me, Henrietta, but a desire to have you with me every moment, to feel your softness close to me and to claim you as my own.'

Henrietta stared at him in speechless wonder. His words were but a ploy to break down the barriers she had erected between them. Still, they were effective in bringing to mind a similar awareness of her own desires. Being with him day after day had made her acutely aware of how deeply she felt about him. He was there when she closed her eyes, haunting her with his presence, and she yearned to have him hold her and kiss her without restrictions. But no matter how hard he tried to lure her into his arms, into his bed, she would not lower the barriers she had erected between them.

His gaze met hers without wavering, promising more than she, in good conscience, could accept. Her hands trembled as she focused her attention on changing his bandages. Though she worked diligently and with care, she was aware that all the prodding and pulling must be painful for him, yet he never twitched a muscle, and when she glanced at his face, there was always that odd, inscrutable gaze that seemed to probe her inner mind and an enigmatic smile playing upon his lips.

When she began wrapping the clean bandages around his muscular chest, in the next instant his hand rose and pulled her close, capturing her lips with his own. Off balance, she could not immediately withdraw and was held snared by a fevered kiss that scorched her cool-minded resolve to resist him. His mouth moved slowly over hers with a hunger that greedily sought for a like response. A rush of excitement flared through her and the need was there to answer him, but the sudden intrusion of who he was and how she had vowed never to become involved with a Jacobite—especially one who was being hunted as a traitor—made her push away with a sudden gasp. She stood up, her cheeks ablaze with shame of her own ardour.

'Please don't do this, Simon. You take too many liberties in my uncle's house. You will destroy yourself and me and my uncle along with you if you continue to indulge in such foolery.' Her rebuke only seemed to amuse him, for his grin deepened, making her doubt that she would ever be effective in discouraging his amorous tendencies. Regaining some measure of control, she collected the soiled bandages and placed them in the bowl at the side of the bed. 'I've finished dressing your wound. It looks healthy and improves all the time. I will go and get you something to eat and then you can settle down for the night.'

Without waiting for him to reply she left him then, a gnawing disquiet descending on her. She was disturbed by his presence, yet she could hardly order him to go. He was wounded, his wound still in need of attention. Yet she did not know how much longer she could tolerate being near him. He was a constant reminder of what she had done, what they had done together, when she had failed to hold her passions in check, carelessly forgetting the future.

Her stay with her uncle had made her more aware of how far she had strayed. She was an unmarried woman of respectable birth, and what she had done—done in a night of abandon and again on the moor—could not bear repeating.

The day finally came when Simon could get out of bed. He was weak and unsteady as he began to move slowly about. Matthew would come in the morning, carefully help him to his feet and then let him shuffle unassisted around the narrow confines of the cave. The first day the pain in his chest and back proved so fierce, he almost passed out, and would have pitched forward had Matthew not been there to grab his arm.

With each passing day his strength returned, though he tired easily and would return to bed and fall asleep, unmindful of the aches the punishing exercises had awakened in his body.

Finally he began to bathe and dress himself, a most notable triumph, he thought wryly when he was at last allowed into the house and he eased himself into the bathtub. With English patrols never far away, he never left the cave until Matthew came to tell him it was safe. Then he would slip like a shadow from his rocky home and come to the house. Now Moira did not come to the cottage, Matthew had taken the cart into Inverness for news and provisions.

As he splashed water over his body and vigorously soaped his limbs, he felt the days of being confined disappear. At that very moment, he was free of his injured body, his heavy spirits, and he was coming alive once more, shedding the lethargy that had encased his limbs since he'd been shot.

As the water began cooling, he carefully eased himself out of the tub and began drying himself with a large bath sheet. At that moment the door opened and Henrietta entered. In her arms she held a basket of linens she had hung out to dry earlier.

Her eyes widened when she saw him and the breath caught in her throat. His body was as lean as ever, his shoulders just as wide, his hips just as narrow. In all he was a splendid specimen of a man. Few men could lay claim to such an exceptional physique. She felt her own body glowing with sensual warmth as her eyes fed upon his nakedness. The sights were there for the taking and she devoured them. Raising her eyes to his face, she saw a wicked, knowing smile quirk his lips. Embarrassed to be caught looking, colour flooded her cheeks and she became flustered.

'Oh—I forgot you were… I should have used the back door into the scullery… Pray forgive me…'

He gave her a lopsided grin. 'Perhaps I should not have been so hasty in getting out of the tub. You could have washed my back.'

'I think you are quite capable of washing your own back.'

In painful embarrassment, turning her back on him, she crossed the room to the scullery. When she had tended him in his bed he had been weak and in no condition to render her helpless with his amorous desire, but now he was almost well and able to tend himself he was as dangerous to her sensibilities as ever and she was frightened he intended to continue his pursuit.

When she had yielded to him before, her whole being had burned with the fire that he had torched. His hands on her body, his lips on hers, his forceful persuasiveness had been her downfall. She had not been able to withstand his ardour and her pride had toppled beneath his deliberate attack on her senses. He had brought her to that moment of sweet ecstasy, knowing full well what he was doing to her, and now she would for ever hunger for that same devastating bliss.

Aware of the thoughts passing through her mind Simon went after her, reaching her in a moment. Taking the basket from her, he set it down and clasped her in his arms.

'Please, Simon, don't do this. I cannot.'

Pulling back, he looked down at her, letting his eyes sweep the flushed cheeks and the rounded orbs of her breasts beneath the soft fabric of her bodice. 'Then speak a lie, Henrietta, and say you want no part of me.'

Though her mouth opened, no words formed and she could only stare up at him, helplessly caught in the web of her own desires. She had already sinned both in the flesh and in the mind, and even as she felt guilt seize her, she knew she would go to him again and again, that no irritating voice in the back of her mind could stop her overwhelming need for this man.

Slowly he lowered his head and placed his lips upon hers to possess their softness leisurely and languidly. He met no resistance, and with a sighing moan her mouth opened under his and their breaths mingled.

Henrietta lost track of time in the circle of his arms. It was as if they had never been parted, as if they had always been together. His kisses were strong yet tender, and, conscious of his naked body pressed to hers, she returned them with a fervour she had forgotten she had ever possessed.

Raising his head, Simon smiled down at her and ran a fingertip down her cheek, tracing the line to her jaw. 'I want you,' he said huskily. 'Here. Now. I am impatient, Henrietta.'

For answer she reached up and kissed him on the lips. 'I want you, too, Simon. But not here, not in the parlour.'

He nodded just once. 'Upstairs. In your bed.'

Without a word, knowing she was indeed lost, Henrietta took his hand and led him to the stairs and up to her bedroom. Aware of what was about to happen, she was suddenly shy of him.

Simon sensed her nervousness and smiled. 'Am I the only one permitted to stand here shivering, or do you mean to undress sometime soon?'

She laughed. 'Help me.'

He stood before her and delicately began removing her clothes, his touch as gentle as any maid's. His hands lingered as he removed her dress and chemise, brushing her shoulders and hips, and as each layer of clothing was removed, she could feel her skin tingling, her breath catching as her clothes rustled to the floor. At last she was as naked as he.

His gaze swept across her, taking in every

detail of her slender, petite body, and he smiled. 'You're still as beautiful as ever. More so,' he said, raising her chin. 'So beautiful that I ache when I look at you.'

'Flatterer,' she murmured.

'No. I have no need to flatter you.'

Closing her eyes, she lay back on the bed, feeling it creak and dip beneath his weight when he finally covered her.

'Your uncle?' he asked as he nuzzled her neck.

'He won't be back for ages,' she murmured. 'But…' She turned her head from him, her hair fanning across the pillows.

Gently he took her chin in his strong fingers and turned her face towards him. 'Look at me, Henrietta,' he said in a low voice. 'What is it? Are you afraid I will hurt you?'

Slowly her eyes opened and she stared at him for a long moment.

'Is that what it is?'

She shook her head.

'Then what is it?' he asked as he bent his head and placed a soft kiss on her shoulder, following its curve to the hollow in her slender throat.

'I—I am ashamed of what we did—before. Of what we are about to do again.' Her eyes closed once more, as if she could not look at him as she uttered these words.

'I would not force you.'

'I know.' She took a deep, ragged breath. 'But—but I have thought about it, and although I have tried to fight it and failed miserably, that this might be the damning of my soul, I do not care. I want you, Simon—while you are here with me. For as long as it lasts.'

Again their mouths melded in warm communion, turning, twisting, devouring, until their needs became a greedy search for more. Passions flared and their hunger grew, mounting on soaring wings. Simon uttered hoarse, unintelligible words as he pressed fevered kisses along her throat, sending her world toppling into a chaos of sensation. The white-hot heat of his mouth on the pink peak of her breast and the licking flames that consumed her was a sudden shock that made her catch her breath. She writhed under his hands, her own caressing his body, but she was always careful not to touch his back where he'd been wounded.

His fingers, so capable, so sure of their path, traced down her flat stomach to her satiny thighs. Pleasure jabbed through her, and the heat was growing until she was sure she would burst into flames. It was so wonderful to have him here, to be with him, to be loving him, to be loved by him. Without hesitation she brushed her hands across his body, feeling the ridges, the scars obtained in battles fought. But she also felt the hardness of his muscles, the strength of his body, the power of it. She ran her hands through the hair on his chest, let them wander down across his taut belly and then up once more to grip his shoulders.

She opened beneath him, arching her back, and Simon smelled the fragrant, womanhood scent of her. With an intense moan, he thrust deep into her. Wave after wave of emotion and passion battered him and he felt her shudder beneath him. She moaned and cried out, her voice mingling with his, and tears of wonder and awe ran down her cheeks. For a while she lay quietly in his arms, her head against his chest, listening to his heartbeat, which matched her own. After a while he rolled onto his side and, propping himself on his elbow, gazed down at her wonderingly.

'You are very beautiful, Henrietta,' he whispered and bent his head to kiss her inflamed lips.

'You flatter me, Simon.'

'It is no flattery, my love.'

She sighed and said nothing. He bent his dark head and kissed the soft skin of her shoulder, touching it with his tongue. She shivered and moaned. His hand traced her waist and hip.

Catching his hand in hers and placing it on her stomach, she whispered, 'Just hold me, Simon.'

Nodding, he let his hands rest. Her head fit

perfectly into the hollow of his shoulder. The warmth of her next to his body comforted him. He breathed deeply, completely at ease for the first time in months.

Some time later Henrietta stirred, waking him from his light slumber. 'We must get dressed before Uncle Matthew gets back. Do not forget that this is not my house.'

'Yes, I know.' After all Matthew's kindness and the danger Simon had placed both Matthew and Henrietta in by being there, the thought of him returning and finding them in bed together was like a dash of cold water on him. He seemed to sober instantly. Reluctantly, he released her and left her to dress.

Henrietta watched him go before resting back on the pillows. With tears blurring her vision, she closed her eyes. She was a fool, she told herself, a fool for having gone to bed with him again. She was no saint, that she well knew. Perhaps she should send him away now, this day, tell him that he could no longer stay at the cottage. But, no, she knew he was not well enough to travel just yet. He would leave her soon, of that she had no doubt. *Please, God, do not let him end his life on the gallows. Let him make it to France.*

But then she would be left alone, having given

him her heart. Fresh tears formed in her eyes as she thought of not ever seeing him again. *You cannot have it both ways,* she told herself with disgust. *You cannot have him, but not want him.*

There was no time or place for love in her life, she asserted to herself. No room for it as long as the issue concerning Baron Lucas's will remained unresolved and Jeremy wanted to kill her.

No room, she thought bitterly. *I am a fool. A fool...for having fallen in love with Simon Tremain, a rebel, a fugitive, a man accused of seditious, traitorous acts against King George.*

Letters arrived irregularly in the Highlands. Sometimes, considering the lengths to which messengers had to go to deliver mail in the outer reaches of Scotland, Henrietta thought it incredible that anything arrived at all. Crossing the yard from the stable, Matthew saw the messenger riding along the road to the cottage. Immediately he went to warn Simon, who had left the confines of the cave to enjoy a little time in Henrietta's company. Unwilling to risk being seen, yet reluctant to leave the cosy fireside chair as he watched Henrietta go about her chores, Simon made a hasty retreat to his lonely dwelling place. Matthew greeted the messenger, who had brought a packet of letters and books. Matthew thumbed through until he came to a letter addressed from London.

'At last. I was beginning to wonder when we would hear from Baron Lucas's lawyer. I think this is what we've been waiting for.'

He cleared his throat sharply as he settled himself in a nearby chair. Opening the letter, he began to read. After a moment a troubled frown creased his brow.

Henrietta became uneasy. 'What is it, Uncle Matthew? Is something wrong?'

'It would appear so. The letter is from Mr Goodwin's son, Christopher Goodwin. He has written in response to my letter and to inform me that his father is missing. With no leads as to his whereabouts, it is assumed that he may have met with a tragic accident.'

'But—but that is terrible news. What can have happened to him?'

'Heaven knows. Christopher Goodwin goes on to say that he has since taken over his father's law practice and will look into the matter I raised in my letter concerning Baron Lucas's will. He does stress that there should be a copy of the will, and if this is the case then claiming your inheritance will be a straightforward matter.'

'I see. Well, one thing is certain. Nothing can be resolved while ever I remain in Scotland. I must go back to London.'

'I agree—and soon. I said in the beginning that I will not let you deal with this alone. We will make arrangements to leave as soon as Simon leaves.' Glancing out of the window, he saw Simon crossing the yard to the house. 'Here he comes now. I'll leave you to inform him of the contents of the letter. I must feed the horses. Thank goodness he's a lot stronger and fit enough to travel. I can only pray he will evade the Redcoats.'

The following day Henrietta returned from a short walk over the moor and let herself into the house. Simon was resting in the cave and Uncle Matthew was visiting a neighbour to inform him of his journey south and to ask him to keep an eye on his property. He was expected back at any time.

He had brought news from Inverness the week before that Prince Charles had abandoned the Jacobite cause and was trying to flee Scotland. So far he had managed to evade capture. It was thought that he was hiding out on the moor, where there would be many still loyal to the cause who would aid him in his escape. There was a price on his head of thirty thousand pounds, but as yet no one had come forward to claim the reward.

He also told them that Cumberland had emptied the prisons in Inverness, people imprisoned by Jacobite supporters, replacing them with Jacobite prisoners themselves. Some prisoners were being taken south to stand trial for treason.

Removing her cloak, Henrietta crossed to the fire to warm herself.

'So this is where you're hiding. I knew I'd track you down eventually,' a voice jeered behind her.

The sound made Henrietta freeze. She knew it too well. Its caustic tone evoked dark memories and suddenly she was afraid, enough that the hairs on the back of her neck stood on end. She swayed in a stunned daze, then, drawing a deep breath to steady herself, she turned slowly and reluctantly responded in like manner.

'Jeremy. Do forgive my surprise. I'm sure you can believe that your visit here is most unexpected. In fact, you're the last person I anticipated seeing today.'

Despite the moment she had been allowed to compose herself, Henrietta realised she hadn't been expecting the sudden surge of abhorrence that had swept through her when she settled her gaze on Jeremy Lucas. She only wished Simon was here with her now, or Uncle Matthew, watching over her with his usual care. Jeremy's clothes were ill-fitting, rumpled and travel stained—far different from what his dandified appearance had been in London. He was thinner and his face had grown leaner. At least his ordeal had proved exhausting to him, she thought with some pleasure.

With a growl Jeremy stepped from the shadows into the room, outraged at this young woman whose disappearance had left him wallowing in debt and dragged him all this way to seek her out. He raked his gaze scathingly over the object of his hatred and felt a bitter disappointment as he took note of the confident girl. His lips twisted downwards snidely as he made comment. 'Life on the run certainly seems to agree with you.'

'I've stopped running, Jeremy. How did you find me?'

'That, my dear, Henrietta, was a relatively easy task. I knew you had an uncle in Scotland. When my enquiries in London failed to locate you, I knew this was where you would come, so I followed you.'

'How did you get here?'

'I left my horse by the rocks in the lane.'

'I see. So you intended taking me by surprise. Well, welcome to Scotland. I trust it is to your liking.'

With a sneer he conveyed his distaste. 'I've seen nothing so far but sheep and marauding

Highlanders—nothing that would make me ever want to venture so far north again.'

Henrietta managed her most tolerant smile. 'But Edinburgh and other Scottish cities are most impressive. As for myself, I treasure the space and freedom of Scotland. The spirit of adventure thrives in this land and appeals to my heart. I found the journey to Inverness a very enlightening experience.'

Jeremy wasn't very appreciative of the tenets of a born Scot, especially one who was the daughter of a traitor. 'I'm sure you must feel quite at home in this savage wilderness, but I much prefer the civilised refinement of London. Of course only an Englishman would esteem his cultural heritage.'

'Arrogant men who think themselves knowledgeable beyond the common man. Granted some are, but many are not, and I think such views they express originate from a narrow-minded prejudice. What do you want, Jeremy? It must be important for you to follow me all this way.'

'My uncle's will would be a start—the one you stole—the one he had drafted on the sly behind my back.'

Henrietta shrugged. Her poise amazed her. She had never dreamt that she could remain calm in the face of so much danger. She had always been afraid that she'd panic when she finally came face to face with Jeremy and fall to pieces. Silently she thanked heaven for her aplomb.

'I do have the copy of the will. Mr Goodwin has the original in his possession—which I am sure you will know all about otherwise you wouldn't be here now. Before you threw me onto the street you were too busy blustering to give me a chance to explain that your uncle had acquired the services of a new solicitor while Mr Braithwaite was out of the country, having him draft a new will.'

'Which excluded me completely.'

'Not quite. He left you a few artefacts.'

'Artefacts! What use are artefacts to me?' he sneered contemptuously. 'With creditors snapping at my heels day and night I needed that money. I held them off as long as possible, praying for my uncle's demise so I could inherit. I grew tired of having to grovel and beg for every penny he threw me.'

'But he didn't die, did he, Jeremy? And you became desperate, which is why you killed him and your aunt—and their coach driver—to acquire their wealth.'

Jeremy's face became suffused with rage. 'I've never heard anything so preposterous,' he flared indignantly. 'I don't understand your purpose, Henrietta, but I do know your accusation is a vicious, slanderous lie.' His eyes flared with unsurpassed fury. 'I'm surprised at the lengths you will go to see me shamed.'

'You shame yourself. You abuse others out of malice and then judge them by your own despicable character. I assure you that whatever shame or slander you reap in this world, you will have brought it on yourself.' Henrietta cast a glance at Jeremy. In all her years she had never seen anyone look so mean or turn such an ugly colour. 'I overheard you and your wife confess to their murder, Jeremy, so please don't take me for a fool by denying it.'

'Aye,' he roared crazily, uncaring what she thought, since she would soon be out of the way. 'I admit it. Tired of waiting, I took matters into my own hands. It was easy. All I had to do was think how rich I'd be once they were out of the way. I ran their carriage off the road and finished them off, making it look like an accident. My one regret was that you weren't in the carriage with them.'

'I can imagine,' Henrietta said, her mind reeling. 'How disappointed you must have felt when Mr Goodwin presented you with the new will. Even then you didn't give up, did you? What do you hope to achieve by coming after me?'

'I want that copy.'

'So you can destroy it?' She smiled thinly. 'It

will do you no good. Mr Goodwin has the original draft. Uncle Matthew has written to him on my behalf explaining what has transpired. Unfortunately he has mysteriously disappeared. His son has taken over his father's law practice. We will meet when my uncle and I arrive in London.'

'Do you think I would allow such a meeting to take place?'

With a sense of premonition, Henrietta turned suddenly cold. 'What do you mean? What have you done?'

'Goodwin and the new draft have been removed.'

Henrietta's brows gathered in confusion. It took a moment for her to comprehend his meaning. She had known Jeremy was evil, but she hadn't counted on him actually admitting to another murder. 'You—you mean you killed him?'

'Not immediately.'

'Do you think to frighten me with a simpering account of your murders?'

'Frighten you?' Jeremy snorted derisively, his pale eyes raking her boldly. 'Why, of course not.' He slowly paced the carpet and instructed her further in the most casual and offhanded tone, 'I did consider coming after you and taking you back to London, ensconcing you in the house and then rendering you feeble and incapable of communication with strong medicines. Then I'd have buried you. Without a legal heir to your name, Braithwaite would have drafted your will and after forcing you to sign it before I killed you, all of the old man's wealth would come to me. But that would take time—time which I could ill afford. When I have snapped that beautiful neck of yours and destroyed the copy of the newly drafted will, no one will be able to contest its authenticity in a court of law. It will be as though it had never existed and the earlier draft leaving everything to me will be the only one.'

Henrietta's skin crawled as he casually talked of her death. Slowly, carefully, she backed away from him. 'You would have had difficulty taking me to London. My uncle would not have allowed it.'

Jeremy chortled smugly. 'He would have been taken care of. The area is swamped with dead Highlanders who did not survive Culloden. One more dead man would not be noticed. Now hurry and get the will. Do not make this any harder for me.'

Henrietta shook her head, becoming quite obstinate. 'If you think I'm going to give it to you and then let you kill me, you're insane.'

The speed of Jeremy's movement took her completely by surprise.

His face twisted with hatred as he grabbed her wrist and jerked her arm behind her back. 'Tell me where you have hidden the copy of the will, or I'll break your arm.'

He increased the pressure, making Henrietta cry out in agony. Her shoulder felt on fire and tears stung her eyes. Too late, she realised the depth of Jeremy's hatred of her.

'Tell me,' he snarled. The pressure on her shoulder brought her to her knees in agony. 'Tell me, or I'll have your uncle hanged from the nearest tree. Perhaps that will loosen your tongue.'

'I—I won't tell you while you're hurting me,' she uttered bravely. 'The—the pain—my arm… Please…' The leverage was lessened slightly, but his grip remained firm. And then he released her with such violence that she fell flat on the floor. Jeremy's eyes blazed down at her. 'If you don't tell me, it will be the worse for you and your uncle.'

Henrietta struggled to her feet, still trembling with shock. Sensing a small movement behind her, she turned from the shadows of the room to find Uncle Matthew standing in the doorway.

Chapter Nine

On returning to the cottage Matthew had come across the horse that had wandered into the lane from the concealing rocks. He entered as Henrietta was getting to her feet, her distress testament to the intruder's assault. It was the threat the stranger uttered that sent his temper soaring, but before he could cross the room and take the stranger by the throat, the man had drawn the pistol he carried in his coat, cocked it and aimed it steadily at his chest.

'Back away,' Jeremy hissed. 'Stay back, or I will kill you. So help me I will.'

In the face of such a threat, Matthew could do nothing but come to a halt, but it took a fierce effort of will for him to curb the goading temptation to drive his fist into the man's face. All the reasons for refraining from such an assault were there before him in the shape of a gun levelled at himself and Henrietta.

Quite suddenly, the door was swung wide and Simon appeared. Emerging from the cave and also seeing the horse, wary of the nature of the visitor within the house, he'd glanced in at the window. On seeing Matthew and Henrietta being held at gun point, alarmed for their safety and with little time to form any kind of plan, he'd cocked one of the two pistols he carried for such an occasion as this and for the sake of safety before entering the house.

Jeremy glanced around in sharp surprise and immediately swept his own weapon around and centred its bore on Simon's chest, not having expected the old man and Henrietta to have company.

Henrietta could see that every muscle of Simon's body was tensed, hard and motionless as stone, but pulsing with furious energy, ready to explode into action. She glanced at him with alarm. 'Have a care, Simon. This is Jeremy Lucas—the man I told you about. He does not make idle threats.'

Comprehending, Simon narrowed his eyes dangerously. 'So, the wretch has managed to track you down.'

'As you see,' Jeremy ground out. 'Put down your weapon—on the floor—or I will shoot the old man.'

'He will, Simon,' Henrietta gasped, moving

closer to her uncle as if to protect him. 'Do as he says.'

After a moment of indecision, reluctantly Simon placed his pistol on the floor. Without lowering his aim, Lucas kicked it out of reach. Simon studied the man who had made such a misery of Henrietta's life from his superior height with a cold and barely controlled anger. He realised he was not entirely defenceless, but the time it would take to draw the pistol from his belt would take longer than for Lucas to carry out his threat and shoot Matthew. The air crackled with tension as the two men glowered at each other. Simon wanted to launch an assault right then, but he just couldn't dismiss the dreadful prospect that Matthew or Henrietta might come to harm. For once, better judgement took precedence. All he could hope to do was to gain time until circumstances could be turned in his favour.

'Stay back,' Jeremy barked, reading what was going through his mind and tightening his grip on the butt of the gun. 'I know how to use this thing, so don't think I won't.'

'Oh, I'm sure that you're able to, Lucas,' Simon replied, slowly straightening to his full height. 'You seem very cold-blooded about getting what you want out of life.'

'He is, Simon,' Henrietta remarked angrily.

'More than you realise. Not content with killing his aunt and uncle, he has just confessed to killing Mr Goodwin. You planned it all, didn't you, Jeremy, yet except for your aunt and uncle's death, none of it will ever come to pass now. Did Mr Braithwaite help you in your murderous deeds?'

'He knew nothing about that. He only became an accessory when I offered him part of the inheritance if we could prove the validity of the original will.' He laughed sneeringly. 'Braithwaite is partial to the little luxuries in life.'

'Little wonder your uncle never liked the man.'

'Like I said, two options were open to me. I could either find you and destroy the copy of the will—you along with it—or take you back to London and force you to sign a new will leaving everything to me before I got rid of you. The latter seemed a little far-fetched and long winded. Better to kill you here and be done with it. So you see, Henrietta, either way, you'll be dead.'

'You have to get hold of the copy before you can do that,' Henrietta retorted.

'If you mean to shoot any one of us,' Simon said, 'be assured that I won't stand here and take it meekly. I'll finish anything you start, believe me.'

The cold gaze piercing the dimly lit cottage

cooled Jeremy's temper effectively. The memory of the pain he had suffered when he'd been set upon by two ruffians intent on stealing his horse on the road from Inverness was too fresh in his mind for him to willingly invite further injury. But he held the gun and could shoot both these men whenever he liked.

'You're proud of what you've done, aren't you?' Henrietta said. 'You actually boast when you talk of your aunt and uncle being killed and how you planned it all. But you're not as clever as you think. Truth has a way of coming out eventually. The three of us know what you are guilty of.'

Jeremy waved the pistol threateningly, beginning to run out of his short supply of patience. 'Then I'll have to kill you all.' He looked at Henrietta. 'Now get me that will, or your life will end right this very moment.'

'You're going to have to shoot me. And if you kill me like that,' Henrietta gritted out, 'it will be difficult for you to get your hands on it, because I am the only one who knows where it is.'

'Then maybe I should shoot your lover—because that's what he is, is he not, Henrietta? In fact I'm beginning to wonder what he's doing here at this time. Is he one of those damned Jacobites who escaped Culloden?' Henrietta's sudden pallor gave him his answer. He laughed low in his throat. 'Good God! What a turn-up.' His eyes held Simon's in a cold, level stare. 'I don't have to shoot you after all. A far worthier death awaits you. After I have spoken with the captain of the Dragoons and they hang you for being the traitor that you are, I shall make my way back to London. They might even hang the two of you side by side. That would even be worth hanging about in Inverness a while longer—if you'll pardon the pun.' He laughed.

Simon made a sudden move, his expression one of aggression, but he halted when Henrietta put her hand on his arm in alarm, fearful he was about to get himself killed.

Though they never wavered from Simon, Jeremy's eyes gleamed in eager invitation, as if he anticipated such a move. 'Try it and I will blow your head off.'

'Stop it,' Henrietta cried. She knew only too well that Jeremy was accomplished with sword and pistol. In fact, there were many things Jeremy was adept at, not the least of which was the skill of verbally baiting men who antagonised him.

'And you would like that, wouldn't you, Lucas?' Simon uttered coldly. 'But I don't intend letting you kill me or her uncle so you can drag Miss Brody back to London.'

'I have told you that I have no intention of taking her back. Although,' he said, a plan of how he could get his own back on this upstart beginning to form in his mind, 'I think the Redcoats might be interested in knowing who she really is. That her father was hanged for treasonable and seditious acts against the king. It should be interesting hearing her defend herself, and with tempers running high in the Highlands as the English search out escaping rebels, I doubt they will be convinced of her innocence.'

Jeremy noticed a slight movement. Having allowed his attention to become firmly fixed on Simon, he suddenly became aware that the old man had moved stealthily to one side, his eye firmly fixed on the weapon Simon had thrown down. Jeremy swung his pistol aside to aim at Uncle Matthew. In swift reaction Simon withdrew his pistol from his belt. It took only a split second to pull back the firing mechanism and fire.

Blood flew outward from Jeremy's chest as the lead shot burrowed deep. He convulsed forward, and a wry smile twisted his lips as he peered at Henrietta, who, surprised by what had happened and the speed of it, could only look death in the face as Jeremy centred the weapon on her.

'Nooo...' she cried out, her heart all but stopping. It was a fleeting moment of terrifying, wrenching suspense as she waited for the hammer to fall. But as quick as a flash, Simon launched himself forward, sending Henrietta sprawling on to the floor and at the same time knocking the gun out of Jeremy's hand. The gun barked in an ear-numbing explosion, projecting the small leaden ball through the air and becoming embedded in the roof.

Jeremy swayed and stared down at his rapidly reddening chest before slumping to his knees. Then he turned his head up and looked at Henrietta, who was scrambling to her knees. His thin lips stretched awkwardly.

'I should have killed you before you left London—you…you…'

He collapsed forward to the floor and breathed his last.

Unable to believe what had just happened, Henrietta froze while her uncle bent over the dead man. Quickly Simon went to her and, taking her hand, raised her to her feet and held her trembling body close.

'It's over,' he murmured, his mouth close to her ear. 'He can't hurt you any more.'

'I—I thought he was going to shoot me,' she whispered.

'Rest easy, Henrietta,' he gently soothed. 'His intent was to kill all three of us and he paid for it with his life.'

'I knew this was Lucas the minute I laid eyes on him,' Matthew murmured. Straightening up, he eyed Henrietta and Simon anxiously. Henrietta was visibly shaken. 'Are either of you hurt?'

'No,' Simon replied, 'although one, or both of us, might have been had you not distracted him when you did.'

'I already knew he'd killed his aunt and uncle and their coach driver, but I cannot believe he killed Mr Goodwin, too,' Henrietta said, trying to wipe away her tears with the back of her hand.

'We all heard him confess to the crime, Henrietta,' Simon said. 'We also heard him say that Braithwaite colluded with him in the cover up in order to line his own pockets. I have no doubt that where he is concerned, justice will have its day.'

Henrietta's face threatened to crumple once more with pent-up emotion, but she promptly sucked in a breath, willing herself not to break down. 'What shall we do with him?' she asked in a small voice.

'Bury him,' Simon answered with contempt.

Matthew shook his head. 'That's the easiest thing to do, but I'll take him into Inverness in the morning. I'll spin some yarn to whoever's in charge of the Redcoats, about how he's been living out on the moor and tried to steal from me and threatened to shoot me if I didn't hand over my horse and some money. I doubt they'll waste time trying to discover the identity of one more dead rebel from Culloden Field.'

'But he isn't, is he?' Henrietta said quietly.

'No, but better for us if they think he is,' Matthew told her.

Matthew was right. No questions were asked when he hauled Jeremy Lucas's body into the cart and took it into Inverness.

Two days after Matthew had taken Jeremy's body to Inverness, rising from her bed and glancing out of the window, Henrietta saw Simon looking out over the open moor. Clutching her shawl about her shoulders, she left the house. Reaching his side and looking at his strongly marked features, it suddenly seemed to her that she was looking at another man, a man she did not know. What was it? Was it in the hard twist to the mouth, a certain weariness in the eyes or something distant in his whole attitude? It was as if he had suddenly removed himself into another world.

'You're deep in thought, Simon.'

Without taking his eyes off the moor, he nodded.

Silence fell between them, broken only by the occasional bird soaring high above them. Henrietta was struggling to still the frantic beating of her heart. It seemed to have become colder all at once, although the wind had dropped, but then she realised that the cold was inside herself. It was spreading from the numbness round her heart.

'You are leaving, aren't you, Simon?' she asked after a moment. He had reached his decision—Henrietta could see it in his shadowed face, resignation and determination mingled. There was grief there, and sadness, too, but those had been put aside—he had no time for sentimentality now.

'Yes. I must. I have wasted too much time already.'

She gave a tiny laugh. 'Yes, you're right. You have wasted too much time.'

Did he sense the bitterness in her tone? Abruptly he took her arm and drew her close. 'Henrietta, why do you say that? You know very well how things stand and that I cannot remain here indefinitely. Until I leave Scotland and find out what is happening, I am not my own man. It's true I have wasted too much time, for my time is my country's and my country is still suffering. We always knew that this moment would come. We agreed that I would leave. You have not forgotten that?'

'No, I have not.'

Henrietta had been too afraid to think that this

day would arrive. While knowing there was no future for them together, despite this, she had hoped and prayed for so long that it never would. And now it had. Hearing what he was saying, she stood still, feeling her heart break, her vision blurring, the wind grieving in her ears.

He smiled then and looked down at her with great tenderness. The smile faded from his face as he again glanced at the moors and the shaded hills beyond. The sun was on them now, but Henrietta would feel the menace of them when night came.

He stood behind her and wrapped his arms around her. They were silent for a long time as the day lengthened. It was quiet now—she could hear nothing but Simon's breathing close to her ear.

'When?'

'Tonight.'

'So soon.' Her heart fell. So little time left. Each moment must be savoured and remembered and treasured against a future empty of him.

Later, when the horse was saddled and all that was left was to say farewell, Simon looked down into Henrietta's pale face, her eyes large and dark with apprehension. Taking her in his arms, he placed a kiss on her forehead.

'It must be faced, Henrietta.' His voice

dropped to almost a whisper and his arms tightened around her. 'If I am taken—if you find yourself to be with child, it will be all that is left of me. I ask you to keep it safe. I will give you the address where my mother is staying in Paris. Go to her. Do you promise me?'

For a moment she was unable to speak for the tears blocking her throat. She swallowed them down, knowing she had to be strong for them both. At length, she said, 'There is no child, Simon, which is as well.' Drawing herself from his arms, she looked up at him, stepping back. 'Nothing has changed. Because of what you are, should you succeed in reaching France, we cannot be together.'

'But we can—if I survive this. Be honest with yourself and admit it. We are caught up in something that cannot easily be cooled and I doubt distance or time will have any effect on the heat of our emotions.'

She shook her head with infinite sadness. 'I will never forget the suffering my father brought to me and my mother with his support for that wretched Stuart cause. You, too, are of the same persuasion. I cannot—will not—live with that. My head is still too troubled with the cruelties of the past. It cannot be ignored.'

'The whole world is drowning in troubles, both past and present,' Simon countered, his mien softer now. 'My uncle, my father's brother, is a staunch supporter of King George. Yes, my father was a Jacobite, but my uncle did not hold it against him. I have friends who are loyal to King George. Like me, they do their duty as they conceive it must be done. But I know well that they bear me no personal animosity. There are times when things are strained, I admit that, but at the end of the day we are all Scots or Englishmen wanting naught but the best for our country.'

His words were words of reason, but Henrietta was not prepared to listen to such calming talk. 'I hear what you say, but for myself I cannot feel the same. My life is in London. I have things to do. It cannot be dismissed.'

Bitterness seared his heart. 'And what will you do there, Henrietta? Become a socialite and marry some handsome bachelor who is unable to resist you?'

'Probably. But in truth, beyond setting my house in order, meeting with Christopher Goodwin and informing him about what Jeremy did to his father, I haven't given it much thought.'

Simon eyed her relentlessly, his jaw tight and his mouth a resolute line. Searching the green depths in the eyes of this proud young beauty, he would go to any lengths to keep her from the life she planned in which he had no place. He was astounded how the image of her coupling with any other man but him tore him to shreds.

His jaw hardened and a glint of anger showed in his eyes. 'Look at me.' He put a finger under her chin and tilted her face upwards. For a moment she resisted and then she raised her eyes and looked him straight in the face. 'Have it your way for now, Henrietta, if it makes you feel better. We have loved one another, and no matter what you say we are meant to be together.'

'You are taking it for granted that because we made love I will marry you. It's not like that for me.'

'Then remember this. I know how you feel when you are in my arms. I have seen it in your eyes and felt how you reacted when we made love, and if you think you can watch me walk away and forget me, you are mistaken.'

There was a warning underlying the lightness of his words and Henrietta knew that he spoke in all seriousness. Simon was a man who must conquer whatever the odds against him and she knew she could expect no mercy from him, that his passion would never be satisfied until she had surrendered her love to him absolutely. The deep timbre of his voice reverberated in her breast and she gave up trying to discern what his faults might be.

'I won't stand against you, Simon, not ever.

But it has to be this way. How are we supposed to have any kind of life together if you continue to support Charles Stuart and follow wherever he leads?'

Anger came to add to the bitterness of Simon's disappointment. He knew, had always known, that she was fanatical in her hatred of Jacobites, but he had hoped that she would not allow her fanaticism to affect how she felt about him. He grasped her forearms hard. 'You have got to trust me, Henrietta.'

'How can I?' she cried, shaking off his touch. 'I don't even know you. How can you ask me to be a part of it by making me your wife?'

'You don't understand. I have a duty.'

'One that apparently matters to you more than I do,' she retorted as tears flooded her eyes.

'No!' He put out a hand to restrain her, but she shook him off. 'Henrietta, you are the most precious thing to me in this world and my main concern is for your safety.'

She shook her head. 'I think you should go. It seems we cannot agree.'

Simon stepped back. He stared at her for a long moment. For the first time in his life he found himself beginning to resent his duty to the Stuart cause. After all Henrietta had gone through with her father, it wasn't fair to ask her to become a part of it once more. Yet he could not see himself ever shirking his duty for the cause. It was too deeply ingrained in him. Maybe he should not have hounded her so relentlessly, he thought. Maybe he should have spared her all this. Then again, he could not imagine his life without his lovely Henrietta. She was the most important thing in the world for him, and because he loved her, until this whole thing was resolved, he would not drag her into a life as a fugitive.

At last he gave her a grim and hardly perceptible nod. 'Very well. I accept what you say. I won't fight you over this. I don't have all the answers and it's too early to see what the impact of our defeat on Culloden Field will have on the cause. Maybe the conflict I am duty-bound to fight will go on.'

'I sincerely hope not, but maybe it will. Who is to say?'

'I am being selfish. I can't have it both ways. Taking everything into consideration, I suppose you will be better off without me. At this time I have nothing to offer you. I have no right to ask you to share the life of a fugitive—outlawed from my homeland for ever.'

Henrietta heard the anguish underlying his words and her heart went out to him. How she wished she could accept his devotion to aiding Prince Charles reclaim his father's throne, but everything in her recoiled from her attempt to wave it away. 'I'm sorry it is to be this way. But I cannot...'

'I understand. I wish with all my heart I didn't have to leave you. I don't want to leave you—and in a way, come what may, I'll never be free of you. I won't write to you, so should I survive this, don't expect a letter. Letters will make me hope and dream, and if I don't stop doing that, I will die of wanting you. I love you, Henrietta. I loved you at Barradine. I love you here. I will always love you. Everywhere and always. Always remember it. But if you send me away without hope, then I won't come back. Believe me, I am not a man to beg.'

'Stop it,' she cried wretchedly. 'Don't threaten me, Simon.'

His face softened for a moment, since he adored the very ground she walked on. 'It's no threat, Henrietta. I mean what I say. But I would have a kiss to remember, to keep me warm on the cold nights to come.'

He bent to kiss her, and despite her resolution she clung to him. All at once he was again the passionate lover she had come to know. His arms tightened around her and his breath was warm on her face, but she did not return his embrace. Something inside her remained frozen. When he removed her hands from around his neck, she held them stiffly by her sides.

Simon turned resolutely and, making his way to Matthew, bowed gravely. 'I'm no great hand at thanks,' he said, 'but while I live you may command me as and where you like. I am your most grateful servant.'

Matthew offered him his hand unreservedly. 'Thank you,' he said simply. 'Don't worry over Henrietta. I shall be watching her.' He added for his ears alone, 'Try to come back for her. She's worth it.'

'I have known that for a long time. But your niece is stubborn, more unbending than I ever thought,' Simon said with a fleeting smile.

'Ah, but love moves mountains and can turn even the wisest heads.'

Mounting Matthew's pony, which he was willing to let Simon take since he would have no further need of it as he was to journey south, with a final salute Simon rode on to the moor.

With her heart breaking, Henrietta stood and watched until he was swallowed up in the darkness of the moor.

A terrible despondency overtook her. Returning to the cottage, she went upstairs to her chamber. She lay down, her knees pulled in towards her chest. Tears drenched her face and she sobbed as if her heart would break as the awfulness of everything that had happened now engulfed her. The overwhelming sorrow of her parting from Simon that now burst its dam did not abate until every last drop of it had poured out and drained away. Here in this room she wondered how she could go on. She would be better off dead. For a moment it did occur to her that perhaps she was dead, since hell could not be worse than facing life without Simon.

How long she remained there she was not sure. When she could cry no more she opened her eyes and for several moments her body seemed unwilling to move. It was with every ounce of her will that she raised herself off the bed and swilled her face with cold water.

Going outside in search of her uncle, she found him looking out over the moor. She moved to stand close to him. He placed his arm about her shoulders.

'Will I see him again, do you think? I do so want to be with him, but…'

'But there are too many issues holding you back, I know. My advice to you is to put aside what your father did to you and your mother. Do not forget that he suffered the ultimate punishment for his crime—if that is indeed what it was. Who is to judge? *You* have to go on, Henrietta. Too much looking back can make you blind to the present—even to one's own heart. If Simon succeeds in escaping the Redcoats and manages to get to France, then despite what he said to you I think he will write to let you know he is safe—so take care of yourself. Do you want to die before you can prove your love?'

Matthew spoke to her with such an air of grief and regret that it moved Henrietta to fresh tears. Already the instinct for life was reviving in her, willing her to go on towards the goal which at this moment eluded her.

'How did you know?'

'He loves you. I have no right to interfere in your life. You are in love with him. I knew from the first day I saw you together.' He squeezed her shoulder. 'Everything will work out—sometimes for the better, sometimes not. You'll see.'

On the point of leaving, Henrietta looked into the cave where Simon had stayed. Nothing showed that it had been occupied for weeks. It was empty of him, empty of feeling.

Had he been taken? The terror of such a thing happening, a terror that would travel with her from Scotland and stay with her rose now to engulf her, choking, drowning her. Her ears rang with her own pulse beat and her throat closed so tight that she felt she could not breathe. A sadness like a weight settled over her. Turning, she left the cave.

* * *

Simon took the most direct, available route to the west coast, skirting lochs and following treacherous tracks through bogs and outlaw-infested forests. Tormented by weariness and cramped limbs and the ache in his chest from the wound inflicted at Culloden, he welcomed the discomfort for it prevented him dwelling on thoughts of Henrietta. Her loss was as fresh to him as the void inside him that was as mortal as only death can be.

He had no outlet for his emotions and the emptiness inside him was so total that it eclipsed everything. With that thought he slammed a door on her image, for he knew otherwise it would never let him rest again.

Many times he came upon Redcoats searching the forests and it was only by his cunning and tenacity that he escaped discovery. Entering the western Highlands at Fort Augustus, he met up with other Jacobites, some fleeing the Redcoats and desperate to get to France. Simon had nothing but admiration for their perseverance. The native courage that Highlanders had inherited from their Celtic ancestors was preserved unimpaired.

Simon was not alone when he boarded a small boat and escaped to the Outer Hebrides. Here he met up with Prince Charles. His loyal supporters still gave him shelter. Pursued by government supporters and local lairds who were tempted to turn him in for the thirty-thousand-pound reward, for weeks they crossed from one island to another.

Finally they were taken out of Scotland by a French frigate after a rendezvous at Loch Uamh, Prince Charles's starting point between Fort William and Arisaig, which ferried them away from Scotland. They arrived in France in September of '46.

In the grey, rainswept light of the early evening, Henrietta and her uncle arrived at Whitegates. There was despair in her heart and it was echoed within the hearts of all those who had flocked to Prince Charles's banner. Culloden was on everyone's mind. The swift and bloody defeat and the ignominious flight of the Highlanders had demoralised them all. The cause of the Stuarts was now lost.

The estates of those lords and clan chiefs who had supported the Jacobite rebellion were stripped from them and the Highland tartan was banned from everyone in Scotland except as a uniform in the British army.

It was amazing, Henrietta thought as she entered beneath the entrance portico and stepped into the house, that nothing seemed to have changed. The servants, all wanting to welcome her back home and crowding into the hall, lifted her spirits.

'Forgive me if I appear somewhat surprised,' she said to Coleman, who had been the butler at Whitegates long before Henrietta had come to live there, 'but I thought I'd be returning to an empty house.'

'Not at all, Miss Brody. When Mr Lucas left London, he made it clear that when he returned he would have full control over his uncle's affairs. We were to refer to Mr Braithwaite should anything untoward arise.'

'I see. Well, I can tell you that Mr Lucas met with an unfortunate—fatal—accident in Scotland. He will not be coming back. As for Mr Braithwaite—I should tell you that Baron Lucas changed his solicitor twelve months before he died. He drafted a new will, leaving everything to me should his wife not survive him. Should Mr Braithwaite call, he is not to be admitted. Now,' she said, smiling at her uncle, 'I would like to introduce my uncle, Matthew Brody. He is going to stay with me for a while, so please have a room made ready. In the meantime some refreshment would be nice.'

Henrietta was about to turn towards the drawing room when she was alerted by a look that passed from servant to servant. She paused, frowning. 'What is it? Is something amiss?' She glanced at Rose hovering close. 'Rose? Are you going to tell me why everyone suddenly appears jumpy?'

'It's Mr Lucas's wife, Miss Henrietta. She's been living here ever since he left.'

'I see. Then I will speak to her.'

'She's not here just now. I believe she had a theatre engagement.'

'Then I'll speak to her when she returns. If she's very late, then it can wait until morning.' She turned to her uncle, leading the way to the drawing room.

'We must see Mr Goodwin first thing in the morning to straighten matters out,' Matthew said as they entered the drawing room. 'The sooner the better, I think.'

'Yes, yes, of course. But first I have Claudia to deal with.'

At the sincerity and warmth of the servants' welcome, Henrietta was pleased to be home. This opinion lasted until Claudia returned later that night. One look at Jeremy's wife, who was wearing too much make-up and jewellery for good taste, made Henrietta's heart sink.

Having been informed of Henrietta's arrival by Coleman as she entered the house, Claudia stood poised in the doorway of the salon, her nose tipped high, her eyes hostile. Her hair was dishevelled, her face flushed. 'So, you're back.'

'As you see,' Henrietta replied stiffly. 'I would have returned sooner, but what with one thing and another I was unable to do so.' She watched Claudia saunter further into the room. She looked as though she had been drinking. 'Perhaps you should sit down,' Henrietta suggested.

'I have no wish to sit down with you.' She moved closer, her movements unsteady, and she lurched slightly and grabbed on to the edge of a chair for support.

Henrietta rose. 'You are unwell.'

'I am drunk, but quite well—quite well indeed, and will be even better when you leave.'

'But I'm not leaving.'

Claudia remained unmoved. A sneer twisted her Cupid's-bow mouth as she fingered a curl of her dark hair. 'You should.' Her voice was rising. 'You are a scheming Scottish witch. I saw through you at the beginning—how you wormed your way into the household. Jeremy saw it, too, just as others know what you really are.'

Henrietta sighed wearily. 'Say what you like, Claudia, your words cannot hurt me. The house is mine as well you know. I will not go into explanations since you already know the gist of it.'

'Jeremy discovered how his uncle double-crossed him when that man Goodwin called at the house. That was the reason he set off after you to Scotland—to get his hands on the copy of the will and destroy it—you, too, afterwards. Did he manage to track you down?'

'Oh, yes,' Henrietta replied drily. 'I swear your husband had the nose of a bloodhound.'

Claudia's eyes narrowed suspiciously. 'Had?'

'Jeremy is dead, Claudia.'

Claudia stared at her in confusion, then shock. 'Dead? But he can't be dead. You lie. He can't be dead.'

'I assure you he is—quite dead. He was shot. Scotland is in turmoil. It was not a good time for him to be there. With government troops and Highlanders at war, he really should have had more sense. He threatened me.'

'So you killed him.' Claudia's eyes were filled with hate as they looked at Henrietta. 'Damn you! I'll report you…'

'I wouldn't do that—and I wasn't the one who shot him,' Henrietta said coldly. 'He killed four people in cold blood. He got what he deserved.'

Claudia's eyes narrowed venomously. 'What are you talking about?'

'I know Jeremy killed his aunt and uncle—and later Mr Goodwin, his uncle's lawyer—not forgetting the coach driver. Before he died he confessed his crime to me—and my uncle, and one other. Both can be called upon to give evidence.' Henrietta's stomach churned. Please God there was truth in what she said and that Simon would survive to provide evidence should he be asked to do so.

Claudia paled beneath the rouge on her cheeks. 'Jeremy wouldn't do that.'

'He did. So if you do not wish to be implicated, to save your neck I suggest you leave this house. I intend speaking to the authorities in the morning.' Claudia looked at her with sudden fear in her eyes. Henrietta knew she had her.

Claudia fought down panic. If she delayed leaving the house, she might die at the end of a rope. At that moment any tender feelings she might harbour for her husband died. She cursed him for getting himself killed, for getting it all wrong, just when she was beginning to enjoy living in the lap of luxury. 'I'll go and pack my things and have Coleman bring the carriage round. I have friends I can go to.'

Henrietta watched her wend her way out of the room with no attempt at dignity. Only when the door was closed did she sink down into the chair she had vacated a moment earlier and closed her eyes.

Henrietta waited impatiently for the weeks to pass as her uncle wrote one letter after another to his extensive circle of friends in France, asking if they had news of any Jacobites who had taken part in the rebellion arriving back in France. In the beginning his friends answered each one the same. They had heard nothing.

And so Henrietta continued to wait, unable to think or care about anything else. Once more the old passionate and painful longing, which ebbed when she knew she could not even hope to see Simon, had revived. Now she remembered with aching clarity all the small separate things about him—the deep blue of his eyes, the gentle wave in his dark hair, the attractive cleft in his chin, the smooth texture of his skin, the feel of his hands touching her, and the warm timbre of his voice, which gave her a real sense of physical pleasure.

She was restless, tormented, for those piecemeal memories could not make a whole. Simon eluded her to the point where she was beginning to wonder if he had ever existed. She desperately wanted to hear he had made it to France.

Finally that wish was granted. In early October one of her uncle's friends wrote to say that Lord Simon Tremain was one of the gentlemen who had arrived in France with Charles Stuart.

Matthew watched her, worried about her. Now she knew Simon was safe she never spoke of him. Her smile was always bright, her conversation animated. But she smiled too much and talked too much. At any other time he would have said it was a good sign, but it didn't mean a thing, except she was trying to hide from her memories.

'You look tired, my dear,' he said one night over dinner. She'd had a particularly tiring day with Christopher Goodwin, answering questions about what she knew about Baron Lucas and his wife's death, and what Jeremy Lucas had confessed to them both before he died. 'It's been a long day. I think you should rest.'

She glanced at him. She loved him dearly. He was so good to her. 'Later, perhaps.'

'Your heart is not here, Henrietta,' he said, wiping his mouth on the napkin and placing it on the table. 'It is in France with Lord Tremain, I think.'

She sighed dejectedly. 'Yes, it is. I can't seem to help it. What can I do?'

'Sell Whitegates, for a start.'

'Sell Whitegates?' Henrietta was horrified that he should suggest such a thing. 'But—I can't do that—at least...'

'Think about it, my dear. There is nothing for you here any more.'

'But there is no reason to sell the house.'

'Yes, there is. Make a clean break of it. You love Simon,' Matthew said gently. 'Does that not seem to you a sufficient reason?' Henrietta did not answer, but her expression told Matthew more than any words. He put out a hand to his beloved niece and when he spoke his voice was torn with sorrow, yet what he said he felt was right and true. 'Lord Tremain is a good man, Henrietta. I really believe that.'

'Do you, Uncle Matthew? Even though he is a Jacobite?'

He nodded. 'Even so. He will not harm you, Henrietta, for you will not let him. You have spirit. You are strong and you are so like your father. Your father hurt you and your mother, I know, but he followed the dictates of his conscience, knowing it would end in his downfall. We did not share the same convictions, your father and I, but we were as close as brothers could be and I admired him for staying true to what he believed in. You do not belong here. Go to France. Make this decision and be proud.'

'I told Simon we could never be together.'

'The cause is lost. Now it is a matter of survival for those who followed Charles Stuart. I believe you are putting yourself and Simon through hell for no reason. Can you really turn your back on him and forget him, a man who loves you and needs you as much as you need him? If you do that, then you will spend the rest of your life hating yourself and blaming yourself because you were afraid to take a chance. You were meant to be together. I believe that.'

Henrietta lay in bed in the semi-darkness. The night was still and humid. Hearing the clock strike two o'clock, she climbed out of bed and went to the window and opened it wide. The moon and stars illuminated the ground and the trees. She peered down into the garden, her heart aching.

Ever since Simon had left her she had been unable to still the confusion of thoughts in her head, to still the tempest of her emotions Simon had stirred in her. He had aroused her, angered her, made her think and feel, and when he had gone he had left a vacuum in her life that nothing and no one could fill.

On a sigh she turned and looked at the room, noting the lovely things, items she had grown accustomed to and cherished through the years. But they were possessions, objects, and no matter how much she had loved her guardians, she could not shake off the feeling that this house and every precious object did not belong to her.

They were not Simon, not the man she loved, the man who was irreplaceable, the man she adored, the man who meant more to her than anything in this house.

I want him, she thought miserably to herself.

Why had she not realised the depth of her love? Why had she not gone with him over the moor that night, riding side by side? She had been so blinded by her own foolish notions, determined not to have anything to do with the rebellion, that she had lost the man who loved her.

After a sleepless night, no longer able to ignore what her heart was telling her, at breakfast Henrietta informed her uncle that she had decided to do as he suggested and put the house up for sale—but on one condition.

'Come with me, Uncle Matthew. I am fluent in French, but I don't think I could face France completely alone.'

Matthew looked at her with great fondness. She would never know how glad he had been to see her that day when she had appeared at his cottage out of the blue, and although she was of his blood, he was struck afresh each time he looked at her, by the glory she had brought with her. She was like the sun coming out after dark days. She had come at a low point in his life, when all he could see coming towards him was the spectre of death through loneliness, and he felt the sadness of it and its slow chill. Despite the unsociable face he showed to the world, this dear girl had brought him to life again and taken him out of his loneliness.

'As if I would let you go alone. I have missed France for some time, but with all the disturbances over the years I did not think I would be able to return. I never envisioned that I would.' He frowned on seeing her pensive look. 'What is it, Henrietta? It is a big step you are about to take and it's perfectly natural for you to be apprehensive.'

'What if I sell the house only to find Simon doesn't want me? What then?'

'Should that happen, my dear Henrietta, then you and I shall go on an extended tour of Europe. You are now a wealthy young woman, don't forget. I shall enjoy showing you everything I saw in my youth—Venice, Rome and Verona to name but a few of the wonderful cities of note and culture. And when we are tired of travelling we shall take respite wherever we happen to be.'

'But—about a house. Where shall we live when we are in Paris?'

'Forgive me, Henrietta, but I shall take care of that. I shall contact a dear friend of mine, Armand de Valeze, to make all the arrangements. He has been long hankering for me to visit Paris again. You are not to worry about the cost of the house, for all the funds will be provided by me. But fear not. Simon will not turn you away. He loves you. Of that you can be sure. Will you write to him and tell him what you intend?'

A mischievous smile curved her lips and her eyes glowed. 'Oh, no. I will surprise him. He mustn't know I'm in Paris until I'm ready to show myself to him.'

Chapter Ten

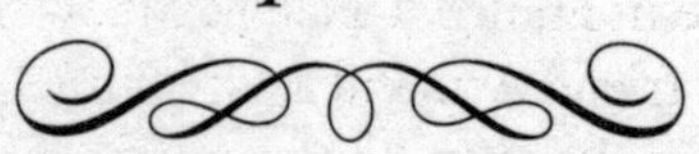

Henrietta watched as the shore of France grew larger and closer. White-capped waves slapped against the hull of the ship, rocking it vigorously as it ploughed on. She gripped the rail as the deck swayed. Soon she would set foot on soil again. But it would not be the soil of her native country. She had left that land in search of her heart's desire.

Before they had left England Christopher Goodwin had come to the house to inform them that Mr Braithwaite had been arrested for colluding in Jeremy Lucas's crimes. Even though he professed his innocence most vocally to anyone who would listen, he was in prison awaiting his fate. He had not been charged with murder, but he faced a long term in prison.

Most of the servants at Whitegates who had been loyal to Baron Lucas and his wife had found it impossible to serve under Jeremy and had found positions elsewhere. When Henrietta told them she was selling the house, she was relieved they had somewhere to go. Thankfully Rose, who had no familial ties, had come with her, excited at the prospect of beginning a new life in France. Uncle Matthew had written to his friend Armand asking him to arrange lodgings in the city. And so arrangements had been made. Armand would hire a coach to take them to Paris. It would be waiting when the ship docked.

During the crossing Henrietta had thought much of what she was doing and was nearly overwhelmed by the enormity of her mission. To be sure she wanted to see Simon again, to feel his arms around her once more. Please God he still wanted her.

Eventually the ship shuddered as it neared the dock at Calais, and the sails drooped as the wind died. Ropes were thrown and tied, securing the ship, and the gangplank was lowered. Henrietta turned to her uncle and he smiled, taking her arm.

'Come, Henrietta. The coach will be waiting for us—unless, of course, you are tired and would prefer to delay for a day while you rest.'

His words were solicitous, as was his tone, but Henrietta was impatient to be on her way.

They faced a long journey and the sooner she reached Paris, the sooner she would be with Simon. 'Thank you, Uncle, but, no. There will be time to rest when we are settled in Paris.'

The coach was waiting and they were soon under way. They faced a long journey, staying each night at country inns.

The journey had proved tiring and Henrietta was exceedingly glad when they finally arrived at the house, a lovely stone mansion, known in Paris as a *hôtel*. The coach entered a circular driveway and Henrietta saw smartly clad servants standing in line to greet them.

'Armand informed me that the house's situation is ideal to go into the city,' Matthew explained, 'but its location will prove restful. Apparently it belongs to a minor nobleman, who is travelling extensively abroad and is not expected to return to Paris for at least a year. Inside it is furnished with comfortable elegance and, as you see, is well staffed. I'm sure you will like living here.'

'I don't doubt it,' Henrietta replied, squeezing his arm fondly. 'Since you are the one who insisted on paying for it, I would not expect anything less. It will do perfectly until you leave to embark upon your exotic journey to other foreign parts.'

* * *

'Welcome,' Bertrand, the *maître d'hôtel,* said when he brought them wine in the blue-and-gold salon. 'No doubt you wish to rest, *mademoiselle,* after such a long journey.' He turned back to the door. 'I hope that I may put to rest any fears you may have about the isolation of the house. I do not think you will have to wait very long for the invitations.'

Henrietta raised an eyebrow. 'No?'

He nodded. 'There is a tray in the hall. Already numerous cards are arrayed there.'

Later when Henrietta studied the names, she saw they were addressed to her uncle from friends and acquaintances, inviting him and his niece to several society events. She smiled, thinking that becoming reunited with Simon would not be as difficult as she had thought.

Between acclimatising himself to Paris—which was a world away from his little house in the Highlands of Scotland—and the daily meetings with Armand and other friends and acquaintances he had not seen for many years, and chaperoning Henrietta about Paris to show her the places of interest, her favourite being the great Cathedral of Notre-Dame de Paris, Matthew suddenly found life full and satisfying. After a week he arrived home in an animated mood.

'Henrietta, I have been invited to a ball and I would like you to accompany me.'

She glanced up from the letter she was writing to Christopher Goodwin. 'Whose ball are we attending?'

'The king will be there—also Prince Charles Stuart and one of his close friends—no other than Lord Simon Tremain.'

Henrietta felt a sudden thump of excitement in the pit of her stomach and exchanged a quick glance with her uncle. He merely shrugged, as though this were nothing startling, but his eyes sparkled with anticipation as he looked at her.

'It is to be a grand affair and will be the perfect occasion for you to show yourself, do you not agree? It will also mark your official entry into Parisian society.'

Henrietta sighed happily and sat back in her chair. 'Yes, Uncle Matthew. Perfect.'

Immediately she began fretting over what to wear for such a grand occasion. Simon had only ever seen her dressed as an unkempt youth and in clothes borrowed from members of his family, and later in the plain and practical woollens of a Highland girl. For his first glimpse of her in Paris society, she wanted to dazzle, to be as mysterious and alluring as possible.

* * *

Rose helped her prepare for the ball. After she had bathed in lilac-scented water, she sat in front of the vanity. Humming softly to herself, Rose smoothly drew back her mistress's red-gold hair and deftly pinned it. Henrietta studied herself in the mirror, turning her head this way and that. The simple hairstyle accentuated her high cheekbones and made her green eyes seem even larger and wider. She also noticed with approval how it showed to good advantage her long white neck.

She had chosen her gown with great care, for she wanted Simon never to forget how she looked tonight.

Nearly an hour later she had finished dressing. Having decided upon a new gown of brocaded gold, she turned slowly in front of the large bevelled mirror. The neckline was square and low-cut, and the fitted bodice and hem of the full skirt were embroidered in an intricate pattern of tiny pearls. A silk shawl in matching gold was draped over her arm and she wore a set of antique pearl earrings that matched the strand at her throat.

'Oh, my dear.' Matthew, awed by his niece's appearance, beamed down at her. 'I swear you are the most beautiful woman I have ever seen. I know you will outshine all the other women tonight. The gentlemen will have eyes only for you.'

'Nonsense, Uncle Matthew,' she said, though not unkindly, for she was pleased with her uncle's praise. 'But thank you anyway.'

At last the *château* south of Paris loomed in the distance, white, ornate and mysterious on the edge of a lake. To Henrietta, who had known the modest homes in London, the sumptuous abodes and palaces of Paris were indeed something to behold. One after another, at slow pace, the carriages turned into the long avenue of poplars leading to the entrance.

Matthew smiled as he glanced at his niece's awestruck face. 'The *château* is very beautiful, is it not, Henrietta? It is good you see it before the light fades from the sky. But perhaps later you will slip away with Simon and stroll through the gardens.'

'I would like that,' she said as a thrill of excitement went through her. She envisioned a moonlit walk through the exquisite gardens on Simon's arm, stopping in some private place to share a kiss.

On stepping out of the carriage, she set foot on the acres of red carpet that covered the steps. There was a great bustle all around the *château,* for the multi-coloured liveries of the footmen mingled with the guests. King Louis himself was to be present and, what was more to the point, Prince Charles Edward Stuart, in whose honour the party was being held, so that the thousand or so guests felt themselves highly privileged persons.

They climbed a vast white marble staircase that rose from the centre of the hall. Busts and statues everywhere were to be seen in a state of magnificent whiteness. The rooms were choked with people, men and women wearing the latest Paris fashions and filling the air with their strong perfumes and their wig powder. Entering a large white-and-gold salon, they found it awash with candlelight and resounding with laughter and conversation. The elite of Paris and some of the court were present. Henrietta walked among them, a smile on her lips. An orchestra was playing in the adjoining ballroom and numerous, glittering couples were already dancing. She glanced around, feeling a small knot of expectation and apprehension in her stomach.

A group of gentlemen appeared at the other end of the salon. Suddenly her eyes became riveted on one of them standing on the edge of the group, leaning against an outsized urn filled with flowers. Even at that distance, she had no trouble in distinguishing the imposing figure of Simon Tremain. Her eyes devoured the keen features, that fine-boned face with the deep-set twinkling blue eyes and firm lips crooked into a half-smile, and the thick unruly black hair that always looked slightly windblown. Surely there could not be another man like that in all the world.

Henrietta was not even conscious of the radiant spectacle she presented in the middle of this light-filled salon in her magnificent gown and full-blown beauty. The brilliant chandeliers spread a halo around her. Matthew stood back and watched her walk towards Simon Tremain. She was unaware of the subdued murmur that followed her passage or how all these strangers devoured her with their eager curiosity. Her heart had started beating a wild tattoo as she slowly advanced, with that strange sensation of helplessness and fatality which one sometimes has in a dream. In the surrounding haze she no longer saw anyone but Simon. She looked at him fixedly, as if drawn by a magnet. Had she wanted to lower her eyes she could not have done so, for to see him again brought to her heart an almost unbearable overload of feeling.

Quite suddenly her heart gave a joyful leap and cried out his name long before her lips could bring themselves to frame the word—'Simon!' She was now almost as close to him as she had been when they had parted in Scotland and everything went blank for her except that terrible memory.

When at last he looked her way, he did not seem to recognise her.

She gave him a puckish smile. 'Why, have you forgotten me already, Lord Tremain?'

Simon jerked erect and stared at her. A world of feelings flashed for an instant across his set face—surprise, disbelief, admiration, happiness—but only for an instant. Then he was moving forward very coolly to bow before her.

'Henrietta!'

The sound of her name on his lips stirred her, forcing roiling emotions out of the depths of her soul.

'This is indeed a surprise,' he went on. 'I did not expect to find you here in Paris—and looking so different. I hardly recognised you. Allow me to compliment you—you are exquisite tonight.'

Thrown completely off balance, Henrietta stared at him uncomprehendingly. When she had come to meet him with a heart overflowing with gladness and love, within an ace of throwing herself into his arms, his tone was coolly formal. What could have happened to turn him into this polite stranger?

'I thank you. I am surprised to see you also.

I am relieved you succeeded in getting out of Scotland. It—cannot have been easy.'

'There were moments when I thought I might not.'

The words were nothing, the merest commonplace such as might have been exchanged by virtual strangers. Henrietta found herself wanting to weep. Could this handsome stranger be the same man who had loved her with such passion, who had told her he wanted her to be his wife? Even as she sought to say something that would not be either stupid or inept, she was aware of his eyes scrutinising every detail of her face. She lowered her gaze as the silence between them grew uncomfortable despite the music and the conversations going on around them. She dared not raise them to his now, for fear he should see the tears in them.

Sick with disappointment and unable to stand the tension a moment longer, she was about to excuse herself and move away, when she was aware of someone coming to stand beside him.

'Simon, here you are,' a feminine voice trilled. 'You promised to dance with me, remember?'

Henrietta raised her eyes and stared with all the horror of one seeing a ghost at the slender young woman with hazel eyes.

'If you will allow me,' Simon said, drawing the young woman closer. 'Miss Brody, I should like to present an acquaintance of mine. Miss Vanessa Wallace. Miss Brody is an old friend, Vanessa.'

Stiffened by pride, Henrietta managed to stifle her disappointment and accept the slap that fate had dealt her. Miss Wallace was an acquaintance, he had said. She was also beautiful and delicately exquisite with masses of dark silk hair arranged in a froth of glittering curls. Schooling her features into a smile, Henrietta managed to inject the necessary social politeness into her voice.

'I am delighted to meet you, Miss Wallace.'

Miss Wallace gave Henrietta a more-than-suspicious look. With a faint inclination of her elegantly coiffed head she said with a frosty smile, 'I am happy to make your acquaintance, Miss Brody. Are you from Scotland?'

'Yes, although I have spent most of my life in London. Do you live in Paris, Miss Wallace?'

'For the present. My father was a supporter of Prince Charles in the recent rebellion. We are unable to return to Scotland, you understand.'

'Yes—yes, I understand perfectly.'

'What are you doing in Paris?' Simon asked.

Henrietta drew a tortured breath, determined not to let him see how much her heart was breaking. Whether she was pretty or not, this woman who had stepped from the shadows had shattered her happiness. There was no room in her heart but this one vast disappointment which became an aching pain.

'I am here with Uncle Matthew. We—we are to reside in Paris for a while—and later, perhaps, do some travelling.'

'How is he? Is he well?'

'Yes, he is, very well. I know he would be glad to see you again.'

'And I him. I will seek him out shortly.'

Taking a step back, Henrietta forced a smile. 'Forgive me. I am keeping you from your dance. Excuse me.'

Denying herself so much as a glance at Simon, with anger simmering in her breast, she inclined her head slightly and then turned away from them to go in search of her uncle.

Hovering in the background, observing his niece's meeting with Lord Tremain, their body language had told Matthew that things were far from well. The sudden appearance of the beauty at his side made him genuinely concerned for Henrietta.

As she walked away, angry and hurt by his cold rejection of her, Henrietta faced the truth. Physically, she was no more immune to Simon Tremain than she had been six months ago. Her heart was beating hard, as though it were trying to get out of her ribcage, to escape the bewildering pain it felt, and she found it hard to draw breath. But she did, just enough to keep her conscious, to keep her upright, smiling, though her face felt as though it would crack. Her whole body was suffering such a torrent of physical anguish she found herself walking quickly to escape it.

So this was heartbreak, then, she thought. How was she to survive it? But she must—she would. No matter what came next, she must bear her pain in silence. But she refused to wallow in self-pity. Simon no longer wanted her. He had just made that clear. But it was her own fault for believing he did. To think he had found someone else!

As had happened once before when she had fled from London and Jeremy Lucas, she was seized by the old longing to run away. It was a primitive urge, which overcame her whenever she was unhappy. It was not cowardice. She was not afraid to face her troubles, but felt a need to hide her feelings from prying eyes and seek her own cure in silence and solitude.

'Are you all right, my dear?' Matthew said quietly.

The anger simmering inside her had increased to such a pitch that it was all she could do to hold back her temper that was making her tremble. Taking hold of herself, she gave him a tight smile from behind her fluttering fan, lifting her head to a queenly angle. 'Of course.' She laughed. 'Why ever would I not be?'

'That's my girl, Henrietta. Don't let what has happened get you down. Come, some wine to fortify you and then you must enjoy the ball.' They were not the most felicitous of words. He smiled when he saw his niece's scowl. 'I want to introduce you to some of my friends who have expressed their desire to be introduced to you—unless you would prefer to slip away?'

'I have no desire to leave just yet, Uncle. The king has yet to arrive and it would be impolite to leave. But one thing I have learned tonight is that coming to Paris was a mistake. There is nothing for me here. I think I would like to move on.'

'Leave Paris? But—my dear, we have only just arrived—and Lord Tremain—'

Henrietta's voice was cold as she answered, 'Lord Tremain no longer concerns me. His attentions are directed elsewhere—but I admit his presence in Paris is my chief motive for wishing to leave. If you will not take me away from here, then I shall leave anyway. I will go to any lengths to erase Simon Tremain from my life.'

Her uncle must have realised she meant what she said for even as she saw him blanch, she was aware of something else, a curious pride glowing in his usually gentle eyes.

'Do you have anywhere in mind? Italy, perhaps?'

'Perfect,' she quipped. 'I will instruct Rose to begin packing my things in the morning.'

Though her heart throbbed and she felt inclined to shiver despite the warmth of the room, Henrietta knew she must get through this night without making a fool of herself. Without anyone knowing how she suffered.

Simon was not as unaffected by Henrietta's sudden appearance in Paris as she thought. As he escorted Vanessa on to the dance floor, he could think of nothing else but the young woman he had left in Scotland. He had been startled to see her, and looking as magnificent as only she could.

He reflected on the joy he had felt when they had become lovers. It had come to him and filled him up the moment he had held her and felt all his passions reciprocated in her. Seldom was the ardour of two lovers equal. There was always one who felt more. But with Henrietta, they had taken their pleasure with a kind of exquisitely matched respect, strong and tender, for each other, and whispered all the while words of passionate attachment. He longed for that again and knew he would experience it with no other woman but Henrietta.

What the hell was she doing in Paris? Why had she come? When he'd parted from her, her rejection had almost sent him over the edge, and tonight, seeing her again, magnificent in these grand surroundings, a beautiful, glittering world she was created for, when the joy had overwhelmed him, he had wanted to hurt her as she had hurt him.

It had been with a great effort, his large frame trembling with the tension of it, that he'd managed to master it and treat her with indifference. He'd had to get away, before Henrietta saw what was in him, what was still buried deep inside, locked away in a safe in which to keep it. But it was a poor, weak thing that was in danger of collapsing at any time and he must guard it against her rejection.

But now she was in Paris she wouldn't let him.

As the evening wore on Henrietta found she could look everyone directly in the eye and smile as though she hadn't a care in the world. She had hoped, of course, to have Simon's arm to cling to, his protection about her, for she knew how he felt about her. But that was before. It had disappeared now, that barrier of security he had erected about her on their journey to Scotland and thereafter, in the icy chill of what appeared to be his total indifference.

The king's arrival with his courtly entourage caused much excitement. As his dark, hooded eyes swept restlessly over the crowd and he raised his haughty Bourbon nose, Henrietta saw he was not a tall man. As he nodded in gracious acknowledgement of his bowing subjects, the richness of his attire, his backswept wig and the attitude of those around him enhanced his stature.

It was to the young man hovering on the periphery of his entourage that Henrietta's eyes were drawn. His head was bent close to a pretty woman eager for his attention. Instinctively she knew this was Prince Charles Edward Stuart. A wave of bitterness swept over her. Handsome, yet slightly effeminate, with soft pink lips and powdered hair, he was not exactly as she had imagined him to be.

This was the man whose head had once been full of great revolutionary ideas, whose eagerness to reclaim the crown for his father had driven him to associate with those who had turned the idea of a revolution into a bloodbath on Culloden Field. He had fled to safety in France, leaving those who had supported him to face the brutal retribution of his enemies.

The rest of the evening passed in a blur of introductions, conversing and consuming more champagne than she was accustomed to. She stayed close to her uncle. When the firework display ended in a blaze of glory, much as she'd been looking forward to this fabulous pyrotechnic display, she regarded it with a jaundiced eye.

Among so many people she did not see Simon again. He made no attempt to approach her or her uncle.

Midmorning the following day found Simon at Matthew Brody's residence. It had not been difficult to locate. His impatience to see Henrietta and to discover her reason for coming to Paris was eating away at him. He could not bear another hour, let alone another day, of this awful suspense.

Matthew put down the newspaper he was reading and rose from the chair when the visitor was admitted. He watched Lord Tremain enter the room, having half expected him to call and heartily relieved that he had. But after his cold treatment of Henrietta at the ball, Matthew had no intention of making it easy for him.

The two men shook hands and exchanged polite greetings. Matthew offered him a chair and the two men sat facing each other.

'I trust you are well, Matthew?' Simon said, sincerely glad to see him again and to express his gratitude once more for providing shelter for him in Scotland.

Matthew was studying him. 'I am well and I can't tell you how relieved I was to learn you had managed to reach France safely. But I do not think it is me you have come to see. You wish to see Henrietta.'

'That is the purpose of my visit.'

'Then it is as well you have called today. We are leaving for Italy shortly,' Matthew stated, standing up and walking to a table where he poured some Madeira into two glasses and handing one to Simon. 'The climate in Paris at this present time is not to my niece's liking.'

The glass in Simon's hand froze halfway to his lips. 'Why? She's only just arrived.'

'I think your behaviour of last night has something to do with her decision.' Matthew watched in satisfaction as Simon tossed down half the contents of his glass as if he wanted to wash away the disappointment of the news.

'Will you allow me to see her? I would like to.'

'That's a pity. I don't think Henrietta wants to see you. The welfare and happiness of my niece is paramount to all else, which is why I've agreed to take her to Italy.'

'Where she will no doubt be a huge success and meet eligible young men with all the prerequisites required of a husband,' Simon remarked savagely, his voice laced with uncharacteristic sarcasm. Draining the glass, he set it down with a thud before getting to his feet.

'She might—although since encountering you, marriage to anyone else is the last thing on her mind. Wealth, titles and all the trappings that accompany them, are not important to her. Given your treatment of her last night—which was undeserved, I might add,' Matthew said, determined to have his say, particularly in matters of morality or justice, 'she was under the influence of the most formidable temper I have ever seen. While I was not present at your—reunion—although my eyes did bear witness to it—I got the gist of it, and if what Henrietta told me is true, then it is obvious that you are completely without either heart or conscience. My heart breaks when I think what she has gone through to come here. How she—'

'Why? What has she done?' Simon interrupted shortly, turning and walking to the window.

'She sold everything, everything Baron Lucas had left to her, and all because she loves you and could not live without you. She turned her back on England and the security of her home to come to you.' With grim satisfaction Matthew observed the muscle that was beginning to twitch in Simon's rigid jaw.

'Despite what I am? That I have nothing to offer her?'

'In spite of all that. She suffered greatly when her father was executed. She was a child, bewildered and hurt—unable to understand—and then…'

Simon turned sharply. 'What? What happened?'

'Her mother could not endure life without my brother. Henrietta will probably berate me for telling you this, but if you are to fully understand the situation then I feel you should know the whole of it.'

'Go on,' Simon urged, his eyes fixed on him intently when he fell silent.

Taking a deep breath, after a moment Matthew continued. 'The brutality of her husband's death my sister-in-law could not endure. Demented with grief, she entered into a state of madness where no one could reach her. Gradually, her behaviour became more and more irrational—her moods erratic. Fearing that something would happen to Henrietta and that she, too, would be taken away from her, she became obsessive and hated to let her out of her sight for a moment. It broke Henrietta's heart when she saw what was happening to her mother.

Quite how it happened we will never know, but one day she left the house and drowned herself. Henrietta found her. The double tragedy was almost too much for the heart and mind of someone so young. Her father's execution had a terrible impact on her—her mother's suicide turned her life into a living hell.'

Simon's brow drew together in a frown of disbelief at what he was hearing. His heart began to hammer in deep aching beats. He was caught between torment and tenderness over what Matthew had divulged. 'I didn't know,' he said hoarsely. 'She didn't tell me this.'

'She could never bring herself to talk about it. When I saw her, her eyes were filled with so much pain—I'll never forget the torment in her eyes.'

Simon stared at him, trying to deny what Matthew was telling him, and then, with his heart bursting with compassion, he closed his eyes as he tried to blot out the image of a little girl with red-gold hair and green eyes being subjected to so much pain and sorrow.

'I did what I could for her,' Matthew went on, 'and when she was stronger I placed her in the care of Baron Lucas and his wife. I believe she was happy, but what happened to her as a child has never left her. She needed someone—something—to blame. Perhaps now you will understand fully why she focused all that hate on the Jacobites and their cause.'

A muscle moved spasmodically in Simon's throat, but he made no effort to defend himself. Bracing his hands on either side of the window, he stared out, Matthew's revelations about Henrietta's mother pounding in his brain with the torment of his own cruelty to her. Little wonder she felt as she did with him being a Jacobite.

He saw her as she had been in Scotland, courageous and lovely, filled with innocent passion in his arms, and he heard her words from last night—*Have you forgotten me already?* Dear God, if he lived to be a thousand he could never forget her. With a fresh surge of remorse, scolding rage at his own blindness and stupidity poured through him. His last words to her in Scotland had been spoken in anger—that if she sent him away without hope, then he would not come back. And now this—she had sold everything to come to him.

Bile rose up in his throat, suffocating him, and he closed his eyes. She was so unselfish, so sweet. She had done that for him.

Matthew hadn't moved. In taut silence he watched Simon standing at the window, his eyes clenched shut. At length he relinquished his stance and turned and faced him.

Paralysed with a mixture of urgency and

fear, he said, 'Can I see her now?' His voice was rough with emotion.

'Only if you promise me not to hurt her.'

'I would kill myself before I would harm one hair on her head.'

Matthew could scarcely conceal his happy relief. His stern features softened. 'I know that. Perhaps I should not be speaking to you like this, except that in you I seem to find a spirit kindred to mine. My life, you see, has been a somewhat solitary thing and I fear this makes me too bold. I have no right to interfere in Henrietta's life. I know that. She is in love with you. It broke her heart when she watched you ride away from her in Scotland. She tried to fight it, but it was hopeless.' He smiled, accompanying Simon to the door and opening it. 'There are worse things than marrying a young woman who has the excellent judgement to fall in love with you—but I must warn you,' he said with humour. 'There's a good chance she will tell you to go and jump in the river.'

Simon grinned. 'I'm a strong swimmer.'

As he made his way to the salon where he knew he would find Henrietta, Simon's mind was preoccupied with the explanations he intended to make to her. She was angry. No doubt she wanted to get a little of her own back by pretending she didn't want him, but that was one thing that didn't concern him. They had wanted each other from the time she had thrown off her disguise and exposed herself as the beautiful woman she was. They had wanted each other every time they'd been together since then.

From the window Henrietta had seen Simon arrive and for what seemed an eternity she had existed in a state of jarring tension. Now, as she watched him enter the room and close the door behind him with an ominous thud, realising that for the first time in six months she was completely alone with him, she fought to appear completely calm, clinging to her composure as if it were a blanket she could use to insulate herself against him.

With that same natural grace that seemed so much a part of him, with a growing sense of unreality and with yards of Aubusson carpet stretching between them, she watched him start towards her with long, purposeful strides. With his clear eyes and energetic movements, he seemed to bring the whole wide world with him into the salon. He grew larger as he neared, his broad shoulders blocking her view of the room, his deep-blue eyes searching her face, his smile one of uncertainty.

'You must have come to visit my uncle, otherwise I cannot see the purpose of your visit?'

Simon observed her pallor and the accusation and ire shooting from her lovely eyes. With one eyebrow raised and a saturnine grin, he said, 'As a matter fact I am here to see you—although being able to reacquaint myself with Matthew is an added bonus. He's a wise man, your uncle.'

'Yes, he is. However, I am very busy at this time—preparing to leave for Italy, you understand, so you will do me a great service if you leave.'

'I will do anything but that.'

'Nevertheless, considering your relationship with the woman you were with last night at the ball, to remain here with me for any given length of time would not be wise.'

Simon gave her a solemn smile. 'Nothing we have ever done has been wise. Let's not spoil it now.'

Reluctantly she met his gaze. 'Why?'

'Because,' he said, smiling tenderly into her eyes, 'I have no wish to hurt you further and I wish to apologise to you for my behaviour last night. It was unforgivably rude of me to treat you so appallingly.'

Still slightly mistrustful of his apparent change of heart, Henrietta eyed him warily. 'Yes, it was.'

'Am I forgiven?'

Already softening, she said, 'It would be no less than you deserve if I don't.'

Laughing softly, Simon moved closer to her. 'I praise God that your spirit is unharmed. Since last night I have been living with the fear that it might be.'

Tipping her head to one side, she regarded him quizzically. 'Really? But why?'

'Because,' he said seriously, 'the woman I saw at the ball was not the woman I knew in Scotland, the girl I remember.'

Despite her resolution not to capitulate to his allure, a rush of warmth pervaded Henrietta's whole being, reawakening the nerve centres that had been numbed by despair. 'Beneath the finery I am still the same woman. You will never know how I wanted you—to the last moment. And then, when I saw you with someone else at the ball, I realised it was too late.'

As quickly as Simon had come to her, he tore himself away, not looking at her, hating himself with a virulence for what he had put her through. 'Vanessa is the daughter of a friend—she means nothing to me, Henrietta. You have to believe that. When I left you in Scotland I didn't know if I would survive—let alone see you again. I believed I had lost you for ever,' he said grimly. 'Your heart was adamantly set against me and the cause.'

'No, Simon—never you. The cause—yes.'

'And I know why. I already knew about your father—but your mother? Your uncle told me about what happened to her. My God, Henrietta, why didn't you tell me?'

Henrietta paled. 'Because I have never been able to speak of it. The tragedy was twofold and too much for me to take in—to bear. Perhaps now you can understand the depth of my abhorrence for the Jacobites. Had my father not been a Jacobite, prepared—honoured, even, to give his life for the cause, none of it would have happened. But when we parted, when I went to London, I could no longer go on running away from it—not if it meant losing you.'

'You would do that—for me, Henrietta?'

'I would die for you,' she whispered, her eyes holding his filled with all the love that was in her heart.

'And I for you, my love. You knew damned well how much I loved you—and still do. If you don't believe anything else I've ever said to you, at least believe that.' He thought she might argue, but she didn't, and he realised that, despite her youth, she was very wise. 'What of Whitegates—your home in London?'

She laughed, a light-hearted sound. 'What of it?' She reached up and stroked his cheek. 'Uncle Matthew will have told you that I sold it—along with every stick of furniture and carpet and useless vase. I realised that possessions are nothing more than that. When you left me my heart was broken. I had to see you again. You could not return to England, so I came to you. You—do still want me, do you not?' she whispered.

In answer he pulled her to him and held her tightly in his arms. 'I have never stopped wanting you. I have missed you so much.'

'I can't believe you are here,' she whispered. 'A few hours ago everything seemed so...'

'Empty?' he provided in his deep, compelling voice. 'And meaningless?' he added.

She nodded. 'And hopeless.'

'Not any longer. I love you from the bottom of my heart. I have loved you from the beginning.'

She smiled up at him and a look showing she had never really doubted the constancy of his love glistened in her eyes. 'And I love you—even when you berated my slovenliness as an unkempt youth. But what of Prince Charles? Will he rebel some more, do you think?'

He shook his head. 'The rebellion failed miserably. Since then the Highland way of life—particularly the clan system—has been dismantled. Even the wearing of the tartan has been banned. The Crown policy to subdue the Highlands has been carried out regardless of the politics of individual clans—not all of whom were Jacobite sympathisers.'

'And Barradine? Has your transfer of the title from you to your younger brother been successful?'

'It caused some confusion in the English court, but they have accepted that the deed is legal. The fact that my uncle—whose loyalty to King George is absolute—is to administer the estate until my brother Edward comes of age, was in our favour.'

'Is it likely that your brother is of the same persuasion as yourself?'

'Edward is not like me. He is a serious boy who devotes himself to his studies. Unfortunately he does not possess the best of health—he has a weakness of his heart—the same weakness that our father died of shortly after Ewen was born. He will be happy to lead a quiet, orderly life back in Scotland, which will satisfy the English. Besides, it's difficult to prove a young boy to be a traitor. At ten years old, Ewen is from a different mould entirely. There is a wild impatience to my young brother's nature. With a mind and will of his own and his mind bent on a military career, it is perhaps as well he was the last born. I thank God Barradine remains in the family.'

His voice was grim. 'I am a fugitive from the

law, Henrietta, and in disgrace, with no name or land. What future could I possibly offer you? None at all. And yet anyone who says we can ever escape our destiny is a fool or a dreamer! We can never break free from the mistakes we have made. We must carry them with us for ever. Because we loved each other, we have done everything we could to bend fate to our will. We parted in Scotland and went our separate ways, but however far we've travelled fate has caught up with us. It is stronger than we are.'

'I love you with all my heart, Simon. You know that.'

'And it does not concern you that I cannot return to Scotland or England now?'

'That matters little to me. I will go where you go. As long as I am by your side that is all that matters.'

'Will you become my wife and come with me to share unknown and unforeseen adventures—and hardships, I dare say?'

Henrietta smiled up at him, loving him. 'The choice, I think, is quite obvious.'

'Then it is a choice we have to make together. Barred from Scotland, we will have to find a place to make a future together, either in Europe or by emigrating to America.'

'You have strong ties with France, Simon.

Besides, your mother and brothers will want to visit.'

'I would like you to meet them before they leave for Scotland. My mother is impatient to meet the woman who has captivated my heart at last. She was beginning to despair it would ever happen. Since my father died she spends most of her time in France.'

'She—has never considered marrying again?'

He shook his head. 'She has been alone for a long time. It is my dearest wish that she marries again, but she has never met anyone who could live up to my father.'

'I look forward to meeting her and your brothers, which is why I really do think we should stay here. France is closer than America.'

'It is also teeming with Jacobites, don't forget.'

She smiled. 'How could I? I shall be married to one. So we will live in France, in the south, I think.'

'I would like that.'

'They say the south is a wonderful place to live,' she murmured placidly and a flicker of the old fire shone for a moment in her green eyes. 'And I have heard it said that in those southern parts it is never cold. I think I should like that very well.'

He gazed down at her, searching her eyes for confirmation of the truth of what he already knew yet scarcely dared to believe. 'With no regrets?'

'With no regrets.'

Arriving at Simon's residence in Paris where he lived with his mother and two brothers, Henrietta stood for a long moment in the doorway to the salon and observed Simon with his family. His brothers, two dark-haired, handsome youths, were laughing heartily at something amusing their elder brother had said. Then this elder brother raised his gaze to her, and she saw all the love she had ever desired within those deep-blue eyes. He came to her and took her hand to lead her to his mother.

'Mother, I would like you to meet Henrietta.'

Lady Mary, a small, slender woman with pale blonde hair, rose and clasped her future daughter-in-law's hands. Tears filled her eyes as she drew back and smiled with satisfaction. 'God answered my prayers and sent a beautiful young woman for my son at last. Welcome to the family, my dear.'

Simon stepped to Henrietta's side and slipped his arm about her as she smiled into his warmly glowing eyes. 'And I have reason to be grateful to him. I could not have wished for a more worthy protector on my journey to Scotland.'

'I suppose I was, in truth,' Simon agreed, gazing lovingly down at his soon-to-be wife. 'Once found, I couldn't bear to think of losing you.'

'And you must love my son very much to have given up everything to be with him.'

'Yes, I do, but it has always been rather hard for me to tell him that.'

'Well, you needn't worry about it any more, Henrietta. You proved your love far better with your actions.'

Taking her uncle's arm, Henrietta drew him forward. 'Lady Mary, I would like to present my uncle, Matthew Brody. It was at my uncle's house that Simon sought shelter after he was wounded at Culloden.'

Lady Mary flicked a quick, hesitant glance upwards, but upon meeting eyes that were calm and as clear as the sky on a summer's day, she searched his lean, still-handsome visage. Interest lit and softened her eyes and she smiled sublimely, holding out her hand to him. 'I am indeed happy to make your acquaintance, Mr Brody.'

Matthew took her hand and raised it to his lips, a merry twinkle lighting his eyes. They roamed across her delicate, refined, still-youthful features and he smiled with the same cajoling charm his niece had mastered. 'Enchanted, *madame*.'

Lady Mary inclined her elegant head ever so slightly, but the shine in her eyes was dazzling.

'I must thank you for the hospitality you showed Simon after Culloden. You will never know how indebted I am to you. Come, sit by me. I think you and I have much to talk about.' She gave no time for replies and took her smiling admirer gently by the arm and led him to a sofa by the window.

Their minds traversing along the same track, standing side by side Henrietta and Simon looked at each other and smiled.

Henrietta's lips mouthed a silent question. 'Do you think…?'

Simon pressed his lips near her ear and spoke in a hushed whisper. 'Indeed I do. But for the time being we will bide our time and watch.'

They were to be proved right. But that was for another day.

* * * * *

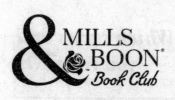